GALAXY'S EDGE

CREATED BY MIKE RESNICK

ISSUE 47: November 2020

Lezli Robyn, Editor
Martin L. Shoemaker, Assistant Editor
Taylor Morris, Copyeditor
Shahid Mahmud, Publisher

Published by Arc Manor/Phoenix Pick
P.O. Box 10339
Rockville, MD 20849-0339

Galaxy's Edge is published in January, March, May, July, September, and November.

Please check our website for submission guidelines.

ISBN: 978-1-64973-074-9

SUBSCRIPTION INFORMATION:
Paper and digital subscriptions are available (including via Amazon.com) . Please visit our home page: www.GalaxysEdge.com

ADVERTISING:
Advertising is available in all editions of the magazine. Please contact advert@GalaxysEdge.com.

FOREIGN LANGUAGE RIGHTS:
Please refer all inquiries pertaining to foreign language rights to Shahid Mahmud, Arc Manor, P.O. Box 10339, Rockville, MD 20849-0339. Tel: 1-240-645-2214. Fax 1-310-388-8440. Email admin@ArcManor.com.

CONTENTS

EDITOR'S NOTE

by Lezli Robyn

For readers of ours not living in the United States, you would be right in thinking that Americans appear to be living the prologue chapter of some near-future apocalyptic novel. Sure, the rest of the world is also going through its own kind of hell with the COVID-19 pandemic—well, except for New Zealand, that is—but in the United States the pandemic has hit during the stirrings of great political, civil, and economic upheaval, dividing a once (usually) united country. I wouldn't be surprised if a lot more people have escaped into a good book or a favorite comfort movie to forget the reality of a life that currently appears more alien than fiction.

This November issue greets our readers with new articles from regular columnists L. Penelope and Gregory Benford, and reviews of the latest and greatest fiction by Richard Chwedyk. We have another Mike Resnick short story for our readers, this time written with celebrated French writer Jean-Claude Dunyach. Nancy Kress also returns to our pages with "Machine Learning," which tells the tale of a researcher and his partner teaching an AI to train others as depression overtakes the researcher following the loss of his family.

In "The Ecology of Broken Promises," Andrea Stewart gifts us a thought-provoking and confronting magical realism story that depicts the journey of a woman grappling with the guilt of all the vows she has broken in her life. If you haven't yet read Andrea's debut novel, *The Bone Shard Daughter*, published by Orbit this past September, you're missing out! I would not be surprised if we see her name on some award ballots in the coming year.

We welcome Joe Haldeman back to our magazine, with "The Monster," and J. Scott Coatsworth will dazzle our readers with "Lamplighter," about Fen, a member of a fantasy world guild whose selfless attempts to relight a city and find a way to keep his love will spark a revolution. "Night Folk," by Barb Galler-Smith, also takes part in the absence of daylight, where some aging creatures of the night put aside their walking canes to battle some geriatric hunters. It's not often that we read about retired supernatural creatures, and this story doesn't disappoint, flipping well-known tropes in this unexpected read.

If you are wanting something witty and entertaining, you can't go wrong with "A Farmboy, a Wizard and a Dark Lord Walk into a Tower" by Dantzel Cherry. And who doesn't like a time traveling story? William and Tyler travel into the past to save the life of William's first child in "Saving Sarah," a science fiction story by newcomer John Haas. With an ending that brought this editor to tears, this piece will show you how far a father will go to protect his child, and remind you that you can't escape the consequences of your actions.

With the holiday season upon us, this issue showcases several pieces with a festive flare. "A Midwinter's Tale" by Michael Swanwick tells a story within a story, about a soldier recalling an incident in his youth when an alien revealed the secret of how their species met. "To Hell with the Stars" is a charming tale by Jack McDevitt about a boy's dream to travel into space, just like his favorite characters did in the thousand-year-old science fiction novels he loves to read so much. And last, but not least, Larry Hodges returns to the pages of *Galaxy's Edge* with "The Untold Christmas Carol," which explores Tiny Tim's real origins, and the frustrations the Devil experiences when his hauntings don't go according to plan.

Now, more than ever, when the United States is so divided, is the time we should come together to curl up with our family and loved ones in front of a roaring fireplace, sipping hot cocoa or eggnog as we celebrate Thanksgiving and Christmas, grateful for surviving the shitstorm that was 2020.

But before that, on the day this issue is published, the United States' presidential election will be looming. Vote. Urge others to vote, whether they identify as red or blue. That way, when we ring in the New Year, we can remind ourselves that like the many brave characters of this issue's science fiction and fantasy stories, we too have the ability to reshape our lives, and the lives of others around us, for the better.

We can't be the heroes of our own story if we don't step up, take a chance. Hold ourselves accountable.

Andrea Stewart is the daughter of immigrants, and was raised in a number of places across the United States. Her debut epic fantasy, THE BONE SHARD DAUGHTER, *is out with Orbit. In addition to writing, she can be found herding cats, looking at birds, and falling down research rabbit holes.*

THE ECOLOGY OF BROKEN PROMISES

by Andrea Stewart

The undressing is always the hardest part. Lisa makes sure that it happens in the dark, but even so, no matter how much she contorts and evades, a stray brush of his finger reveals her secrets.

The man stops, and in that moment, she can't breathe or even remember his name. All she feels is fear, white and electric as a lightning bolt. His fingers brush the place on her ribs again, lingering over the threads she used to bind the tiny mouth shut. Flesh-colored thread, of course, not that he can see in the dark.

"Is this the only one?" Jason whispers. That's right; his name is Jason. His breath tickles her cheek. It smells like mint and alcohol.

She knows without looking, without touching, that he is blemish-free—just from the way he says those words. He's young, she supposes. It makes sense.

"There's another," Lisa says. She guides his hand to a second set of stitches on the opposite hip. And one more, though she doesn't add that aloud. That one, the result of her infidelities, her broken vows, lies on the bottom of her right foot. He doesn't need to know about it. "Does it bother you?"

Now she wishes it wasn't dark, so she could see the expression on his face.

"No," he says. "At least you know better now. At least you know what not to ask of other people. What's too much, too far."

He leaves the rest unspoken—that she knows not to ask too much of *him*—and kisses the juncture between her neck and shoulder. For a moment she hesitates, because she's accustomed to more. She

wants more. But then she leans into his chest, guiding his hands so they do not touch the mouths on her hip and ribs.

One step, and another, and then they fall onto the bed together, their mouths, the real ones, pressed lip to lip.

☼

He doesn't call her back.

Lisa stows the secret phone back between mattress and box spring. The screen showed only the time, nothing more. She should have known the mouths would bother Jason. Maybe he's talking to his friends right now about sleeping with her, about how it was a one-time thing.

"She had two extra mouths," he might say.

"That's nothing," a friend would reply, "I once fucked a girl with *five*."

The mattress squeaks as Lisa's husband shifts beside her. She glances over, but he's still asleep. When they bought this bed, they joked about the sexual gymnastics they'd undertake on its wide surface. Now that surface feels like an ocean, his slumping shoulder the mountain of some other continent.

One mouth mars his shoulder, and Michael never bothered to sew it shut. Its lips probe the empty air, like a baby searching for a teat. He told her, on their twelfth date, how he earned it: a promise to his mother that he'd become a doctor.

He'd tried, of course, and he'd wept when his MCAT scores were too low, and he told Lisa of the itching and the dread as the mouth grew on his shoulder—a red, patchy rash expanding into a hole to signify his failure; his broken promise.

Lisa rolls onto her back, staring at the blank expanse of the ceiling, wishing that were her skin. She never told Michael about her mouths, and even when the third one appeared on her foot, he didn't ask.

It's private.

☼

The silence in the car presses on her eardrums, making her tap her foot on the brakes. The tapping fills the air, and Michael sighs. He rests his head against the window, his breath fogging the glass. "Do you have to do that?"

She stops, reaching for the radio instead. As soon as she turns it on, it blares, the strumming of a guitar magnified a thousand-fold.

"Fuck, that's loud!" Michael covers his ears and glances at her, and she reads it on his face: *Can't you do anything right?*

Her chest tightens as she mutters an apology, and she dials the volume down to an acceptable level. She checks his expression the way she checks her mirrors. His lips are pressed together, and she can see the vein throbbing at his temple.

"Should I turn it off?" she asks.

He says, just as quickly, "Does it matter what I want?"

"It matters to me."

His gaze goes out the window again. "Really? Are you sure?"

That shuts her up. She doesn't know what to say, what to do, to assuage his anger. She's not sure what caused it in the first place. He couldn't possibly know about her infidelity; she's never left a sign. He would never know the reason for the mouth on the sole of her foot.

When they married, she wouldn't have dreamed of going outside their marriage, of breaking her vows. Things have changed. Every time they talk, it seems to lead to more fighting. It's exhausting, and she needs some sort of release. Sometimes, when they're yelling at one another, Lisa imagines just digging her fingers into his scalp, peeling back skin and flesh and bone to reveal the thoughts beneath.

She could use that sort of insight.

"At least your flight is on time," she says, lamely. It's all she can manage.

Michael just grunts a reply.

When they pull up to the airport, she watches him visibly brightening. He lifts his head, his hands passing over his shirt, his tie. He straightens in his seat; he clears his throat.

It's just a business trip, Lisa reminds herself, for what feels like the hundredth time. But she sees his colleague waiting for him just inside the sliding glass doors—her long, supple legs, her white-toothed smile, the perfectly coiffed hair that Lisa smelled in passing once: all ocean breeze and lavender. She'd bet that woman has skin as smooth as a cultured pearl. She'd bet that woman has only ever made small promises, easily kept.

There haven't been any new mouths on Michael's skin; she's checked. But it won't be long, Lisa can feel it. Maybe this time Michael will return with an angry welt on his chest—a welt that grows into a pair of lips, a tongue, a gaping orifice that cannot be filled.

"Have a good trip," Lisa says as her husband reaches for his bag. "Love you." *Promise you'll think of me while you're away.* But she doesn't say it.

"Love you too," he says. He doesn't kiss her or even meet her eyes. The words are hollow, the rote repetition of a parrot.

As Lisa watches her husband greet his colleague with a smile, all of her mouths ache at once and she feels them straining at their stitches.

In the next breath, they're quiet once more.

She stops by a bar on the way home. Sure, it's only two p.m., but the whole drive and drop-off has her anxiety levels through the roof. Michael would never hit her, would never call her names. But when they're alone, she feels the tension between them and it's somehow worse.

She almost wishes he'd hit her, just to clear the air. Just to give her a good reason.

Smoke fills the inside of the building; it stinks of beer and tobacco. The soles of her shoes stick to the hardwood floors as she walks. It's not any place she's been before. "A Bud Light, please," she says as she sits on one of the barstools. A couple of regulars occupy other seats. They glance at her and then their gazes stray back to the television. The bartender, a middle-aged woman, nods and grabs a bottle from the fridge.

"Troubles got you down?" a voice says from behind her.

Lisa turns and does her best not to gape. A young woman stands behind her, one hand on the back of Lisa's barstool. She's lanky and borderline hollow, like a greyhound that's seen one too many races around the track. Her chestnut hair is pulled into a messy bun, and she's wearing a cropped black tank top and jean shorts that reveal not one, not two, but *eight* mouths. None are sewn shut. The one on the woman's left shoulder opens, a small pink tongue lolling out. A musky scent hangs around her, like moist soil and rotting wood.

It's *grotesque*.

"It's rude to stare, y'know," the woman says. "Just wanted to know why you're here. Never seen you here before."

The bartender slides the Bud Light in front of Lisa, and she grips it, the coolness of the glass bringing some clarity to her thoughts. She gathers herself. "Sorry. I didn't mean to stare."

"Troubles got you down?" the young woman says again.

Normally, Lisa would just shrug, or tell the young woman it was none of her business, but everything about this encounter has her off balance. "Husband problems," she says. She takes a swig from the bottle.

The young woman sits in the barstool next to Lisa. "Imogene," she says. "That's my name."

"Lisa."

"I know all about husband problems," Imogene says. She points to the mouth on her shoulder, and then to the one next to her belly button. "Two divorces."

"You *chose* to get married again?" Lisa says. She picks at the corner of the bottle label. "You'd think once would be enough." A lot of people don't get married at all, but the two Lisa knows who've divorced have vowed to never marry again. It's just not worth the risk.

Imogene shrugs. Despite her disheveled appearance, her cat-eye eyeliner is perfectly applied. "My mom and dad were married thirty-five years before he kicked it. They were so fucking in love—every day. Always wanted what they had. Always kept hoping for it." She laughs. "Still hoping for it, really."

Lisa doesn't ask about the other mouths, but Imogene answers anyway. Their lips strain for her finger as she points at them. "Swore I'd be friends with someone forever. Promised to be nice to my homophobic coworker. Made a pact with myself that I would never, ever be so stupid again…" Imogene lets out a long breath, her shoulders caving in on themselves.

Lisa wraps both hands around the bottle. The scratched surface of the bar chafes her elbows. "Three," she says.

Imogene only nods. "Can't be avoided."

"I mean, it can," Lisa says. "You just have to avoid making promises in the first place."

"Sure," Imogene says, but Lisa feels her sidelong glance. "That's not worked well for you, it seems."

Why is she letting this stranger get under her skin? She shrugs. "Knowing what I have to do and doing them are two different things. I never should have gotten married."

"And I never should have lent money to Natalie 'cause she bailed and now I'm short for this upcoming week's rent. High hopes. We've got them. Clink." Imogene touches an imaginary bottle to Lisa's. "Life's a bitch."

Lisa smiles for the first time today. Misery *does* love company. "Sounds like Natalie's the bitch."

Imogene laughs—a husky, throaty sound. "Damn right."

"Let me buy you a drink," Lisa says, even as she wonders if Imogene gets drinks by latching onto people, or if Imogene is an alcoholic. But the bartender is standing in front of them and it's too late to worry about enabling.

"Same as what she's having," Imogene says.

☼

"Are you sure this is okay?" Imogene grips the doorframe as though it's the only thing holding her upright. Maybe it is.

"Yes, yes." Lisa waves her in. The hallway swims before her eyes. Two beers, three shots, some horrible bar food and a cab ride later, it's nine p.m. She'll have to go back for the car tomorrow. "Michael's gone for five days, anyway. Another business trip with his beautiful, perfect coworker." More bitterness leaks into the words than she intended. It's the alcohol.

"But you don't even know me." Imogene's voice sounds plaintive.

"You've got two sisters and a brother," Lisa says. "You like Thai food and pizza, and you fucking *hate* Natalie."

"Sure do." Imogene pushes off from the doorframe and swaggers into Lisa's apartment. She swings an arm around Lisa's shoulders, and Lisa doesn't even mind when the mouth on Imogene's wrist probes her skin. Imogene's words slur together. "Michael doesn't goddamned deserve you, you know that? You're *so* pretty, like a princess. But not a stuck-up one. Like, a warrior princess." Her eyes widen. "Like, you're fucking Xena."

"I'm not really interested in fucking Xena."

Imogene throws her head back so hard when she laughs that Lisa loses her balance. They stumble together into the wall. "Owwww," Imogene says.

"You okay?"

Imogene disentangles from Lisa. "Yeah. Just the mouths. They make everything more sensitive."

Lisa takes Imogene's elbow and guides her to an armchair. "You could sew them shut, you know."

Imogene sinks into the plush cushions. "I did, once. But it hurt too much. Couldn't be bothered." She reaches for the bowl of pistachios on the coffee table, shells one, and pops it into the mouth on her shoulder.

"You *feed* them?" Lisa collapses onto the couch.

"Sometimes," Imogene says, her voice small.

"Well, what happens to the—that is," Lisa circles a hand in the air, "you know."

"It's not a full separate being like you or me," Imogene says, "so it just, sort of…comes back out later." Lisa's disgust must have shown on her face, because Imogene scowls at her from beneath dark brows. "Yeah? Well, what do you do? Just pretend they're not there? Pretend you never made those promises in the first place?"

Lisa thinks of Jason's lips on hers, his hands hot against her skin. "Sometimes." She still remembers her first affair—Caleb. He plied her with compliments, with caresses, with the sort of sweet attentions that Michael no longer seemed interested in giving. When they fell into bed together she thought, *This is real*, and she hadn't even minded the mouth that grew on the bottom of her foot.

But no. Reality was three months later, when Caleb met a tattooed barista named Adira and lost Lisa's number. After that, what had it mattered? She was already scarred.

"Should I leave him?" Lisa wonders aloud.

"You're asking the wrong person," Imogene says. She reaches back and pulls out the pins holding her bun in place. Her hair falls in waves about her face, softening the angles. "Can't anyone make that decision but you."

"Is that what someone told you about your two husbands?" Lisa can't help the sharpness in her words.

Imogene gives her a wry smile. "Nobody told me nothing. My mom passed soon after my dad, and

I'm the eldest child. I didn't have anyone to give me advice. But my heart said 'stay,' and my head said 'go,' and between the two of them, my head's always been the smarter one."

"And you'd marry again?"

"If I found the right guy, yeah."

Lisa blinks, trying to keep the room from spinning. "I don't think I would. This marriage—this is my one and only chance to get things right."

"There's always another chance."

"And how many chances for you until you're covered with the consequences?"

Imogene makes a sound halfway between a cough and a sob. "That's kinda mean, don't you think? I know what I am, what I have on my skin. I think about it all the time." She presses a hand into her forehead, like a headache has started there.

"I'm sorry," Lisa says quickly. She pushes herself to her feet. "Let me get you some water."

When she comes back with the glass of water, Imogene is lying across the couch, her knees up, one arm over her eyes. She doesn't reach for the glass. When she speaks, it's an imposition into the silence. "Well, you must have gotten married for a reason. If you could go back, would you do things differently?"

Freedom, a chance to begin anew. "Yes." Lisa stands over the couch, watching the way her shadow creeps up the side of Imogene's cheek. The mouths across her body are still. "You?"

"No," Imogene says. "I made these choices. I'll suffer for them, one way or another." Her lips press together. "It's my lot in life."

"It sounds like a miserable way to live."

Imogene peeks at Lisa from beneath her forearm. "Who are you, my shrink?"

Lisa kneels and runs a hand over Imogene's hair, spilling over the couch cushions. She weaves her fingers into the silky strands. "No. Just a friend."

"Oh," is all Imogene says.

Lisa watches the way her throat moves as she swallows. There's power in this—a power she doesn't have as a wife, when she can't do anything right. She flicks her gaze to Imogene's. The ends of Imogene's cat-eye makeup smudge into her eyelids. Deliberately, Lisa curls her fingertips at the base of Imogene's neck and tugs.

Imogene gasps.

Without a thought for the consequences, Lisa leans over and kisses her. Imogene's lips give way before hers, Imogene's hands seize the front of Lisa's shirt. Lisa's heartbeat races; it pounds in her ears. She climbs atop the other woman and runs a hand up her thigh. All of Imogene's mouths fumble at Lisa's skin, leaving wet trails in their wake.

Imogene pulls back for a moment, her shadowed eyes troubled. "I don't really know you," she says. "I don't really know you at all." But then she hooks her fingers around Lisa's ears and drags her back down.

Their limbs tangle together. Clothes become obstacles, things to be discarded in haste. Lisa grabs the bottom of her shirt and pulls it up over her head. It catches at her shoulders, and as she struggles to wriggle free, something on her hip tears.

It burns. Imogene tugs the shirt off, and they both look down. The stitches on Lisa's hip have torn, freeing the mouth beneath. Scars and frayed thread mark the circumference. A tongue emerges, hesitantly, swiping across the upper lip, licking away little pinpricks of blood.

Lisa presses a hand to the mouth. "It hurts," she moans.

"I know," Imogene says. "Shh…I know." She rests her palms on Lisa's waist and kisses her hand. "Here. Let me." When Lisa slowly draws her hand away, Imogene presses her lips to the mouth.

The world swims. Lisa can't be sure what she sees, but she thinks the mouth on her hip kisses Imogene back. She thinks she can *feel* it—the mouth of a broken promise, Imogene's mouth, tongues twining together.

"Imogene," Lisa whispers.

Imogene opens her arms. "Come here, love."

✿

Light falls through the blinds in horizontal slats. Lisa cracks an eye open. Her mouth feels as though she's swallowed cobwebs. The back of her throat still tastes like the Jack Daniels she drank the night before.

She tries to stretch and finds her neck sore from spending the night on the couch, propped on an armrest. For a moment she thinks Imogene is gone, but then she hears humming from the kitchen and the scrape of a spatula against a pan.

As Lisa rises to her feet and dresses, the stretching and pulling makes the mouth on her hip sting. It hangs open, the skin around it loose, as if years of being sewn shut means it can't close on its own anymore. Lisa gropes beneath the couch and finds the metal tin she keeps her sewing supplies in. The needles and buttons rattle as she brings it to her lap.

Her fingers move with a learned repetition. She has to replace the stitches every so often as they dissolve. She threads the needle, ties a knot at the end, grits her teeth, and begins. The scar tissue shields her from the worst pain. Each loop pulls the lips together, getting her closer to some semblance of normal.

Imogene emerges from the kitchen, the spatula in hand. She watches the process for a moment as something pops on the pan behind her. "Looks like it hurts."

"Yes," Lisa says. She pinches the skin and pierces both sides with the needle.

"You're not perfect, you know. Anyone who expects you to be is spouting bullshit." Imogene punctuates her words with a thrust of the spatula.

Lisa runs out of thread and ties the end. She's managed to do half, so far. "Doesn't mean I should stop trying."

Imogene shrugs and turns back to the kitchen. "It's too late. You do this for Michael? Why torture yourself for him?"

Not for Michael, not anymore—for all the others. With shaking fingers, Lisa unspools more thread. No matter how hard she tries, she can't seem to thread the needle. Frustrated, she throws everything back in the tin. Her phone, the non-secret one, catches her eye from the side table. When she picks it up and hits the button at the bottom, she finds her screen blank.

No new messages. No calls.

Two years ago, when Michael first began traveling for work, he texted her several times a day and never ended a night without a call. After a year it was just a phone call at night, and now she gets nothing. She still remembers the day she met him, playing Frisbee on the campus greens, his hair wild, eyes bright. The Frisbee hit her as she was on her way to class, and she remembers his hand at her forehead—as if touch and concern could stop a bruise from forming. She had the uncontrollable urge to kiss him, right then, and though she refrained, she had another chance at it two days later, on their first date.

Back then she had no concept of "forever."

On an impulse, Lisa sends a text to Michael: "Thinking of you. I miss you. Wish you were here."

Imogene walks into the living room with two plates and Lisa drops the phone. "Figured the least I could do was make you breakfast."

They eat scrambled eggs and pancakes in silence, as though they both used up all their words the night before. As soon as they're finished, Imogene gets up, her eyes darting to the clock on the wall. "I should go. Got work in a few hours."

Lisa reaches out, her fingers grazing the mouth on Imogene's wrist. "Stay," she says. "I have the day off."

"I don't think that's a good idea."

"Can I at least get your number?"

The mouth on Imogene's wrist finds Lisa's index finger, lips latching onto the end. Imogene gently pulls away. "I don't think that's a good idea either."

Lisa's heart feels heavy as a stone. "Did I do something wrong?"

Imogene smiles, leans down, and kisses her. Her warm breath gusts past Lisa's cheek. "Thanks for letting me stay the night." And then, without a backward glance, she picks up her purse and goes to the door.

The click of the latch echoes across the hardwood floors, and all of Lisa's mouths feel hungry and hollow, empty as her apartment.

☼

She doesn't finish sewing up the mouth, not for the entire day and the day after. At work, the freed half nips at her blouse each time it flutters close enough. She pulls up the waistband of her pants to cover it.

When Lisa gets home, she sits on the bed and kicks off her heels, delighting in the feel of the rug beneath her sore toes. She reaches between the mattress and the box spring and removes her hidden phone.

There's a message. In an instant, her heartbeat quickens. For a moment she thinks, impossibly, that it must be Imogene, but then she reads the name. Jason.

"Sorry I haven't called," it reads. "Can I see you?"

He never promised to call; she didn't expect it of him. She texts back that he can come over now, that her husband is gone, that she's alone. As soon as she presses "send," she remembers the mouth.

Hastily, she goes to the living room, grabs the sewing kit, and starts to bind the rest of the mouth shut. She wants it to be smooth, seamless but for the soft, downy feel of thread. It's hard and painful work. She barely has time to wipe the sweat from her brow when a knock sounds.

Lisa shoves the sewing kit back beneath the couch and answers the door.

Jason stands there, still wearing his work suit, his jacket unbuttoned, his hands in his pockets. He smiles when he sees her, and his dark eyes fix on hers. "Hope I'm not bothering you."

She stands to the side to let him in. "Come in." As soon as she shuts the door he presses up against her, hands tangling in her hair, the stubble on his chin grazing her cheek.

"I've missed you," he says, but the words mean nothing.

Reaching up, she takes his hands and removes them from her hair. She wants to put his fingertips to her scarred, sewn-up mouths, to force him to acknowledge what she is, what she's done. But she just holds them in front of her, not quite able to meet his eyes.

"Lisa?"

She starts to unbutton his shirt, just to give herself time to think. With each button, she backs him up a step. He gives way, his chest heaving. Once she has him up against the couch she removes the cufflinks from his shirt and sets them on the side table, then moves to his jacket.

"If you had to break a promise," she says quickly, "what would it be?"

"Babe," he says, "if I had to make a promise, it would be to you." He reaches for her, but she sidesteps his grasp.

"And then you'd break it."

A frown mars his face, his single, only mouth. "Come on, what's the deal? Why does it matter?"

"It matters to me."

Jason closes a hand over her wrist, moves it up her arm, fingertips caressing her skin. "Let it go."

She feels the words on the tip of her tongue: *promise me*. But she lets him draw her in, lets him cover her mouth with his, lets the words drown. As his hands find their way beneath her shirt she can't help but notice—he never touches the mouths.

☼

Lisa wakes to the sound of a car pulling up to the sidewalk outside. The engine idles, never turning off, and a spike of dread worms its way into her heart. She throws the blankets off, disturbing a murmuring Jason, shrugs on her robe, and goes to the window.

The streetlamps illuminate a taxicab at the curb. The door opens and a man steps out. Michael. He reaches back inside for his suitcase. "Jason," Lisa hisses. "Jason, get up."

He moans, so she stalks back to the bed and pulls the rest of the blankets off of him.

"What the hell?" he says, his voice sleepy.

"My husband is here," she says. "He's back early."

For a moment, he says nothing, and then, *"Shit."*

The room becomes a whirlwind as he explodes out of the bed. Lisa tosses him his pants and his belt; she kneels to feel around on the rug for his socks. Jason reaches for the lamp, but she stops him. "Are you *crazy?*" she whispers. "He'll see."

He diverts the movement into pulling on his shirt, grabbing his jacket from the back of a chair. "Why'd you tell me it was okay to come over?"

"Because it *was* okay," she bites back. "Go out the fire escape. Quickly."

His shoes in hand, he darts out of the room and to the back of the apartment. Lisa has to help him lift the window; it sticks a little once it's open halfway.

A key turns in the lock.

"Go go go," Lisa says.

Jason shakes his head a little, and she knows this time he won't be calling her back. She finds she no longer cares. And then he's gone, just as Michael steps inside.

Lisa takes a deep breath, as though she's taking in the night air. "You're home early."

"It's dark in here." Michael flips on a switch. "Couldn't sleep?"

"No," she says. She leans on the top of the window to shut it. Below, in the alley, Jason is hopping as he puts on his shoes. She turns to face her husband.

He sets his rolling case on its base and pushes the handle to retract it. Just as he pivots to hang his jacket on the hook by the door, Lisa notices Jason's cufflinks on the side table. Bright silver against dark brown. Her breath catches. But then Michael looks at her and she snaps her gaze away.

"I got your text," he says. "I've been thinking about you too."

He has? A memory pops into her head—of the time Michael's mother dropped a not-so-subtle hint about his MCAT scores, about how little she thought of his current profession. And Lisa felt the blood rising to her cheeks, the pounding of her pulse in her neck as she called his mother—his *mother*—a bitchy nag. Michael worked damned hard for a living, thank you very much. He was good at it too. And if his mother couldn't recognize that, then she should keep her mouth shut.

She remembers the way Michael kissed her later that night and told her how fiercely he loved her. There are so many memories like this one; they clutter her mind.

Michael's expression hardens. "You haven't texted me in ages," he says. He marches into the living room. "What's the deal? What do you want?"

"I just wanted to tell you I was thinking of you." Imogene. The mouths.

"Bull*shit*," he spits out. "It was manipulative. You knew I was busy. You wish I was here?" He spreads his arms. "Well, I'm here. You might as well just say whatever's on your mind."

Speaking against his anger is like swimming upriver. If she shouts back, they'll fight again and then they'll stop talking and nothing will be solved. She turns her head, as if that will give her the chance to breathe. Lisa's gaze slips once again to the cufflinks. Michael doesn't seem to notice; he's too fixated on her.

What if he notices? What if he finds out?

She realizes then: it doesn't matter. She doesn't want this anymore. Doesn't want the fighting, the silences, the marriage. An itch starts between her shoulder blades. "I don't want a divorce," she blurts. The cufflinks blur in her vision as her eyes fill with tears. Her throat aches; her mouths ache.

Michael sighs, and he seems to deflate. "I don't want a divorce either." His feet scuff against the floor as he shuffles closer. He sinks into the armchair that Imogene sat in only two nights before.

"Maybe," Lisa says, her voice trembling, "maybe we can go back to the beginning. Make things right between us?"

He sags, leaning his head into his hand. "I don't know you anymore, Lisa."

"You could get to know me again." It's pointless, useless, but she tries anyway.

Michael straightens, untucks his shirt, and lifts it. A welt marks the soft flesh just below his ribs. "I love her," he says, and Lisa knows he's not referring to his wife. The words cut, even though Michael hasn't loved her for a long time. "We don't have to get divorced," he tells her. "We could just carry on as usual. Dani doesn't want to get married."

The itch sharpens. Another mouth if she gets divorced. Four of them. Carrying on as usual would be easy, simple. She could keep just the three mouths. Not perfection, but closer to it. She could live without making any more promises, without hoping for better.

The thought is smothering.

Lisa unties the belt of her robe, letting it fall to the floor. She stands in front of Michael, leans down, and takes his hand.

"Lisa," he says, his voice choked, "don't—"

She presses his hand to the stitches on her hip. The first time he touched her there, he did not pull away or hesitate. There's so much shared history between them, and too much left unsaid. "This one," she says, her voice low, "is for the promise I made to my brother, to always protect him." Michael stills at the touch, his gaze on the stitches. She guides his hand to her ribs. "This one is for the promise I made to a friend, to always listen." She lifts her foot and the ache in her mouths ease, though the ache in her throat does not. "And this one is for the promise I made to you."

✿

Her duffel bag weighs on one shoulder as she steps into the night. Michael listened as she spilled her secrets, and wept at the last mouth, the one on the bottom of her foot. He hadn't the right to tears, but then, neither had she.

Lisa doesn't need to look at the itch between her shoulder blades to know it's now a welt. She told Michael she wanted a divorce, and she meant it. The

welt will grow a pair of lips when she sends him the papers; it will grow a tongue when they finalize it. Another mouth to mar her skin, to broadcast the failure of her hopes.

As she strides down the sidewalk, the air cool against her neck, she recalls that day, nine years ago, when Michael took her hands in his, his smile a little lopsided. She could smell the sweet roses from the flower arrangements, and she remembers the cold, heavy feeling of the ring on her finger. Michael's voice trembled only a little when he spoke his vows, and he looked down at her with a surety that made her heart pound as he promised to be with her to the end. To love her forever.

She concentrates on putting one foot in front of the other. Maybe someday she'll sew this new mouth shut. But for now, she'll let it be.

Like her, it needs a chance to breathe.

Nancy Kress is the author of thirty-four books and over one hundred short stories. Her work has won six Nebulas, two Hugos, the Sturgeon, and the John W. Campbell Memorial Award. Her most recent work is Sea Change, *a stand-alone novella from Tachyon (2020) and* The Eleventh Gate, *from Baen (2020).*

MACHINE LEARNING

by Nancy Kress

Ethan slipped into the back of the conference room in Building 5 without being noticed. Fifty researchers and administrators, jammed into the room lab-coat-to-suit, all faced the projection stage. Today, of course, it would be set for maximum display. The CEO of the company was here, his six-foot-three frame looming over the crowd. Beside him, invisible to Ethan in the crush, would be tiny Anne Gonzalez, R&D chief. For five years a huge proportion of the Biological Division's resources—computational, experimental, human—had been directed toward this moment.

Anne's clear voice said, "Run."

Some people leaned slightly forward. Some bit their lips or clasped their hands. Jerry Liu rose onto the balls of his feet, like a fighter. They all had so much invested in this: time, money, hope.

The holostage brightened. The incredibly complex, three-dimensional network of structures within a nerve cell sprang into view, along with the even more complicated lines of the signaling network that connected them. Each line of those networks had taken years to identify, validate, understand. Then more time to investigate how any input to one sub-structure could change the whole. Then the testing of various inputs, each one a molecule aimed at the deadly thing near the center of the cell, the growing mass of Moser's Syndrome. All this hard work, all the partnering with pharmaceutical companies, in order to arrive at Molecule 654-a, their best chance.

So far, no one had noticed Ethan.

The algorithm for 654-a began to run, and in a moment the interaction combinations produced the output on the right side of the screen. Only two outputs were possible: "continued cell function" or "apoptosis." The apoptosis symbol glowed. A second later, in a burst of non-realistic theatrics, the cell drooped and sagged like one of Dali's clocks, and the lethal structure at its heart vanished.

Cheering erupted in the room. People hugged each other. A lab tech stood on tiptoe and kissed the surprised CEO. They had done it, identified a possible cure for the disease that attacked the bodies of children, and only children, killing half a billion kids worldwide in the last five years. They had done it with molecular computation, with worldwide partnerships with universities and Big Pharma, and with sheer grit.

Someone to Ethan's left said, "Oh!" Then someone else noticed him, and someone after that. Ethan's story was company-wide gossip. The people at the front of the room went on burbling and hugging, but a small pocket of silence grew around him, the embarrassed silence of people caught giggling at a wake. Laura Avery started toward him.

He didn't want to talk to Laura. He didn't want to spoil this important celebration. Quickly he moved through the door, down the corridor, into the elevator. Laura, following, called "Ethan!" He hit the DOOR CLOSE button before she could reach him.

In the lobby he walked rapidly out the door, heading in the rain toward his own facility. Buildings of brick and glass rose ghostly in the thick mist. MultiFuture Research was a big campus and he was soaked by the time he reached Building 18. Inside, he nodded at security and shook himself like a dog. Droplets spun off him. What the hell had he done with his umbrella? He couldn't remember, but it didn't matter. The important thing was to get back to his own work.

He didn't belong at a celebration to defeat Moser's Syndrome.

Too late, too late. Way too late.

✿

Building 18 was devoted to machine learning. Ethan's research partner, Jamie Peregoy, stood in their lab, welcoming this afternoon's test subject, Cassie McAvoy. The little girl came with her mother every Monday, Wednesday, and Friday after school. Ethan took his place at the display console.

That end of the lab was filled with desks, computers, and messy folders of printouts. The other end held child-sized equipment: a musical keyboard, a video-game console, tables and chairs, blocks, and puzzles. The back wall was painted a supposedly cheerful yellow that Ethan found garish. In the center, like a sentry in no-man's land, stood a table with coffee and cookies.

"The problem with machine learning isn't intelligence," Jamie always said to visitors. "It's *defining* intelligence. Is it intelligence to play superb chess, crunch numbers, create algorithms, carry on a conversation indistinguishable from a human gabfest? No. Turing was wrong. True intelligence requires the ability to learn for oneself, tackling new tasks you haven't done before, and that requires emotion as well as reasoning. We don't retain learning unless it's accompanied by emotion, and we learn best when emotional arousal is high. Can our Mape do that? No, she cannot."

If visitors tried to inject something here, they were out of luck. Jamie would go into full-lecture mode, discoursing on the role of the hippocampus in memory retention, on how frontal-lobe injuries taught us that too little emotion could impair decision making as deeply as too much emotion, on how arousal levels were a better predictor of learning retention than whether the learning was positive or negative. Once Jamie got going, he was as unstoppable as a star running back, which was what he resembled. Young, brilliant, and charismatic, he practically glittered with energy and enthusiasm. Ethan went through periods where he warmed himself at Jamie's inner fire, and other periods where he avoided Jamie for days at a time.

MAIP, the MultiFuture Research Artificial Intelligence Program based in the company's private cloud, could not play chess, could not feel emotion, and could only learn within defined parameters. Ethan, whose field was the analysis of how machine learning algorithms performed, believed that true AI was decades off, if ever. Did Jamie believe that? Hard to tell. When he spoke their program's name, Ethan could hear that to Jamie it *was* a name, not an acronym. He had given MAIP a female voice. "Someday," Jamie said, "she'll be smarter than we are." Ethan had not asked Jamie to define "someday."

The immediate, more modest goal was for MAIP to learn what others felt, so that MAIP could better assist their learning.

"Hello, Cassie, Mrs. McAvoy," Jamie said, with one of his blinding smiles. Cassie, a nine-year-old in overalls and a T-shirt printed with kittens, smiled back. She was a prim little girl, eager to please adults. Well-mannered, straight As, teacher's pet. "Never any trouble at home," her mother had said, with pride. Ethan guessed she was not popular with other kids. But she was a valuable research subject, because MAIP had to learn to distinguish between genuine human emotions and "social pretense"—feelings expressed because convention expected it. When Cassie said, "I like you," did she mean it?

"Ready for the minuet, Cassie?" Jamie asked.

"Yes."

"Then let's get started! Here's your magic bracelet, princess!" He slipped it onto her thin wrist. Mrs. McAvoy took a chair at the back of the lab. Cassie walked to the keyboard and began to play Bach's Minuet in G, the left-hand part of the arrangement simplified for beginners. Jamie moved behind her, where she could not see him. Ethan studied MAIP's displays.

Sensors in Cassie's bracelet measured her physiological responses: heart rate, blood pressure, respiration, skin conductance, and temperature. Tiny cameras captured her facial-muscle movement and eye saccades. The keyboard was wired to register the pressure of her fingers. When she finished the minuet, MAIP said, "That was good! But let's talk about the way you arch your hands, okay, Cassie?" Voice analyzers measured Cassie's responses: voice quality, timing, pitch. MAIP used the data to adjust the lesson: slowing down her instruction when Cassie seemed too frustrated, increasing the difficulty of what MAIP asked for when the child showed interest.

They moved on, teacher and pupil, to Bach's Polonaise in D. Cassie didn't know this piece as well. MAIP was responsive and patient, tailoring her comments to Cassie's emotional data.

It looked so effortless. But years of work had gone into this piano lesson between a machine and a not-very-talented child. They had begun with a supervised classification problem, inputting observational data to obtain an output of what a test subject was feeling. Ethan had used a full range of pattern recognition and learning algorithms. But Jamie, the specialist in affective computing, had gone far beyond that. He had built "by hand," one complicated concept at a time, approaches to learning that did not depend on simpler, more general principles like logic. Then he'd made considerable progress in the difficult problem of integrating generative and discriminative models of machine learning. Thanks to Jamie, MAIP was a hybrid, multi-agent system, incorporating symbolic and logical components with sub-symbolic neural networks, plus some new soft-computing approaches he had invented. These borrowed methods from probability theory to maximize the use of incomplete or uncertain information.

MAIP learned from each individual user. When Cassie's data showed her specific frustration level rising to a point where it interfered with her learning, MAIP slowed down her instruction. When Cassie showed interest in a direction, MAIP took the lesson there. It all looked so smooth, Ethan and Jamie's work invisible to anyone but them.

At the end of the hour, MAIP said, "Well done, Cassie!"

"Thank you."

"I hope you enjoyed the lesson."

"Yes."

"See you on Monday, then."

"Okay."

Mrs. McAvoy took Cassie's hand, exchanged a few pleasantries with Jamie, and led Cassie out the door. It closed. In the corridor, the motion-activated surveillance system turned on.

Jamie beamed at Ethan. "That went really well! Mape—"

"I don't want to come here anymore," said the image of Cassie on the surveillance screen.

"Why not?" Mrs. McAvoy said.

"It's no fun. Please, Mommy, can we never come here again?"

Silence in the lab. Finally Ethan said, "I guess we need to work more on the ontology of social pretense."

Jamie looked crushed. "Damn! I thought Cassie liked coming here! She fooled me completely!"

"More to the point, she fooled MAIP."

"All the sub-agents worked so well on yesterday's test kid!"

"There's no free lunch."

Jamie had a rare flash of anger. "Ethan—do you always have to be so negative? And so fucking *calm* about it?"

"Yes," Ethan said, and they parted in mutual snits. Ethan knew that Jamie's wouldn't last; it wasn't in his nature. There they were, yoked together, the Elpis and Cassandra of machine learning.

Or maybe just Roo and Eeyore.

The first time Ethan had heard about Moser's Syndrome, he'd been chopping wood in the back yard and listening to the news on his tablet. Chopping wood was an anachronism he enjoyed: the warming of his muscles, the satisfying clunk of axe on birch logs, the smell of fresh woodchips on the warm August air. In a corner of the tiny yard, against the whitewashed fence, chrysanthemums bloomed scarlet and gold.

"—coup in Mali that—"

Also, if he was honest with himself, he liked being out of the house while Tina was in it. His year-old marriage was not going well. The vivacity that had originally attracted Ethan, so different from his own habitual constraint, was wearing thin. For Tina, every difference of opinion was a betrayal, every divergent action a crisis. But she was pregnant and Ethan was determined to stick it out.

"—tropical storm off the coast of North Carolina, and FEMA is urging—"

Thunk! Another fall of the axe on wood, not a clean stroke. Ethan pulled the axe out of the log. Tina came out of the house, carrying a tray of ice tea. Although her belly was still flat, she proudly wore a maternity top. The tea tray held a plate of his favorite chocolate macaroons. They were both trying.

"Hey, babes," Tina said. Ethan forced a smile. He'd told her at least three times that he hated being called "babes."

He said, "The cookies look good."

She said, "I hope they are."

The radio said, "Repeat: This just in. The CDC has identified the virus causing Moser's Syndrome, even as the disease has spread to two more cities in the

Northwest. Contrary to earlier reports, the disease is transmitted by air and poses a significant threat to fetuses in the first and early second trimester of pregnancy. All pregnant women in Washington and Oregon are urged to avoid public gatherings whenever possible until more is known. The—"

Ethan's axe slipped from his hand, landing on his foot and partially severing his little toe in its leather sandal.

Tina shrieked. In his first stunned moment, he thought she'd screamed at the blood flowing from his foot. But she threw the tray at him, crying, "You took me to that soccer game last week! How *could* you! If anything happens to this baby, I'll never forgive you!" She burst into tears and ran into the house, leaving Ethan staring at the end of his foot. A chunk of toe lay disjointed from the rest, bloody pulp surrounded by chocolate macaroons. Vertigo swept over him. It passed. The newscaster began to interview a doctor about embryonic damage, nerve malformation, visible symptoms in newborns.

Ethan shifted his gaze to the axe, as if it and not a maybe-living-maybe-not molecule was the danger to his unborn child. An ordinary axe: silver blade, hardwood handle, manufacturer's name printed in small letters. Absurdly, a sentence rose in his mind from decades ago, a lecture from his first tech professor when he'd been an undergraduate: *Technology is always double-edged, and the day stone tools were invented, axe murder became possible.*

Then the pain rushed in, and he bent over and vomited. After that, he pushed the chunk of toe back in place, wrapped his shirt around it, and applied pressure.

If anything happens to this baby, I'll never forgive you! They divorced eighteen months later.

✿

Social pretense was not a problem with one of Jamie and Ethan's other research subjects, eleven-year-old Trevor Reynod. He barreled into the lab, shouting, "I'm here! Freakish! Let's go!"

"My man!" Jamie said, giving him a fist bump that Trevor practically turned into an assault.

"Jamie! And Dr. Stone Man!" That was the kid's name for Ethan. Ethan didn't object, as long as Trevor stayed well away from him. Trevor suffered from

ADHD, although most of the suffering seemed to belong to the tired-looking mother who trailed in after him. A member of some sect that didn't believe in medication, she refused to allow Trevor to be calmed down by drugs, but computer games were apparently allowed. Ethan suspected that these thrice-weekly sessions were an immense relief to her; she could turn Trevor over to someone else. Mrs. Reynod poured herself some coffee and slumped into the easy chair in the corner.

Trevor pummeled the air and danced in place, knocking over a pile of blocks. Jamie got the bracelet onto his wrist ("Your super-power ring, dude!") and settled both of them in front of a game console as carefully wired as Cassie's keyboard. Trevor's data began to flow down Ethan's display. MAIP was silent during Trevor's sessions, adjusting his game in response to his frustration or satisfaction levels but not instructing him. Trevor did not respond well to direct instruction.

The game involved piloting a futuristic one-man plane, ridiculously represented as a bullet-shaped soap bubble. Its flight simulator was state-of-the-art, similar to the one used to train USAF jet pilots, who might eventually have MAIP incorporated into their training sessions. While flying over various war-torn terrains, Trevor had to shoot down alien craft to avoid being vaporized and to dodge "falling stars" that appeared from nowhere. Jamie's role was to fire at Trevor from the ground. He almost never hit him, which allowed MAIP more control and Trevor merciless mockery.

"Ha! Missed me again!"

"You're really good, Trev."

He was. Like most attention-deficit kids, Trevor could muster enormous powers of concentration when the activity actually interested him.

They followed their plan of transitioning Trevor from the shooting game to one teaching math in the last fifteen minutes of the hour. Trevor's levels of arousal and engagement fell, but not as far as they had the previous week. This was a new version of the math game, punchier and more inventive. In effect, Trevor was beta-testing Math Monkeys, while Ethan and Jamie gained learning-algorithm data from him.

The session was a success. After Trevor left, shouting about his victory over the Math Monkeys, Jamie said, "Did you catch that? Mape tried a stutter-and-recover strategy on him! We didn't program that!"

"Not in quite that form, anyway."

"Come on, Ethan, she figured out for herself how to apply it! She learned!"

"Maybe." He would have to do the analysis first.

But Jamie danced around the lab in an exuberant imitation of Trevor. "Freakish! She did it, Dr. Stone Man! You did it! Go, Mape!"

Ethan smiled. It felt odd, as if his face were cracking.

☼

At midnight, Ethan let himself into the modeling lab in Building 6. The place was empty, even the most diehard geek having gone out on a Friday night for beer and company. "Lights on low," Ethan said. The lab complied.

He'd told himself he wasn't going to do this again. It only made everything harder. But he could not resist. This was the only place that felt meaningful to him now—or at least the only place where meaning felt natural, like air, instead of having to be manufactured moment after effortful moment.

The lab contained, in addition to its staggeringly expensive machinery, three "rooms," each with the missing fourth wall of a theater stage or a furniture showroom. The largest was an empty, white-walled box, used to project VR environments ranging from an Alpine village to the surface of the moon. The two furnished rooms represented living spaces with sofas and tables, onto which could be projected the VR programs: changing a chair from red velour to yellow brocade, setting out bottles on a table. Old stuff, but it was the starting point for the real challenge of modeling three-dimensional "reality" that could move and be moved, touch and be touched. This lab, already a huge profit-maker for MultiFuture Research, was usually the first one shown to visitors.

Some of the programs, however, were private.

Ethan slipped on a VR glove and put his password into the projector aimed at the smallest room. It sprang to life and Allyson was there, sitting on the floor, holding her stuffed Piglet. This was the Allyson he'd brought to the lab near the end of her illness, when it was clear that the doctors' pathetically inadequate measures could not help her. Four more months, they said, but it had been only two. Ethan was grateful that Allyson had gone so quickly; he'd seen children for whom Moser's Syndrome took its slower, crueler time.

Tina had not been grateful. By that point, she had barely been Tina.

Allyson had loved Winnie the Pooh. Kanga, Roo, and Eeyore had been her friends, but Piglet had been more: a talisman, an icon. Once she'd told Ethan that she "hated Christopher Robin because *his* Piglet can talk to him and mine can't."

The 3-D model of Allyson raised her head and looked up at Ethan. It was a tremendous technical achievement, that mobile action on a holographic projection. Right now, Ethan didn't care. When he'd brought Allyson here, late at night on another Friday, she'd already begun to lose weight. Her skin had gone as colorless as the sheets she lay on at home. Her hair had fallen out in patches. Ethan had known this was his last chance; the following week Allyson had gone into the hospital. When Tina found out what he'd done, she had raged at him with a ferocity excessive even for her. Although it should have been a warning.

The model of Allyson—or rather, the voice recorder in the computer—said, "Hi, Daddy."

"Hi, baby," Ethan said. And she smiled.

That was it. Ten seconds of Allyson's short life, and an enormous expenditure of bandwidth. He hadn't kept his daughter in the lab longer than that; she'd looked too tired. Ethan hoped that the biological division's molecule 654-a could cure Moser's Syndrome. But for him, there was only this.

He called up the overlay programs, one by one. Allyson's skin brightened to rosy pink. Her hair became thick and glossy again, without bare patches. Her little body grew sturdier. Her eyes opened wider. "Hi, Daddy."

"Hi, baby." He reached out with the VR glove and stroked her cheek. The sensation was there: smooth warm flesh.

Over and over he played the enhanced, miraculously mobile model. Throughout, Ethan kept his face rigid, his hands under control, his thoughts disciplined. He was not Tina. He would never let himself be Tina.

No one, not friends or colleagues, had known how to treat Ethan after Allyson, after Tina. "Call us" friends had said while Ethan awaited Allyson's diagnosis, "if anything goes wrong." And later, after Tina, "Call us if you need anything." But there is no one to call when everything goes wrong, when you need what you can never have back.

"Hi, Daddy."

"Hi, baby."

When he'd had his fill, the fix that kept him from becoming Tina, he closed the program and went home.

☼

On Monday, Laura Avery waylaid him as he walked from the parking lot to Building 18. This being October in Seattle, it was still raining, but at least Ethan had remembered his umbrella. She had one too, blue with a reproduction of a Marc Chagall painting, which seemed to him a frivolous use of great art. Laura, however, was not frivolous. Serious but not humorless, she had made important contributions during her months at MultiFuture Research, or so he'd been told. The company, like all companies, was a cauldron of gossip.

"Ethan! Wait up!"

He had no choice, unless he wanted to appear rude.

She was direct, without flirtatious games. Ordinarily he would have liked that. But this was not ordinarily, and never would be again, not for him. Laura said, "I wondered if you'd like to have dinner one night at my place. I'm a good cook, and I can do vegetarian."

"I'm not vegetarian."

"I know, but I thought I'd just show off my fabulous culinary range." She smiled whimsically.

It was an attractive smile; she was an attractive woman. When they'd first been introduced, Laura had glanced quickly at his left hand, and her smile grew warmer. He'd taken off his wedding ring the day after Tina had left him, long before she'd killed herself. Later, after someone had undoubtedly told Laura about Ethan's story, Laura had grown more circumspect. But the warmth had still been there; he hadn't needed MAIP to read her face. Now, a year after Tina's death, this invitation—had someone told Laura it was exactly one year? Was she that coldly correct?

No. She was an intelligent, appealing woman aware enough of her appeal to go directly after

someone she liked. Why she liked him was a mystery; in Ethan's opinion, there wasn't enough of him left to like. Or to accept a dinner invitation.

"Sorry. I'm busy."

She recognized the lie but hid any feeling of rejection. "Okay. Maybe another time."

"Thanks anyway."

That was it. A nothing encounter. But it left him feeling fragile, and he hated that. The only thing that had gotten him through the last year was the opposite of fragility: controlled, resolute, carefully modeled action.

After his encounter with Laura, he threw himself into work, trying to figure out why MAIP hadn't detected Cassie McAvoy's social pretense of enjoying her piano lesson. He found a few promising leads, but nothing definitive.

How far they still had to go was made clear by Jenna Carter.

Jamie was good with the children who came to the machine lab. Sometimes Ethan thought this was because Jamie, brilliant as he was, was still a child himself: enthusiastic, sloppy, saved from terminal nerdiness only by his all-American good looks. Untested, as yet, by anything harsh. Other times Ethan felt ashamed of this facile assessment; Jamie was good with kids because he liked them.

Not, however, all of them equally. While Jamie had no trouble with Trevor Reynod, he had to hide his dislike for Jenna, who wasn't even a test subject, only the babysitter for her little brother Paul.

They came in after school on Tuesday. Paul, at eight years old their youngest subject, went straight to the small table where Jamie had set out a wooden puzzle map of the United States.

"Hey, Paul," Jamie said. "How's it going?"

"Good." Paul had a thin face, a shock of red hair, and a sweet smile.

"Can I put the magic bracelet on you? Have to warn you, though, it might turn you invisible."

Paul looked uncertain for a moment, caught Jamie's grin, and laughed. "No, it won't!"

"Well, if you're sure—let's see if you can put this puzzle together. Recognize it? It's our country, all fifty states. Wow! That's a lot of states! What a challenge!"

"I can do it!"

Jenna pushed forward. "He can't do that! It's too hard! He's only in the third grade!"

"Yes, I can!" Paul picked up Maine and fitted it into the upper right corner of the wooden holder. "See?"

"That one's easy, dingleberry! Anybody can get Maine!" She turned to Jamie. "Our mother said *I* was supposed to do the puzzles today."

Paul looked up, outraged. "No, she didn't!"

"Did to!"

"Did not!" Jenna grabbed her brother by the shoulders and tried to pull him out of the chair.

"Hey! Quit it! Dr. Peregoy!"

Jamie detached Jenna's hands. "Paul, let Jenna try the puzzle. I'll let you do the flight simulator."

Paul's mouth opened and his eyebrows rose: surprise, one of the basic facial-recognition patterns. The flight simulator was a treat usually withheld until the end of each session.

Jenna cried, "No fair! I want to do the flight simulator!"

"Maybe later." Jamie slipped the sensor bracelet off Paul and onto Jenna, and pushed her gently onto the chair. "After all, *your mother* said you should do the puzzle, right?"

Jenna glared at him. "Yeah!"

"Then let's see how fast you can do it."

Jenna hunted for a place to fit Iowa. Paul ineptly piloted the transparent bubble. ("You have crashed the jet, Paul," MAIP said.) Ethan wondered what Jamie was doing. Then he got it: Jamie wanted to see if MAIP could detect the fact that Jenna was lying. Ethan studied his displays.

MAIP worked with what was, basically, a set of medical data. It didn't have the context to interpret what that data might mean. To detect social pretense—which it also couldn't do yet—its algorithms used a subject's baseline data, observed data, and contradictions among the ontologies of emotion. But MAIP hadn't "learned" Jenna, couldn't yet do cold readings without a subject's baseline data, and had neither context nor algorithms to detect lies. So it was no surprise that MAIP didn't recognize Jenna's lies.

"Well," Jamie said after the children left, "it was worth a shot."

"Not really," Ethan said.

"Mr. Negative."

"MAIP didn't even register social pretense for Jenna, no matter how much you led her into lying. We're just not there yet."

Jamie sighed. "I know."

"What you just did was no better than a polygraph, and there's a reason polygraphs aren't admissible in court. Not reliable enough."

"Yeah, yeah, you're right. But there should be some way to do this."

"We need to solve the problem of social pretense first, and with subjects that we do have baseline data for."

Jamie said, "Maybe if we…. No, that wouldn't work. And—oh, God, I just thought of another problem. Jenna clearly knew she was lying, but what if someone has convinced themselves that they feel one thing but are actually feeling something different? Like, say, a woman who convinces herself she's in love, even though all she really wants is to have babies before her biological clock stops ticking? She doesn't really feel love for some poor schlump but thinks she does, to ease her conscience about trapping him?"

Was this a glimpse into Jamie's personal life? If so, Ethan didn't want to know about it. He said, more primly than he intended, "Oh, I think most people know what they really feel."

Jamie gave him a strange look. "Really, Ethan?"

"Yes. But the point here is that MAIP didn't know."

Jamie picked up Texas and fitted it into the puzzle, his head bent over the small table, his hair falling forward over his face and hiding his expression.

☼

December, and still raining. Ethan went to the modeling lab late on a Sunday afternoon. He was alone in the building; it was almost Christmas. Water dripped from his raincoat and umbrella onto the floor. "Lights on."

"Hi, Daddy."

"Hi, baby."

Allyson smiled, and the recording ended. He clothed her in artificial health, pink cheeks, and lustrous hair, and started it again.

"Hi, Daddy."

"Hi, baby."

He stroked her cheek. Soft, so soft in his VR glove. But Allyson had not been a soft child. Not noisy and obnoxious like Trevor or Jenna, not hidden and falsely polite like Cassie. Allyson had been direct, opinionated, with a will of a diamond. She and Tina clashed constantly over what clothes Allyson would put on, what her bedtime was, whether she could cross the street alone, why she drew butterflies instead of the alphabet on her kindergarten "homework." Ethan had been the buffer between his wife and daughter. It seemed ridiculous that a five-year-old had to be buffered against, but that was the way it had been. Allyson and Tina had been too much alike, and when Tina had blamed not only Ethan but herself for exposing Allyson to Moser's Syndrome, Ethan had not seen the danger. Tina, dramatic to the end, had thrown herself under a Metro train at the Westlake Tunnel Station.

Allyson would not have grown up like that. As she matured, she would have become calmer, more controlled. Ethan was sure of it. She would have become the companion and ally that Tina had not been.

"Hi, Daddy."

"Hi, baby."

The recording stopped, but Ethan talked on. "We're having trouble with MAIP's ability to attune, Allyson."

She gazed at him from solemn eyes. Light golden brown, the color of November fields in sunshine.

"'Attune' means that two people are aware of and responsive to each other." And attunement began early, between mother and infant. Was that what had gone wrong between Allyson and Tina? He and Allyson had always been attuned to each other.

Ethan reached out both arms, one in the VR glove and one bare. Both arms passed through the model of Allyson that was made only of light. The gloved hand tingled briefly, but it still moved through the child as if she did not exist.

For a terrible second, Ethan's brain filled with thick, tarry mist, cold as liquid nitrogen. He went rigid and clamped his teeth tightly together. The mist disappeared. He was in control again.

He turned off the recording, wiped the rain droplets from the floor, and left.

✿

Zhao Tailoring didn't open until 10 a.m. on Mondays. Ethan, who'd been there at 8:30, waited in a Starbucks, slowly drinking a latte he didn't want. The *Seattle Times* lay open on the table, but he couldn't concentrate. At 9:50 he threw his paper cup in the trash, left his unread paper, and walked across the street to the tailor shop. He huddled under the roof overhang, out of the rain.

Tailoring was not part of his life. Ethan bought clothes haphazardly, getting whatever size seemed the best fit and ignoring whatever gaps might present themselves. The window of Zhao Tailoring held Christmas decorations and three mannequins. The plastic-resin woman wore a satin gown; the man, slacks and a double-breasted blazer; the child, a pair of overalls over a ruffled blouse. They looked bound for three entirely different events. The sign said ALTERATIONS * REPAIRS * NEW CLOTHES MADE. At 9:58, an Asian woman unlocked the front door.

"Ethan! What are you doing here?"

Laura Avery, under her Marc Chagall umbrella. Ethan felt his face go rigid. "Hello, Laura."

"Are you having tailoring done?" Her voice held amusement but no condescension.

"No. What are you doing here? Why aren't you at work?"

Her brows rose in surprise at his harsh tone. "I had a doctor's appointment across the street. Nothing serious. Are you having a suit made?"

"I already said I wasn't having tailoring done. Please stop asking me personal questions."

Surprise changed to hurt, her features going slack in the blue shadows under the umbrella. "Sorry, I just—"

"If I wanted to talk to you, I would."

A moment of silence. Ethan opened his mouth to apologize, to explain that he was just distracted, but before he could speak, she turned and stalked away.

"You come in, yes?" the Asian woman said.

Ethan went in.

"You want nice suit, yes? Special this week."

"No. I don't want a suit. I want...I want to buy the mannequin in the window." Incongruously, an old childish song ran through his head: *How much is that doggie in the window?*

"You want buy what?"

She didn't have much English. The person who did was late showing up for work. "You come again, twelve o'clock maybe, one—"

"No. I want to buy the mannequin…the *doll*." They had finally agreed on this word. "Now. For a hundred dollars." He had no idea what store mannequins cost.

She shook her head. "No, I cannot—"

"Two hundred dollars. Cash." He took out his wallet.

They settled on two-fifty. She stripped the overalls and blouse off the mannequin, and, to his relief, she put it in a large, opaque suit bag. Ethan watched its stiff plastic form—hairless, with a monochromatic and expressionless face—disappear into the bag. He put it in the trunk of his car, pushing from his mind every bad B-movie about murderers and wrapped-up bodies.

✧

Marilyn Mahjoub was fifteen minutes late for her first testing session. Waiting, Jamie paced, smacking a fist into his palm, dialing the energy all the way up to ten. "You know, Dr. Stone Man, we'd be so much further along with Mape if all the fucking subfields of AI research hadn't been—oh, I don't know—slogging along for sixty or seventy years without fucking *communicating* with each other?"

"Yes," Ethan said.

"It's just such a…oh, by the way, I changed some of our girl's heuristics. What I did was—are you listening to me? Hello?"

"I'm listening," Ethan said, although he wasn't, not really.

"You're not listening. Mape listens to me more than you do, don't you, Mape?"

"I'm listening," MAIP said.

"Why is she so much more *here* than you are? And why is that kid so late?"

If there was a reason, they never heard it. Marilyn Mahjoub arrived eventually, in the custody of a sullen older brother. Her clothing embodied the culture clash suggested by her name: hijab, tight jeans, and crop top. She had huge dark eyes and a slender, awkward grace. In a few years she would be beautiful.

Like Cassie McAvoy, Marilyn played the keyboard. Unlike Cassie, she was good at it. Ethan could picture her in a concert hall one day, rising to cries of "Brava!" However, she did not take well to MAIP.

"Try playing that last section slower," MAIP said in the warm, pretty voice that Jamie had given her.

She was comparing Marilyn's rendition, note by note, to the professional version in memory.

Marilyn's lip curled. "No. It shouldn't be slower."

"Let's try it just to see."

"No! I had it right!"

"You did really well," MAIP said. "Can I please hear the piece again?"

Jamie nodded briskly; MAIP was acting to lower Marilyn's frustration level by offering praise and neutrally suggesting a redo. Ethan studied the data display. Frustration level was not lowering.

"No," Marilyn said, "I won't play it again. I don't *need* to play it again. I did it right already."

"You did really well," MAIP said. "I can see that you're talented."

"Then don't tell me to do it slower!"

"Mare," said her brother, with much disgust, "*chill*."

Jamie stepped in. "What would you like to play now, Marilyn?"

Her childish pique disappeared. Lowering her head, Marilyn looked up at Jamie through her lashes and purred, "What would you like to hear?"

Christ—twelve years old! Were all young girls like this now? Allyson wouldn't have been. She would have been direct, intelligent, appealing.

Jamie, flustered (Ethan hadn't known that was possible), said, "Play…uh, what else do you…what do you want to play?"

Later, after brother and sister had left, Jamie turned on Ethan. "What's wrong with you?"

"With me?"

"You've been distracted this whole session and you made me deal with that little wildcat by myself! Did you even hear me say that I added heuristics to Mape, matching emotion with postural clues?"

"No, I…. Yes."

"Uh huh. Get with it, Ethan! We have to get this right!"

Ethan said, "Don't take your frustration with Marilyn out on me."

MAIP said, "Jamie, you seem distressed."

Startled, Ethan turned toward the computer. "MAIP has your data? Did you give your baseline readings to her?"

"No!" Jamie's irritation disappeared, replaced instantly with buoyancy; it was like a dolphin breaking the surface of gray water. "Well, I gave her some data, anyway—but I think she applied the postural heuristics and the other new stuff and… I don't know, you'll have to do the analysis, but I think she actually *learned*!"

Ethan gazed at MAIP. A pile of intricate machinery, a complex arrangement of electrons. For some reason he couldn't name, he felt a prickle of fear.

✿

It was after 10 p.m. when the last researchers left Building 6. In Building 5, the Biological Division, lights still burned. Perez and Chung clattered out together, talking excitedly. Maybe they'd had another breakthrough, or maybe they just loved their work.

Ethan knew he didn't love his work on MAIP, no more than a castaway loved his raft. Depended on it, was grateful for it, needed it. But love was nowhere anymore, unless it was here.

"Hi, Daddy."

"Hi, baby."

The mannequin from Zhao Tailoring wore one of Allyson's dresses, still hanging in her closet at Ethan's apartment. The mannequin had jointed arms and legs. Ethan carefully positioned it into a sitting position. It was a little too tall for the projection, and he had to wrap the bottom four inches of plastic with his raincoat. That was all right; when he projected Allyson onto the mannequin, it looked as if she had plopped herself down onto his coat. Maybe after playing dress-up, maybe just with five-year-old mischief. Ethan set the lights to low, put the stuffed Piglet into her arms, and added the projected overlays, one by one. Healthy skin, glossy hair, bright eyes.

"Hi, Daddy."

"Hi, baby."

Ethan's knees trembled. Slowly he knelt beside her, the coat buttons lumpy under his calves. Lightly—so lightly, the VR glove on his right hand feeling her skin but not the hard plastic below—he used his left arm to hug his daughter.

"Hi, Daddy."

"What the *fuck*?"

Lights crashed on full; illusion crashed with them. Ethan jumped up. Jamie said, "What the hell are you doing? Laura called me, she saw you go into—"

"Go away. Leave me alone."

He didn't. But Jamie's face, always so confident, turned a mottled maroon of embarrassment. "Hey, man, I'm sorry, I didn't mean to—" Then confusion and embarrassment vanished. "No, I'm not sorry! Ethan, somebody has to level with you. You can't go on like this. I know—we all know—what you've been through. As tough as it gets, yeah. But you have to.… This isn't *normal*. That model isn't Allyson. You *know* that. You have to let go, move on, accept that she's gone instead of.… This is a perversion of technology, Ethan. I'm sorry, but that's what it is. And also a perversion of Allyson's mem—"

He didn't finish the sentence. Ethan crossed the floor in a mad dash and knocked him down.

Jamie looked up at Ethan from the floor. He wasn't hurt or even winded; Ethan was no fighter and Jamie outweighed him by at least forty pounds. Ethan had merely pushed him over. Jamie got up, shook his head like a pit bull hurling away a carcass, and left without a word.

Ethan began to tremble.

His fingers shook so much that he could barely shut down the programs. He left the mannequin sitting in the middle of the floor, a lifeless hunk of plastic, and left his coat and the stuffed Piglet with it. He couldn't bear to touch any of them.

Outside, in the dark and blowing rain, there was no sign of Jamie. Ethan lurched to Building 18. He had nowhere else to go. He couldn't drive; he could barely see. The tarry mist was back in his brain, filling it, chilling him to the marrow. There had never been anyplace else to go, not for a year. It frightened him that he couldn't feel the sidewalk beneath his feet, couldn't hear the raindrops strike the ground.

In the AI lab, lights burned and the flight simulator was running. Jamie must have been working late. But Jamie wasn't here now, and if Ethan didn't do something—anything—he would die. That was how he felt—how Tina must have felt. Thinking of Tina only made him feel worse. He stumbled to the game console and squeezed himself into the small chair in front of it. His hands gripped the controls. At least he could feel them, solid under his fingers: the only solid thing in his world of black mist and tarry cold. Black mist as a train sped into Westlake Tunnel Station, as an unseen virus ate into nerve and tissue…

"You have just crashed the jet," MAIP said. "Let's try again!"

Train speeding forward at forty miles per hour… "Hi, Daddy"…keep going keep going don't give in or you'll explode you will be Tina…damn bitch how could she leave me like that not my fault Moser's Syndrome not my fault…*don't give in*….

"You have crashed the jet. But I know you can do this—let's try again!"

Over and over he crashed the jet, even as MAIP made it harder and harder for him to fail. He smashed the jet into mountains, into desert, into the sea. Again and again and again. Someone spoke to him, or didn't. There was noise again, a lot of noise, there was destruction and death as there *should* be, to classify reality, to match the ontology of everything he had lost—

And then, finally, he realized the noise was his own screaming, and he stopped.

Into the silence MAIP said, "You were very angry, Ethan. I hope you feel better now."

He gave a little gasp, first at MAIP's words and then because he wasn't alone. Jamie stood beside him with Laura Avery.

She said gently, "Are you all right?" And when Ethan didn't answer, she added, "Jamie called me. After I called him, I mean. I saw you carrying something into Building 6 and—"

Jamie interrupted. "When did you input your data into MAIP?"

Ethan said nothing. The tarry cold mist had receded. No—it had vanished. He felt limp, drained, bruised, as if he had fallen off a cliff and somehow survived. *You were very angry. I hope you feel better now.*

"You didn't, did you?" Jamie demanded. "You never gave your baseline data to MAIP! She did a cold reading on you, extrapolating from free-form observation! We didn't teach her to do that!"

"Be quiet," Laura said. "Jamie, for God's sake— *not now*."

MAIP said, "Ethan, I'm glad you feel better. You were both angry and sad before. You were sad even when you smiled."

Jamie drew a sharp, whistling breath. "Detection of social pretense! I'm sorry, Ethan, I know you're upset and I said some things I shouldn't have, but—detection of social pretense! From

cold readings! She's taken a huge step forward— she *knows* you!"

Ethan said, not to Jamie but to the complexity of machinery and electrons that was MAIP, "You don't know me. You're a non-linear statistical modeling tool."

Laura said, "But I'm not." She put a tentative hand on his arm.

Jamie said, "Mape's not, either. Not anymore. She *learned*, Ethan. She did!"

Ethan looked at the flight simulator, which flashed the total number of jets he had crashed. He looked at MAIP. He saw the mannequin, a pathetic lump of plastic that he had left in Building 6.

Ethan rose. He had to steady himself with one hand on the game console. Laura's hand on his arm felt warm through his damp shirt. He didn't, he realized, know any of them, not really: not Laura, not MAIP, not Jamie. Not himself. Especially not himself.

He would have to learn everything all over again, reassess everything, forge new algorithms. Starting with this moment, here, now, to the sound of rain on the roof of the building.

Copyright © 2015 by Nancy Kress.

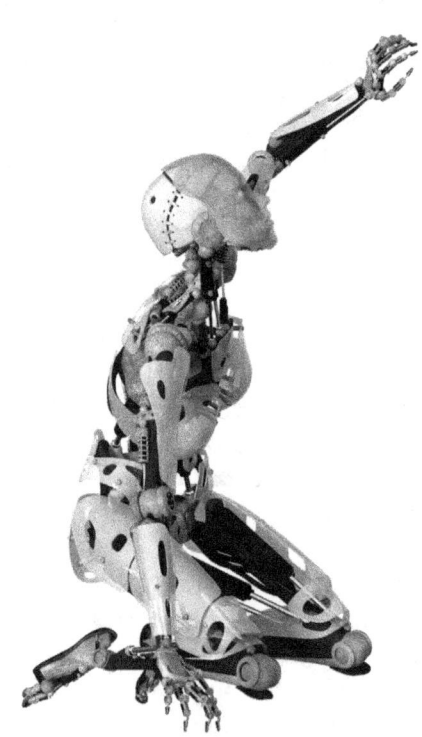

Michael Swanwick is the recipient of the Nebula, Theodore Sturgeon, and World Fantasy Awards and five Hugo Awards. His recent novel, The Iron Dragon's Mother, *completes a trilogy begun twenty-five years ago with* The Iron Dragon's Daughter. *Just out is* City Under the Stars, *co-authored with the late Gardner Dozois.*

A MIDWINTER'S TALE

by Michael Swanwick

Maybe I shouldn't tell you about that childhood Christmas Eve in the Stone House, so long ago. My memory is no longer reliable, not since I contracted the brain fever. Soon I'll be strong enough to be reposted offplanet, to some obscure star light-years beyond that plangent moon rising over your father's barn, but how much has been burned from my mind! Perhaps none of this actually happened.

Sit on my lap and I'll tell you all. Well then, my knee. No woman was ever ruined by a knee. You laugh, but it's true. Would that it were so easy!

The hell of war as it's now practiced is that its purpose is not so much to gain territory as to deplete the enemy, and thus it's always better to maim than to kill. A corpse can be bagged, burned, and forgotten, but the wounded need special care. Regrowth tanks, false skin, medical personnel, a long convalescent stay on your parents' farm. That's why they will vary their weapons, hit you with obsolete stone axes or toxins or radiation, to force your Command to stock the proper prophylaxes, specialized medicines, obscure skills. Mustard gas is excellent for that purpose, and so was the brain fever.

All those months I lay in the hospital, awash in pain, sometimes hallucinating. Dreaming of ice. When I awoke, weak and not really believing I was alive, parts of my life were gone, randomly burned from my memory. I recall standing at the very top of the iron bridge over the Izveltaya, laughing and throwing my books one by one into the river, while my best friend Fennwolf tried to coax me down. "I'll join the militia! I'll be a soldier!" I shouted hysterically. And so I did. I remember that clearly but just what led up to that preposterous instant is utterly beyond me. Nor can I remember the name of my second-eldest sister, though her face is as plain to me as yours is now. There are odd holes in my memory.

✿

That Christmas Eve is an island of stability in my sea-changing memories, as solid in my mind as the Stone House itself, that neolithic cavern in which we led such basic lives that I was never quite sure in which era of history we dwelt. Sometimes the men came in from the hunt, a larl or two pacing ahead, content and sleepy-eyed, to lean bloody spears against the walls, and it might be that we lived on Old Earth itself then. Other times, as when they brought in projectors to fill the common room with colored lights, scintillas nesting in the branches of the season's tree, and cool, harmless flames dancing atop the presents, we seemed to belong to a much later age, in some mythologized province of the future.

The house was abustle, the five families all together for this one time of the year, and outlying kin and even a few strangers staying over, so that we had to put bedding in places normally kept closed during the winter, moving furniture into attic lumber rooms, and even at that there were cots and thick bolsters set up in the blind ends of hallways. The women scurried through the passages, scattering uncles here and there, now settling one in an armchair and plumping him up like a cushion, now draping one over a table, cocking up a mustachio for effect. A pleasant time.

Coming back from a visit to the kitchens where a huge woman I did not know, with flour powdering her big-freckled arms up to the elbows, had shooed me away, I surprised Suki and Georg kissing in the nook behind the great hearth. They had their arms about each other and I stood watching them. Suki was smiling, cheeks red and round. She brushed her hair back with one hand so Georg could nuzzle her ear, turning slightly as she did so, and saw me. She gasped and they broke apart, flushed and startled.

Suki gave me a cookie, dark with molasses and a single stingy, crystalized raisin on top, while Georg sulked. Then she pushed me away, and I heard her laugh as she took Georg's hand to lead him away to some darker forest recess of the house.

Father came in, boots all muddy, to sling a brace of game birds down on the hunt cabinet. He set his unstrung bow and quiver of arrows on their pegs, then hooked an elbow atop the cabinet to accept admiration and a hot drink from mother. The larl padded by, quiet and heavy and content. I followed it around a corner, ancient ambitions of riding the beast rising up within. I could see myself, triumphant before my cousins, high atop the black carnivore. "Flip!" my father called sternly. "Leave Samson alone! He is a bold and noble creature, and I will not have you pestering him."

He had eyes in the back of his head, had my father.

Before I could grow angry, my cousins hurried by, on their way to hoist the straw men into the trees out front, and swept me up along with them. Uncle Chittagong, who looked like a lizard and had to stay in a glass tank for reasons of health, winked at me as I skirled past. From the corner of my eye I saw my second-eldest sister beside him, limned in blue fire.

Forgive me. So little of my childhood remains; vast stretches were lost in the blue icefields I wandered in my illness. My past is like a sunken continent with only mountaintops remaining unsubmerged, a scattered archipelago of events from which to guess the shape of what was lost. Those remaining fragments I treasure all the more, and must pass my hands over them periodically to reassure myself that something remains.

So where was I? Ah, yes: I was in the north bell tower, my hidey-place in those days, huddled behind Old Blind Pew, the bass of our triad of bells, crying because I had been deemed too young to light one of the yule torches. "Hallo!" cried a voice, and then, "Out here, stupid!" I ran to the window, tears forgotten in my astonishment at the sight of my brother Karl silhouetted against the yellowing sky, arms out, treading the roof gables like a tightrope walker.

"You're going to get in trouble for that!" I cried.

"Not if you don't tell!" Knowing full well how I worshiped him. "Come on down! I've emptied out one of the upper kitchen cupboards. We can crawl in from the pantry. There's a space under the door— we'll see everything!"

Karl turned and his legs tangled under him. He fell. Feet first, he slid down the roof.

I screamed. Karl caught the guttering and swung himself into an open window underneath. His sharp face rematerialized in the gloom, grinning. "Race you to the jade ibis!"

He disappeared, and then I was spinning wildly down the spiral stairs, mad to reach the goal first.

☼

It was not my fault we were caught, for I would never have giggled if Karl hadn't been tickling me to see just how long I could keep silent. I was frightened, but not Karl. He threw his head back and laughed until he cried, even as he was being hauled off by three very angry grandmothers, pleased more by his own roguery than by anything he might have seen.

I myself was led away by an indulgent Katrina, who graphically described the caning I was to receive and then contrived to lose me in the crush of bodies in the common room. I hid behind the goat tapestry until I got bored—not long!—and then Chubkin, Kosmonaut, and Pew rang, and the room emptied.

I tagged along, ignored, among the moving legs, like a marsh bird scuttling through waving grasses. Voices clangoring in the east stairway, we climbed to the highest balcony, to watch the solstice dance. I hooked hands over the crumbling balustrade and pulled myself up on tiptoe so I could look down on the procession as it left the house. For a long time nothing happened, and I remember being annoyed at how casually the adults were taking all this, standing about with drinks, not one in ten glancing away from themselves. Pheidre and Valerian (the younger children had been put to bed, complaining, an hour ago) began a game of tag, running through the adults, until they were chastened and ordered with angry shakes of their arms to be still.

Then the door below opened. The women who were witches walked solemnly out, clad in hooded terrycloth robes as if they'd just stepped from the bath. But they were so silent I was struck with fear. It seemed as if something cold had reached into the pink, giggling women I had seen preparing themselves in the kitchen and taken away some warmth or laughter from them. "Katrina!" I cried in panic, and she lifted a moon-cold face toward me. Several of the men exploded in laughter, white steam puffing from bearded mouths, and one rubbed his knuckles in my hair. My second-eldest sister drew me away from the balustrade and hissed at me that I was not to cry out to the witches, that this was important, that when I was older I would understand, and in the meantime if I did not behave myself I would be beaten. To soften her words, she offered me a sugar crystal, but I turned away stern and unappeased.

Single-file the women walked out on the rocks to the east of the house, where all was barren slate swept free of snow by the wind from the sea, and at a great distance—you could not make out their faces—doffed their robes. For a moment they stood motionless in a circle, looking at one another. Then they began the dance, each wearing nothing but a red ribbon tied about one upper thigh, the long end blowing free in the breeze.

As they danced their circular dance, the families watched, largely in silence. Sometimes there was a muffled burst of laughter as one of the younger men muttered a racy comment, but mostly they watched with great respect, even a kind of fear. The gusty sky was dark, and flocked with small clouds like purple-headed rams. It was chilly on the roof and I could not imagine how the women withstood it. They danced faster and faster, and the families grew quieter, packing the edges more tightly, until I was forced away from the railing. Cold and bored, I went downstairs, nobody turning to watch me leave, back to the main room, where a fire still smoldered in the hearth.

The room was stuffy when I'd left, and cooler now. I lay down on my stomach before the fireplace. The flagstones smelled of ashes and were gritty to the touch, staining my fingertips as I trailed them in idle little circles. The stones were cold at the edges, slowly growing warmer, and then suddenly too hot and I had to snatch my hand away. The back of the fireplace was black with soot, and I watched the fire-worms crawl over the stone heart-and-hands carved there, as the carbon caught fire and burned out. The log was all embers and would burn for hours.

Something coughed.

I turned and saw something moving in the shadows, an animal. The larl was blacker than black, a hole in the darkness, and my eyes swam to look at him. Slowly, lazily, he strode out onto the stones, stretched his back, yawned a tongue-curling yawn, and then stared at me with those great green eyes.

He spoke.

I was astonished, of course, but not in the way my father would have been. So much is inexplicable to a child!

"Merry Christmas, Flip," the creature said, in a quiet, breathy voice. I could not describe its accent; I have heard nothing quite like it before or since. There was a vast alien amusement in his glance.

"And to you," I said politely.

The larl sat down, curling his body heavily about me. If I had wanted to run, I could not have gotten past him, though that thought did not occur to me then. "There is an ancient legend, Flip, I wonder if you have heard of it, that on Christmas Eve, the beasts can speak in human tongue. Have your elders told you that?"

I shook my head.

"They are neglecting you." Such strange humor dwelt in that voice. "There is truth to some of those old legends, if only you knew how to get at it. Though perhaps not all. Some are just stories. Perhaps this is not happening now; perhaps I am not speaking to you at all?"

I shook my head. I did not understand. I said so.

"That is the difference between your kind and mine. My kind understands everything about yours, and yours knows next to nothing about mine. I would like to tell you a story, little one. Would you like that?"

"Yes," I said, for I was young and I liked stories very much.

☼

He began:

When the great ships landed—

Oh God. When—no, no, no, wait. Excuse me. I'm shaken. I just this instant had a vision. It seemed to me that it was night and I was standing at the gates of a cemetery. And suddenly the air was full of light, planes and cones of light that burst from the ground and nested twittering in the trees. Fracturing the sky. I wanted to dance for joy. But the ground crumbled underfoot and when I looked down the shadow of the gates touched my toes, a cold rectangle of profoundest black, deep as all eternity, and I was dizzy and about to fall and I, and I...

Enough! I have had this vision before, many times. It must have been something that impressed me strongly in my youth, the moist smell of newly opened earth, the chalky whitewash on the picket fence.

It must be. I do not believe in hobgoblins, ghosts, or premonitions. No, it does not bear thinking about. Foolishness! Let me get on with my story.

When the great ships landed, I was feasting on my grandfather's brains. All his descendants gathered respectfully about him, and I, as youngest, had first bite. His wisdom flowed through me, and the wisdom of his ancestors and the intimate knowledge of those animals he had eaten for food, and the spirit of valiant enemies who had been killed and then honored by being eaten, even as if they were family. I don't suppose you understand this, little one.

(I shook my head.)

People never die, you see. Only humans die. Sometimes a minor part of a Person is lost, the doings of a few decades, but the bulk of his life is preserved, if not in this body, then in another. Or sometimes a Person will dishonor himself, and his descendants will refuse to eat him. This is a great shame, and the Person will go off to die somewhere alone.

The ships descended bright as newborn suns. The People had never seen such a thing. We watched in inarticulate wonder, for we had no language then. You have seen the pictures, the baroque swirls of colored metal, the proud humans stepping down onto the land. But I was there, and I can tell you your people were ill. They stumbled down the gangplanks with the stench of radiation sickness about them. We could have destroyed them all then and there.

Your people built a village at Landfall and planted crops over the bodies of their dead. We left them alone. They did not look like good game. They were too strange and too slow and we had not yet come to savor your smell. So we went away, in baffled ignorance.

That was in early spring.

Half the survivors were dead by midwinter, some of disease but most because they did not have enough food. It was of no concern to us. But then the woman in the wilderness came to change our universe forever.

When you're older you'll be taught the woman's tale, and what desperation drove her into the wilderness. It's part of your history. But to myself, out in the mountains and winter-lean, the sight of her striding through the snows in her furs was like a vision of winter's queen herself. A gift of meat for the hungering season, life's blood for the solstice.

I first saw the woman while I was eating her mate. He had emerged from his cabin that evening as he did every sunset, gun in hand, without looking up. I had observed him over the course of five days and his behavior never varied. On that sixth nightfall I was crouched on his roof when he came out. I let him go a few steps from the door, then leapt. I felt his neck break on impact, tore open his throat to be sure, and ripped through his parka to taste his innards. There was no sport in it, but in winter we will take game whose brains we would never eat.

My mouth was full and my muzzle pleasantly, warmly moist with blood when the woman appeared. I looked up, and she was topping the rise, riding one of your incomprehensible machines, what I know now to be a snowstrider. The setting sun broke through the clouds behind her and for an instant she was embedded in glory. Her shadow stretched narrow before her and touched me, a bridge of darkness between us. We looked in one another's eyes...

✧

Magda topped the rise with a kind of grim, joyless satisfaction. I am now a hunter's woman, she thought to herself. We will always be welcome at Landfall for the meat we bring, but they will never speak civilly to me again. Good. I would choke on their sweet talk anyway. The baby stirred and without looking down she stroked him through the furs, murmuring, "Just a little longer, my brave little boo, and we'll be at our new home. Will you like that, eh?"

The sun broke through the clouds to her back, making the snow a red dazzle. Then her eyes adjusted, and she saw the black shape crouched over her lover's body. A very great distance away, her hands throttled down the snowstrider and brought it to a halt. The shallow bowl of land before her was barren, the snow about the corpse black with blood. A last curl of smoke lazily separated from the hut's chimney. The brute lifted its bloody muzzle and looked at her.

Time froze and knotted in black agony.

The larl screamed. It ran straight at her, faster than thought. Clumsily, hampered by the infant strapped to her stomach, Magda clawed the rifle from its boot behind the saddle. She shucked her mittens, fitted hands to metal that stung like hornets, flicked off the safety and brought the stock to her shoulder. The larl was halfway to her. She aimed and fired.

The larl went down. One shoulder shattered, slamming it to the side. It tumbled and rolled in the snow. "You sonofabitch!" Magda cried in triumph. But almost immediately the beast struggled to its feet, turned and fled.

The baby began to cry, outraged by the rifle's roar. Magda powered up the engine. "Hush, small warrior." A kind of madness filled her, a blind anesthetizing rage. "This won't take long." She flung her machine downhill, after the larl.

Even wounded, the creature was fast. She could barely keep up. As it entered the spare stand of trees to the far end of the meadow, Magda paused to fire again, burning a bullet by its head. The larl leaped away. From then on it varied its flight with sudden changes of direction and unexpected jogs to the side. It was a fast learner. But it could not escape Magda. She had always been a hothead, and now her blood was up. She was not about to return to her lover's gutted body with his killer still alive.

The sun set and in the darkening light she lost sight of the larl. But she was able to follow its trail by two-shadowed moonlight, the deep, purple footprints, the darker spatter of blood it left, drop by drop, in the snow.

✿

It was the solstice, and the moons were full—a holy time. I felt it even as I fled the woman through the wilderness. The moons were bright on the snow. I felt the dread of being hunted descend on me, and in my inarticulate way I felt blessed.

But I also felt a great fear for my kind. We had dismissed the humans as incomprehensible, not very interesting creatures, slow-moving, bad-smelling, and dull-witted. Now, pursued by this madwoman on her fast machine brandishing a weapon that killed from afar, I felt all natural order betrayed. She was a goddess of the hunt, and I was her prey.

The People had to be told.

I gained distance from her, but I knew the woman would catch up. She was a hunter, and a hunter never abandons wounded prey. One way or another she would have me.

In the winter all who are injured or too old must offer themselves to the community. The sacrifice rock was not far, by a hill riddled from time beyond memory with our burrows. My knowledge must be shared: The humans were dangerous.

They would make good prey.

I reached my goal when the moons were highest. The flat rock was bare of snow when I ran limping in. Awakened by the scent of my blood, several People emerged from their dens. I lay myself down on the sacrifice rock. A grandmother of the People came forward, licked my wound, tasting, considering. Then she nudged me away with her forehead. The wound would heal, she thought, and winter was young; my flesh was not yet needed.

But I stayed. Again she nudged me away. I refused to go. She whined in puzzlement. I licked the rock.

That was understood. Two of the People came forward and placed their weight on me. A third lifted a paw. He shattered my skull, and they ate.

✿

Magda watched through power binoculars from atop a nearby ridge. She saw everything. The rock swarmed with lean black horrors. It would be dangerous to go down among them, so she waited and watched the puzzling tableau below. The larl had wanted to die, she'd swear it, and now the beasts came forward daintily, almost ritualistically, to taste, the young first and then the old. She raised her rifle, thinking to exterminate a few of the brutes from afar.

A curious thing happened then. All the larls that had eaten of her prey's brain leaped away, scattering. Those that had not eaten waited, easy targets, not understanding. Then another dipped to lap up a fragment of brain, and looked up with sudden comprehension. Fear touched her.

The hunter had spoken often of the larls, had said that they were so elusive he sometimes thought them intelligent. "Come spring, when I can afford to waste ammunition on carnivores, I look forward to harvesting a few of these beauties," he'd said. He was the colony's xenobiologist, and he loved the animals he killed, treasured them even as he smoked their flesh, tanned their hides, and drew detailed pictures of their internal organs. Magda had always scoffed at his theory that larls gained insight into the habits of their prey by eating their brains, even though he'd spent much time observing the animals minutely from afar, gathering evidence. Now she wondered if he was right.

Her baby whimpered, and she slid a hand inside her furs to give him a breast. Suddenly the night seemed cold and dangerous, and she thought: What am I doing here? Sanity returned to her all at once, her anger collapsing to nothing, like an ice tower shattering in the wind. Below, sleek black shapes sped toward her, across the snow. They changed direction every few leaps, running evasive patterns to avoid her fire.

"Hang on, kid," she muttered, and turned her strider around. She opened up the throttle.

Magda kept to the open as much as she could, the creatures following her from a distance. Twice she stopped abruptly and turned her rifle on her pursuers. Instantly they disappeared in puffs of snow, crouching belly-down but not stopping, burrowing toward her under the surface. In the eerie night silence, she could hear the whispering sound of the brutes tunneling. She fled.

Some frantic timeless period later—the sky had still not lightened in the east—Magda was leaping a frozen stream when the strider's left ski struck a rock. The machine was knocked glancingly upward, cybernetics screaming as they fought to regain balance. With a sickening crunch, the strider slammed to earth, one ski twisted and bent. It would take extensive work before the strider could move again.

Magda dismounted. She opened her robe and looked down on her child. He smiled up at her and made a gurgling noise.

Something went dead in her.

A fool. I've been a criminal fool, she thought. Magda was a proud woman who had always refused to regret, even privately, anything she had done. Now she regretted everything: Her anger, the hunter, her entire life, all that had brought her to this point, the cumulative madness that threatened to kill her child.

A larl topped the ridge.

Magda raised her rifle, and it ducked down. She began walking downslope, parallel to the stream. The snow was knee deep and she had to walk carefully not to slip and fall. Small pellets of snow rolled down ahead of her, and were overtaken by other pellets. She strode ahead, pushing up a wake.

The hunter's cabin was not many miles distant; if she could reach it, they would live. But a mile was a long way in winter. She could hear the larls calling to each other, soft cough-like noises, to either side of the ravine. They were following the sound of her passage through the snow. Well, let them. She still had the rifle, and if it had few bullets left, they didn't know that. They were only animals.

This high in the mountains the trees were sparse. Magda descended a good quarter-mile before the ravine choked with scrub and she had to climb up and out or risk being ambushed. Which way? She wondered. She heard three coughs to her right, and climbed the left slope, alert and wary.

✿

We herded her. Through the long night we gave her fleeting glimpses of our bodies whenever she started to turn in a direction she must not go, and let her pass unmolested the other way. We let her see us dig into the distant snow and wait motionless, undetectable. We filled the woods with our shadows. Slowly, slowly, we turned her around. She struggled to return to the cabin, but she could not. In what haze of fear and despair she walked! We could smell it. Sometimes her baby cried, and she hushed the milky-scented creature in a voice gone flat with futility. The night deepened as the moons sank in the sky. We forced the woman back up into the mountains. Toward the end, her legs failed her several times; she lacked our strength and stamina. But her patience and guile were every bit our match. Once we approached her still form, and she killed two of us before the rest could retreat. How we loved her! We paced her, confident that sooner or later she'd drop.

It was at night's darkest hour that the woman was forced back to the burrowed hillside, the sacred place of the People where stood the sacrifice rock. She topped the same rise for the second time that night, and saw it. For a moment she stood helpless, and then she burst into tears.

We waited, for this was the holiest moment of the hunt, the point when the prey recognizes and accepts her destiny. After a time, the woman's sobs ceased. She raised her head and straightened her back.

Slowly, steadily she walked downhill.

✿

She knew what to do.

Larls retreated into their burrows at the sight of her, gleaming eyes dissolving into darkness. Magda ignored them. Numb and aching, weary to death, she walked to the sacrifice rock. It had to be this way.

Magda opened her coat, unstrapped her baby. She wrapped him deep in the furs and laid the bundle down to one side of the rock. Dizzily, she opened the bundle to kiss the top of his sweet head, and he made an angry sound. "Good for you, kid," she said hoarsely. "Keep that attitude." She was so tired.

She took off her sweaters, her vest, her blouse. The raw cold nipped at her flesh with teeth of ice. She stretched slightly, body aching with motion. God it felt good. She laid down the rifle. She knelt.

The rock was black with dried blood. She lay down flat, as she had earlier seen her larl do. The stone was cold, so cold it almost blanked out the pain. Her pursuers waited nearby, curious to see what she was doing; she could hear the soft panting noise of their breathing. One padded noiselessly to her side. She could smell the brute. It whined questioningly.

She licked the rock.

✿

Once it was understood what the woman wanted, her sacrifice went quickly. I raised a paw, smashed her skull. Again I was youngest. Innocent, I bent to taste.

The neighbors were gathering, hammering at the door, climbing over one another to peer through the windows, making the walls bulge and breathe with their eagerness. I grunted and bellowed, and the clash of silver and clink of plates next door grew louder. Like peasant animals, my husband's people tried to drown out the sound of my pain with toasts and drunken jokes.

Through the window I saw Tevin-the-Fool's bone-white skin gaunt on his skull, and behind him a slice of face—sharp nose, white cheeks—like a mask. The doors and walls pulsed with the weight of those outside. In the next room children fought and wrestled, and elders pulled at their long white beards, staring anxiously at the closed door.

The midwife shook her head, red lines running from the corners of her mouth down either side of her stern chin. Her eye sockets were shadowy pools of dust. "Now push!" she cried. "Don't be a lazy sow!"

I groaned and arched my back. I shoved my head back and it grew smaller, eaten up by the pillows. The bedframe skewed as one leg slowly buckled under it. My husband glanced over his shoulder at me, an angry look, his fingers knotted behind his back.

All of Landfall shouted and hovered on the walls.

"Here it comes!" shrieked the midwife. She reached down to my bloody crotch, and eased out a tiny head, purple and angry, like a goblin.

And then all the walls glowed red and green and sprouted large flowers. The door turned orange and burst open, and the neighbors and crew flooded in. The ceiling billowed up, and aerialists tumbled through the rafters. A boy who had been hiding beneath the bed flew up laughing to where the ancient sky and stars shone through the roof.

They held up the child, bloody on a platter.

✿

Here the larl touched me for the first time, that heavy black paw like velvet on my knee, talons sheathed. "Can you understand?" he asked. "What it meant to me? All that, the first birth of human young on this planet, I experienced in an instant. I felt it with full human comprehension. I understood the personal tragedy and the community triumph, and the meaning of the lives and culture behind it. A second before, I lived as an animal, with an animal's simple thoughts and hopes. Then I ate of your ancestor. I was lifted all in an instant halfway to godhood.

"As the woman had intended. She had died with her child's birth foremost in her mind, in order that we might share in it. She gave us that. She gave us more. She gave us *language*. We were wise animals before we ate her brain, and we were People afterward. We owed her so much. And we knew what she wanted from us." The larl stroked my cheek with his great, velvety paw, the ivory claws sheathed but quivering slightly, as if about to awake.

I hardly dared breathe.

"That morning I entered Landfall, carrying the baby's sling in my mouth. It slept through most of the journey. At dawn I passed through the empty street as silently as I knew how. I came to the first captain's house. I heard the murmur of voices within, the entire village assembled for worship. I tapped the door with one paw. There was sudden, astonished silence. Then slowly, fearfully, the door opened."

✿

The larl was silent for a moment. "That was the beginning of the association of People with humans. We were welcomed into your homes, and we helped with the hunting. It was a fair trade. Our food saved many lives that first winter. No one needed know how the woman had perished, or how well we understood your kind.

"That child, Flip, was your ancestor. Every few generations we take one of your family out hunting, and taste his brains, to maintain our closeness with your line. If you are a good boy and grow up to be as bold and honest, as intelligent and noble a man as your father, then perhaps it will be you we eat."

The larl presented his blunt muzzle to me in what might have been meant as a friendly smile. Perhaps not; the expression hangs unreadable, ambiguous in my mind even now. Then he stood and padded away into the friendly dark shadows of the Stone House.

I was sitting staring into the coals a few minutes later when my second-eldest sister—her face a featureless blaze of light, like an angel's—came into the room and saw me. She held out a hand, saying, "Come on, Flip, you're missing everything." And I went with her.

✿

Did any of this actually happen? Sometimes I wonder. But it's growing late, and your parents are away. My room is small but snug, my bed warm but empty. We can burrow deep in the blankets and scare away the cave-bears by playing the oldest winter games there are.

You're blushing! Don't tug away your hand. I'll be gone soon to some distant world to fight in a war for people who are as unknown to you as they are to me. Soldiers grow old slowly, you know. We're shipped frozen between the stars. When you are old and plump and happily surrounded by grandchildren, I'll still be young, and thinking of you. You'll remember me then, and our thoughts will touch in the void. Will you have nothing to regret? Is that really what you want?

Come, don't be shy. Let's put the past aside and get on with our lives. That's better. Blow the candle out, love, and there's an end to my tale.

All this happened long ago, on a planet whose name has been burned from my memory.

Copyright © 1988 by Michael Swanwick; first appeared in Asimov's Science Fiction.

Scott lives with his husband, Mark, in Sacramento. He started reading sci-fi at nine, and as he grew up, he wondered where all the queer characters were. Eventually he decided to write them himself. A Rainbow Award–winning author with thirty-five publications, he runs QueerSciFi.com and is an associate member of SFWA.

LAMPLIGHTER

by J. Scott Coatsworth

Panting heavily, back against a whitewashed wall, Fen prayed for the shaking to end. He mumbled one of the Guild Cantos:

> *We are keepers of light*
> *In the river of night*
> *when the black tides of darkness advance.*

Then he ran as if Davien the Betrayer were after him. Behind him, walls that had stood since long before he was born crashed to dust, and the smell of char and the metallic tang of blood hung heavily in the morning air. Clouds of smoke and dust blotted out the spindle above, blocking its golden light, and Disembodied voices screamed around him. He needed something to light the way....

Fen Theora'son woke with a start, sweat-drenched, alone. He looked around—his narrow bedroom was empty, with only the whispering of the wind through the open window. He ran his fingers through his black, sweat-drenched hair, unsettled. *Just a dream.*

Why not believe in the world-mind too, while I'm at it? Fen snorted. His mother had spun tales of the creature that made the winds blow and the light of the spindle shine and the rain fall inside this pebble of a world, but he'd always taken it for a fairy tale.

Another of her old stories sparked in his head. The one about liminals, who in his mother's telling were half human and half something else, people who did magical things, like talking mind to mind or communing with the world by touch. Who dreamed strange dreams that often came true.

I'm letting the quiet and the darkness get to me. He laid back and closed his eyes, pulling his blanket up over his lanky form, but the easy rhythms of sleep were lost to him. The hard-straw pallet that was the journeyman lamplighter's only bed for his first year was worn down and flat, but at least he had a bed frame now. And his own small room.

There'd been no new straw for weeks to stuff the mattress with. The scent of Lewin's amber skin was gone too, worn out of the sheets like an old half-forgotten song. Anger creased red at the edges of his mind, but he thrust it away. *I won't let him do this to me.* Slowly it receded.

Sleep eluded him, dream fragments and unwelcome memories and overheard rumors chasing one another in his head like a pack of street dogs. So many rumors, filling the city like worms in a rotten apple.

As the earth shook and the Enders—a wool-headed pack of idiots who claimed knowledge from the world-mind—proclaimed the apocalypse, his own world had shrunk down to almost nothing. Buffoons like Luz Tamars'son, Fen's cousin, who'd follow a sheep to slaughter without thought.

Would the gates still be closed when the spindle lit up the inside of Forever with its golden morning light? The council sat behind closed doors, seeing no one, only sending out pages. Outside Thyre's walls, food was rotting in the fields as farmers were locked out.

Fen's stomach grumbled. Perhaps his vivid dreams were the sign of an upset stomach, fed too little from stores that were stale and old.

Dreams of a morning with no light, of falling walls and unearthly screams. And a room so full of light it hurt his eyes.

Would there be war? It was a word unused since the Chaos Years.

I just want to sleep.

He closed his eyes and drifted off into a troubled rest.

✧

Fen blew out the little candle on the windowsill and looked out at the city. The walls of the world curved up and around to meet over his head, extending north and south like a giant version of the pipes which carried water throughout the buildings of the guild.

The outer walls of the city followed the arc of the world to meet somewhere overhead, forming two tall rings with the quarters of the city carving out smaller rings of their own inside. High above Fen's head, the place where they met was hidden by the faint silver night light of the spindle that ran above him from one horizon to the other.

As he watched, the spindle flared into glorious life, a golden wave of morning illumination riding it past Thyre and on toward Darlith and Micavery, brightening the inside of world.

Morning light crossed Thyre in little steps too as pollen began to glow and the few plants shone with their own morning light. The very air around him shimmered. Night gave way to the golden glow of daylight that leapt over the far wall of the city and crossed into the plains and forests beyond, the trees and grasses beginning to glow.

Guild apprentices were out already, extinguishing the lamps on each street. Lights from windows set in high, white-washed walls blinked out one by one, as did the occasional light on the back of a wagon that passed by below.

Fen pulled on his tunic and breeches and washed his face in the mallowwood basin in one corner of the tiny room. He sat at his tiny wooden desk, where long sheets of parchment, curled at the ends, held the month's ledgers for Master Harmon's accounts. He'd spent hours the evening before calculating the dues owed by the various city merchants to the guild account.

Everyone wanted light at night to fend off the fear in the air, so the numbers were inordinately high, but the prospects of collecting it seemed dubious with counselors and commoners alike shuttered behind locked doors. But that was an apprentice's problem, not a journeyman's. *Why do we even bother to light so many empty streets?*

The need for light is reason enough. The guild maxim came without thought.

Why did I ever want to be a lamplighter? The seven guilds of Thyre were the main source of coin for Thyrian youth. Unless someone's family was wealthy, or their parents were shopkeepers or farmers, one ended up in a guild or the guard.

Fen sighed. He dipped pen to ink and got to work.

A while later, a knock at the door startled him. He was glad he'd set the pen down, or he'd have ruined one of the ledger pages. Master Harmon would skin him alive for the loss, journeyman or no. "Who is it?" Annoyance colored his tone.

The door swung open.

"Alissa…" Half exasperated, his lips quirked in amusement. She didn't respect personal boundaries very well, but he'd gotten used to it.

"At least I knocked, this time." The apprentice grinned, ignoring his annoyance. Like many in the guild, Alissa said she'd been drawn to service by a need to belong to *something* in these strange times. Why would someone whose father was a city councilor *need* to do anything? She'd never said, and he'd never asked. His own father was a master leatherworker who'd raised his family on a minor landholder's farm outside the city walls. Fen hadn't talked to them for years.

"Up carousing with the boys?" Alissa grinned.

"Not last night," His own smile felt pained.

"Too bad. Might have done your sour mood some good."

"As if *you'd* know." His wasn't the only lonely bed. There were few secrets in the packed dormitory of the Guild House. "You didn't come here just to tease me."

She shook her head. "Not *just* for that. Master Harmon sent me to check on your accounting. He's got a task for us to perform, if you're done. A *great privilege.*" She eyed his untidy stack of papers.

"I'm done, for now." He shuffled them into some semblance of organization. No lowly apprentice was going to call him on the carpet. Especially not *this one.* "What did Harmon want?"

She grinned, a look of pure mischief, and he knew he was in trouble. "Better bring your wetboots."

✧

As Fen sloshed through sewer water up to his knees, he tried to concentrate on the *great privilege* he'd been given. The sewer tunnel was filled with the terrible stench of human waste—he was thankful their small lamps didn't cast too much light. Beneath the streets of Thyre, the Underground was a maze of tunnels and sewer lines that even the most experienced journeyman knew little about.

Few outside the Sanitation Guild did, and he was happy to leave it to them.

This was his first time in the realm that few in the city even knew existed. The Lamplighter's Guild kept barrels of luthiel down here in locked store-rooms. Who knew how much there was, and what else was hidden down here?

"You get used to the smell, eventually, they tell me." At least he hadn't been able to see any of the things in the water that brushed against his wet boots, the soles of which squished for the first couple steps out of the water.

"Pay attention to the map, journeyboy. I don't want to get lost." Alissa's eyes were wide as she looked at the dark walls.

Fen shivered at the thought. If you were still here when your light ran out, you might never find your way back to the surface.

They came to the last crossing on the hastily scribbled map. Water flowed along the right-hand tunnel while the left-hand one sloped up in rela-tive dryness. They left the underground river behind, climbing up the passageway until it dead-ended in a flat white wall. Or at least he supposed it must have been white at one time; now it was covered with a thin layer of moss or algae, which gave off a faint greenish glow outside the lanterns' pale light.

"This is the place." He scraped away the muck along the right side of the wall to reveal a recess with a se-ries of metal handles. He pulled them up and down in the sequence Master Harmon had given him.

Nothing happened.

With a sigh, he reset them and tried again. Still nothing.

"Let me try."

With a sigh, he handed Alissa the paper. She flicked the levers, and this time, the wall slid aside with a loud grinding protest.

Fen frowned.

"That one was a six, not an eight. Master Harmon has sloppy handwriting."

Fen snorted. "I'll tell him you think so." He squeezed through the doorway, concerned that it might slam shut on him, and found himself in a room filled with hundreds of sealed wooden barrels. He whistled…so much luthiel. One barrel would

light half the streetlamps in the city—this room rep-resented a stockpile almost beyond imagining.

Why had Master Harmon sent him for this? Fen was still a journeyman. If he wanted, he could steal them and put a large dent in the guild's monopoly, if not ruin it altogether. He wouldn't, but why would Harmon take that chance?

Alissa stared at the vast store of barrels. "Why us?"

"I don't know, 'Liss."

"I didn't know the guild even had this much luthiel." She shook her head. "Father would be apoplectic."

Fen managed a smile. "Their claim of a limited supply would fall apart—they'd have to lower prices." How many other storerooms like this were there? *Too many secrets.*

Alissa's expression hardened. "The guild should light the streets for free at a time like this."

You're not wrong. He was a journeyman, though. Such decisions were above his paygrade. "Come on. Let's get what we came for and get out of here." Time enough to think things over later.

She nodded, but she wasn't satisfied. They'd known each other too long—it was gnawing at her.

Between them, they lifted one of the heavy barrels, turning it on its side, and rolled it out of the vault. He closed the door behind them, and they set off for the surface. "You can't tell anyone about this."

Alissa bit her lip. "Father should know."

He stopped the barrel and held up his lantern to look her in the eye. "You took an oath to the guild. You could get both of us kicked out. Promise me you won't say anything, at least until we have a chance to think this over."

"It's not right—"

"I know. Promise?"

At last she nodded. "Promise."

"Good. Come on, let's get this to the surface. I want to wash off the stench of this place before it becomes permanent."

✧

Something to light the way.

A loud thump outside Fen's door disturbed his sleep, bringing him out of his recurring dream. He brushed it aside, looking around blearily.

His bed was empty, and he felt cold and alone. *I need to see Lewin.*

He got up and pulled on his clothes. He scribbled out a hasty note on one of the precious sheets of parchment he'd saved from his accounting work and folded it neatly, sealing it with a dab of melted wax. Then he crept to the door. It opened softly for once, the wood drier than the desert sand. Even the weather had been odd lately.

Fen slipped out of his room and down the hall, past the other journeymen dorms. All the doors were closed, and only Caswin's had light glimmering under the crack. At the end of the hall, he eased the outer door open just far enough to squeeze out into the central courtyard.

The white fountain at its heart, with its stature of Andrissa Hammond holding aloft a luthiel lantern, trickled quietly in the night. Everything was serene, quiet, normal.

Softly he closed the door behind him and made his way along the inner wall around the courtyard, quiet as a cat. The fountain's flickering lamplight cast slivers of gold light across the open space.

Fen reached the gate that led out into the city, hoping it would be unguarded. When Ersa was on duty, she often slept through the middle part of her shift.

No such luck. He was met at the gate by Archer Tamars'son, who poked his head out of the guard's kiosk at his approach. "Bit late for a stroll, isn't it?" It was well past guild curfew, for journeymen and apprentices alike.

"Sorry, Arch, but I *have* to go out."

"You know the rules, Fen…."

"And I *have* to break them, Arch. It's important… come on, I'll be back well before light."

Archer stared at him. The man had come with Fen and Kerrith on several hunts into the steppe. They respected each other, and Fen had a good reputation in the guild.

"Please, Archer."

The guard sighed and opened the gate. "Go. Be back before shift change. It'll be on *my* head if you're late."

Fen nodded. "Thanks, Arch, I owe you." He slipped out into the cobblestoned city streets. It was quiet, everyone in the city waiting for *something*. Echoes of his dreams haunted him. The shakes had diminished to an occasional background noise, a rumble or groan issuing from the ground beneath his feet. *Not much of an improvement.*

He crossed through the rings that defined the districts of Thyre, making his way from the guild quarters near the desert wall through the normally bustling lower rings. Even there he found silence—a few taverns were open, but most of the patrons looked more lost than drunk. Still, he'd left his pouch behind; this was not a place to wander at night with a sack full of coin.

His fever-dreams had convinced him—he had to talk to Lewin. If things were over between them, let them be over, but he had to know for sure.

At last he reached the alleyway behind the Masons' Guildhouse. Sure no one was watching, Fen slipped into the narrow alley between buildings. The walls were uncomfortably close, and he imagined them crashing down to crush him. He pushed the disturbing image out of his head.

Softly glowing vines grew thickly here, vines that the Lamplighter's Guild would have seen torn down long ago had they not belonged to another guild. Each guild was sovereign, and occasionally they thumbed their noses at one another. Fen snorted. *Like overgrown children.*

Handy for him though. Finding the right spot, he placed the letter between his teeth and took hold of one of the thick ropes, levering himself up the wall.

He froze as noises spilled from an open window above. Someone was violating curfew, in the most carnal way possible. Fen grinned.

The sounds continued unabated, and after a moment, so did he.

Lewin's room was on the second floor, a journeyman's like his. There was no light coming from the window, but the shutters were open. Taking a deep breath, Fen let go of the vine with one hand to swing around the gaping shutters to grasp the windowsill. A flick of his wrist, and the sealed letter sailed into the room.

He didn't wait to see where it landed. With haste, he scurried down the wall, making more noise than he had on the way up. His hand slipped, and he fell the remaining few feet, scraping his hands on the way down and landing on the cobblestone alley hard enough to knock the breath out of him.

He gasped softly until the air returned to his lungs, then wiped the blood on his breeches, cursing the likely stain it would leave. He had no time to waste, and it wasn't safe to linger there. He scrambled down the alley, disappearing into the darkness of the street just as someone popped their head out of a lighted window above.

✧

Back in his own bed, dreams swarmed through his head—images of dark, wet passageways that twisted like snakes beneath the city, full of glowing venom. Fen was lost in their darkness, calling out Lewin's name…

Something awakened him again, bringing him out of yet another apocalyptic dream where the ground shook itself into powder and a woman's screams filled the air. He sat up in the pale light of the spindle's night glow and glanced around the room, looking for the source of the noise that had brought him out of his slumber. It had to be near daylight.

He pulled himself up with a hand on his mattress and winced—his hands were sore from the fall.

A pebble clattered across the floor near the window, skittering to rest beside his cot. *Lewin.*

He nearly leapt out of bed, scrambling toward the window. But just short of that gaping portal, he stopped. He ran a hurried hand through his hair, wincing again. *He came. That has to mean something.* He took a deep breath, and then looked out onto the street below. "Lewin?"

Lewin grinned, his teeth white even in the darkness. "Let me up, Fen."

Like *Rapunzel.* Fen pulled a knotted rope from beneath the mattress, playing it out down the wall.

Lewin was athletic and had used the rope countless times before. Soon he was climbing through the window into the room to give Fen a bear hug. "You took quite a chance, coming up to my room tonight." Lewin's voice was low as he searched Fen's face. "Someone else might have that room by now, and might have read your…sentiments."

Fen blushed. "I'm sorry. I just needed to talk." He sank down onto his mattress, back against the wall. "It's been so long…." He leaned over to light one of the smaller luthiel candles on the floor

beside the bed. It cast a golden, flickering light across the room.

It was Lewin's turn to blush. He sat down on the bed heavily next to Fen. "Yes, it has. I've meant to come. To *talk.*"

Fen was keenly aware of the small distance between them, of the shape of Lewin's unshaven jaw, of his scent. He wanted to reach out, to touch that face. Instead, he kept his hands resolutely at his side. "You're here now."

Lewin nodded. "Your letter…well, I had to come. This hasn't been easy for me either." He reached up to stroke Fen's cheek gently with the back of his hand, and Fen shivered.

"Is it over between us?" *Don't let yourself feel anything.*

Lewin pulled his hand back as if he'd been stung. He stood and moved to the darkened window to stare silently out at the city.

Fen's internal alarm blared at him. *Something's wrong.*

Lewin's head dropped, and his voice was so low, Fen almost didn't hear it. "There's a woman, Fen. I know—I don't want it, but she's a good match. My family wants me to—"

Fen went stand next to Lewin. He stared out the window at the darkness beyond. It was still dark out. Something was very wrong.

Lewin looked at him, eyes narrowed. "Fen, I'm so sorry—"

Fen shook his head in annoyance, barely hearing the words. "Not now, Lew. Listen."

As if in response, the Dawn Tower pealed out its *first light* chimes. They sounded ominous in the unnatural darkness. The sense of wrong vibrated inside him like a plucked string.

"Lew, where's the morning glow?" Panic rose in his gut, but he shoved it down again. "It's first light— why is it still dark outside?"

Above, the spindle's silver night-glow was fading, leaving the city in near-total darkness. Lewin stared at him, lit only by the lone candle in the tiny room.

That's when the wailing began. Disembodied voices screaming and crying out in the darkness outside his window. *It's my dream.* Fen cursed himself for being right. *But how?*

"What in the blazes?" Lewin stared at him.

The door flew open.

Fen gaped, realizing Lewin was still in his room. Like that really mattered right now.

Luckily it was only Alissa. She gave Lewin a cursory glance before blurting out her news. "Fen, the masters are sending everyone out to light all the lamps. There's no daylight!"

Fen nodded. "Lewin is—"

Alissa's smile was grim. "Doesn't matter. Bring him. We can use every hand we've got."

☼

Fen refilled the lantern with luthiel, enough golden liquid filling the small basin to last for at least a day. The golden substance glowed on its own, like the trees and shrubs of the world.

The rumors were flying fast and thick. It was the end of the world. Or the mythical world-mind had re-awoken and was seeking its revenge. Or Davien the Betrayer had returned to rule them all.

Fen didn't know what to believe, so he stuck to his job. He checked the lamp's mantle—it was still in good condition, but if they had to burn the lanterns night and day, they would deteriorate twice as fast. Satisfied, he sparked the lamp, and a comforting golden glow lit up the world around him. It gave off light but no heat.

From his high perch, he looked down the long, winding Merchant's Way—they had a long distance to go yet before they were done for the morning. *More like perpetual night.* He shoved that unhelpful thought aside.

The guild had instructed them to light every other lamp, claiming a shortage of luthiel. People needed light, especially right now when darkness threatened to consume them all. *Greedy bastards.* There was more than enough luthiel hidden away in the sewers.

Along Tassian Way, the next street over, another team was lighting lamps too, a scene repeated across the city. Even the apprentices like Alissa had been pressed into lighting service for the first time. In the distance there was a deep rumbling sound. The shakes were coming more constantly now.

Fen clambered down the pole, his feet finding the stepping bars by instinct. Lew met him at the bottom and filled his pouch with luthiel for the next lamp. "Thanks, Lew."

Across the street, another one lit up, and Alissa waved at them as she descended. "This is a lot of work."

Lewin laughed. "You're telling me."

Fen gave him the side-eye. "You're just carrying the supplies. Try going up and down a lamp pole a few hundred times!"

Lewin laughed, and so did Fen, a welcome release in the tense dark morning.

There were few passers-by in the darkness—most people were staying inside, frightened of the darkness.

They proceeded down the lane, taking turns with the lamps, all the way to the Open Market. The one place that had never needed, nor wanted, the lamplighter's guild's lights before today. The Open Market was a wide plaza in the center of the lowest ring of the city. Merchants from the cities around Forever came here to hawk their wares, and there was always abundant light from the sky above to illuminate their dealings with one another. But not this morning.

The market was desolate today, empty of the colors and smells that usually pervaded it. The vendors had vanished, one by one, over the last few days, and now the space was vast, empty and dark. That, more than anything, rattled Fen.

Alissa looked across the plaza. "Dismal, isn't it? Father says the merchants are afraid to come to market now. No one's buying, and there have been too many thefts."

Fen nodded. There was a darkness in his soul that seemed well-matched to the darkness outside. It was getting colder too, a bitter chill he'd never felt before that worked its way up from his fingers and into his wrists. Fen's ears were frozen too, and his nose was running. He could see his breath in the golden lamp light. They stared at each other in surprise.

"It really is the end of the world." Lewin's own breath made a small cloud of fog.

"Come on. I want to *feel* the darkness." Fen stepped into the marketplace, not waiting for his friends to follow.

After a moment, Alissa and Lewin did. Neither brought a light.

The last streetlamp diminished behind them, becoming only a star's pinprick of light to the darkness. The cobblestone rocks of the plaza were worn smooth by the passage of many feet, cartwheels and horses over the years, but the near-invisible ground felt solid, safe under his feet. The darkness here felt somehow less threatening than the shadows that clung to the streets and alleyways.

At last they reached the center of the plaza, where the pinpricks of light from the lamps of the surrounding streets were equally distant. Fen stopped to stare up at the black night sky.

The spindle was always there, a constant thread of light night or day, as sure as life and breath. Now it had vanished, and his world was cast adrift.

Lewin and Alissa came up beside him, vague shadows, each putting a hand on his shoulder.

"What happens next?" Alissa's voice seemed small in the vast dark space.

"I don't know." He felt better having them there with him in the darkness.

"Look!" Fen felt Lewin's arm shift upward.

"What?" He stared at the inky sky.

"It's *still there*. Faint as hell, but still there."

Fen searched the sky. At last, he saw it—a whisper-thin hairline of silver light. He reached up as if he could touch it, and the darkness inside him melted. "There's hope."

In the darkness, Lewin's hand slid into his, squeezing it tightly.

Light the way.

The city needed light. The guild had barrels and barrels of luthiel stored in the sewers.

Fen frowned. He was bad enough with directions aboveground, let alone in the labyrinthine passages below the city, and Master Harmon had taken back the directions he'd provided for their underground expedition.

The world shook again, so hard that it knocked them to the ground. Fen caught himself, his abraded palms slamming into the hard stone. *Fuck.* As he caught himself on the smooth stones, a tingling ran through him.

The world changed and shifted, and he could *feel* the stones beneath him, not just the ones he was touching, but the whole of the market, each connected to the next in a long chain of slow-moving *life*. And beneath that, the tangled tunnels of the sewers.

Fen. The voice was weak, thready, but determined.

Fen sat up and looked around. "Alissa? Lewin?"

There was no answer.

He stood, and his eyes began to adjust to the darkness. He was in a long valley, the wind whispering through the grass at his feet. He looked up and the sky was full of tiny lanterns.

Stars. His mind supplied the word. He stared at them in wonder—something no one living inside Forever had ever seen.

Fen. The voice filled the air, filled his head, stronger this time.

He turned to find a tall stone tower looming over him, blotting out the sky. "Who are you?"

The world-mind. You can call me Elle. She sounded tired. World weary.

The world-mind was a myth as strange as the stars. Fen looked around for the source of the voice, wondering if he was losing his mind. "What do you want?"

I'm dying, Fen.

The stars above began to wink out of existence, one by one.

Fen frowned. It couldn't be true. He *must* be dreaming again. And yet, he felt the weight of it. The passing of something vast and almost unimaginable from the world. "What can I do?"

Light the way for them, Fen. Get them through the night. The voice was fainter now, as if it came from much farther away.

"Is this the end of the world?"

It is an ending. *But it's a beginning too. Have hope, Fen Theora'son. You know what to do.* Then it was gone, and the strange starlit valley was too, leaving Fen alone in the darkness of the market.

"You okay, Fen?" Lewin's hand was warm on Fen's face, his outline barely visible above him.

"Yeah, just hit my head." They'd never believe him if he told them the truth. The world-mind was real, and she had spoken to *him*. How was that even possible?

Still, Elle was right. There was more to do this night than lighting lamps and cowering behind the walls of the guild. "I know what to do."

He explained what he needed and could almost see the shocked looks on Alissa and Lewin's faces.

"How will we find our way back there?" Alissa sounded uncertain, but somehow firmer. "This could get us thrown out of the guild."

"You just have to trust me. Do you trust me?" He was as sure about this as he'd ever been about anything. Whatever the consequences.

Lewin squeezed his hand. "I'm in. Sometimes you have to take a chance."

Do you mean…? Fen had to let that go, for now. "So we're agreed?"

"Damn it all to hell." Fen could hear Alissa grinding her teeth. "I'm in too."

"Come on then." Fen didn't want to lose his new-found courage. "We have a lot to do."

✡

The walls of the sewer shook around them, the water sloshing up their sides like waves on the sea. Fen stopped to touch the rock, and the strange *sense of place* flooded through him again. It was like touching the nerves of the world; as if he were, however momentarily, a small part of them. It was a strange thought.

He was tired, but he pushed himself onward. They were almost there. He hoped Lewin had managed to round up the other things they needed above ground.

"A few more like that and there won't be any more us." Fen looked around grimly. Ahead, the passageway connected with a cross-shaft. "Almost there."

Alissa nodded. "This looks familiar." She looked as tired as he felt.

During one of the more recent shakes, there had been a distant crash behind them, followed by a rush of water through the passage, bringing the level well up their chests for a moment. Fool chance they were taking, but what else could they do?

The glow of the moss on the walls was stronger here. Strange that the moss was alight while the rest of the world above was dark. Better to think on that than to imagine what was in the muck that sucked at his boot soles with every step. They were filthy enough with the sewer water as it was. He imagined not even his own mother would let him in the door after this, not before he had a long, hot bath.

Alissa followed his thoughts. "Bit of a mess, aren't we? I haven't had this much fun since we played salamander in the rain outside the walls as kids. Remember?"

He laughed, some of the tension broken. "We never smelled this bad." He looked up to see the tunnel branch. "Left here."

Wearily they climbed the slope to the hidden room, where he stared blankly at the opening mechanism. *What was the blazing sequence?* The dying world-mind couldn't help him with that one.

"Let me." Alissa slipped past him and moved the levers, and the door slid noisily open.

"How did you do that?"

She snorted. "I paid attention."

Fen laughed. "Ten barrels should be enough. Come on, let's get them moving."

They took turns putting the barrels on their sides and rolling them down the slope to rest just above the fork in the tunnel.

Alissa was right—they'd be thrown out of the guild for this. They were stealing precious guild property. Fen no longer cared. It was a small enough offense at the end of the world, when everyone needed light and hope.

When they had all the barrels lined up, they tied a rope around one of the small metal loops on each side of the first one and eased it into the water, holding it steady.

Alissa wrestled the second one next to the first, and they tied the two together. In short order, they had all ten in a long floating convoy. "Ready?"

Alissa grabbed the lantern and rejoined him in the fetid water. "Ready as I'll ever be." They started off, hauling the barrels upstream along the slow-moving waters of the sewer. They maneuvered the casks of luthiel carefully around a corner, with Fen checking the way every ten paces.

"Let's hope your boyfriend comes through for us."

Fen stared at her. "He's not…Lewin's not my boyfriend." Cross-guild relationships between journeymen were strictly forbidden.

Alissa snorted. "So our dear mason journeyman was in your bedroom before first light this morning to *inspect the walls?*"

Fen sighed. Alissa was no idiot. "He—we were together. Once. But now—"

The world shook violently, and Alissa fell, grabbing at one of the barrels. It slipped from her grasp and she splashed into the water. The lantern light went out, plunging them into pitch-black darkness.

"Liss! You okay back there?" Fen peered into the darkness from the front of their little caravan of barrels.

Someone spat and cursed. "I think so." Fen heard water dripping. "Sweet Ariadne that's foul." She spat out something—Fen didn't want to know. "It's gonna take a week for me to get the stench out. But how are we going to get out of here now?" Her voice was edged with panic.

"Stay calm." He reached out to find the wall. "Ouch."

"You okay?"

He nodded, then realized she couldn't see him. "Yeah. The rock's rough, is all." His palms were still sore from the fall down Lewin's wall.

He put his palm against the stone, and awareness flooded through him once again. "I can get us home."

Half an hour later, they reached the sewer entrance, cheered by the glow of the luthiel lantern they'd left hanging on the landing. One by one, they untied the barrels and hauled them up out of the water to sit up on dry ground.

I did it. Fen stared back along the pitch-black tunnel in wonder. He'd heard of people like him—liminals, they'd been called—who could speak to the world-mind. It was a strange legend out of the depths of time. *Apparently more than legend. No time to figure it out now.*

Together, they carried the first barrel up the stone stairs and out the once-locked gate onto the city street, where they were greeted by an unexpected multitude.

"You made it!" Lewin hugged him, then backed away, his nose wrinkling in disgust. "And you brought the stench with you."

Fen grimaced. "Not much choice. We were in the sewers, after all." He looked at the assembled crowd under the golden light of the streetlamps. "You brought some friends."

Lewin nodded. "Every one of the journeymen and apprentices I could find from the Mason's Guild. And some of *their* friends too."

Fen looked around at the crowd. They were all his age, give or take. He even recognized a few faces from his own guild—Caswin and Jacob and Tyler.

Cas grinned. "If they kick you out of the guild, they'll have to kick all of us out. It's about time we changed things around here."

There was a general cheer of agreement.

Lewin turned to address the crowd. "There's more barrels down there. We need a few strong bodies to bring them up."

As some of the others streamed past him and into the stairwell that led down to the sewer, Fen whistled in appreciation. "How did you do this?"

Lewin grinned. We're all tired of the guilds, Fen. Things need to change. If we survive the long night, they *will* change."

It was Fen's turn to grin.

"But how are we going to distribute all this luthiel?"

Lewin turned to Alissa and laughed. "You look like a half-drowned rat who took a dip in Shit River."

Alissa grumbled. "Close enough."

"That's a good question." If they could secure a wagon somewhere, they could deliver it from house to house. But that would take forever.

A creaking sound caught Fen's attention.

"Ah, the Potter's Guild is here." Lewin gestured to an arriving wagon loaded with baskets, like an answer to Fen's prayers. "Dera Thessas'daughter's a journeyman in the Potter's Guild."

A woman with silver hair set down the reins and jumped down to greet them. She held out her hand to Lewin. "I'm Dera. You must be Lewin? Del said you were a handsome bastard. Quite a movement you've started here."

"Fen here did it. I just rounded up the troops."

Dera turned to appraise him. "This little thing? Nice to meet you, Fen the revolutionary."

Fan laughed in spite of himself. "Hardly. I just had an idea."

She grinned. "Every good revolution starts with one."

Fen looked over at her wagon. "What did you bring us?"

Dera led them to the back and opened one of the baskets. Inside were bunches of ceramic stoppered vases of all colors, nestled in homecloth.

This was going to work. "I'd hug you, but—"

Desa's laugh was deep and hearty. "Keep your distance, sewer boy. You can thank me later."

Fen's mind was racing. He was born to organize things like this. "We need teams. We have ten barrels—we'll also need dippers, and runners to distribute the luthiel—"

"What in Saint Ana's name is going on here?" The roar silenced all activity.

Fen looked up to see Master Harmon descending upon him, dressed in his nightclothes, his long gray hair waving around his head like a horde of snakes. He took Lewin's hand.

The Guild Master stopped half a meter away and glared at him, and then Lewin, and finally at the barrels and baskets.

"It's—I can explain. Everyone needs light—"

Harmon's gesture cut him off. "I don't want to hear it. You *do* know this is a dismissible offense?"

The other journeymen gathered around them in a circle, their gazes hardening.

Harmon looked around at each of them. The Lamplighters' Guild members blanched but stood their ground.

Harmon muttered under his voice.

Fen stared at him, waiting for the word. Waiting to hear he'd been let go, that he'd be out on the street come first light. If first light ever came again.

Harmon opened his mouth.

Alissa threw herself between them. "It's not Fen's fault. It was all my idea. Dismiss me…sir."

"Liss, no—"

Harmon looked at him, then Alissa, and then back at him again. "I *ought* to dismiss the lot of you. And not just from the Lamplighter's Guild—I could report each of you to your own respective guilds." He looked around the circle. "But sometimes you need to be young to see what has to be done." He eased Alissa aside and begrudgingly put a hand on Fen's shoulder. "You're right, Mr. Theora'son. We need to *light the way.*"

There was a collective sigh of disbelief from the journeymen.

Fen stared at him. Those words—it couldn't be a coincidence. "Yes, sir."

"What can I do to help, son?" A sly grin played across his face but was gone in an instant.

He wanted *me to do this*, Fen thought furiously. He needed a revolutionary movement bigger than one man for change to happen. "We could use some barrel taps, sir. And more runners."

Harmon nodded. "Consider it done. Caswin, Tyler, to me."

As the journeymen organized themselves into work teams, Fen turned to Lewin and Alissa. "Spin be damned, I think we did it."

Alissa laughed. "Not yet. But with the Guild Master's help…"

Fen turned to Lewin. "Lew…things are changing. I don't want to face it all alone. If we survive this long night…."

Lewin took his hand, pulled him in for a kiss. It was long and sweet, and when it was over, Lewin laid his hands on Fen's face and looked in his eyes. "Like I said, sometimes you have to take a chance."

✿

Fen led Lewin down the hall to his room. No more subterfuge. No more hiding.

It had been an arduously long night, and no one knew if daylight would ever come again. If the spindle would ever flare to life. If there was a world-mind, would it ever wake up? It was also bitterly cold. If this was the end, Fen was determined to spend it with Lewin.

The shaking had subsided a few hours before. Fen didn't know if that portended good, or ill.

They reached his room and Fen led Lewin to the open window. He wrapped his blanket around the two of them for warmth, and together they looked out at the lights that burned in every window of the city—golden pinpricks of light that lit Thyre like the fabled stars inside the world-mind.

"The end of the world is more beautiful than I ever imagined."

Fen grinned. "I'd give it all up, just for this moment." Somehow it had all worked out. They'd brought a little hope to the world and he still had his post. For all the good that would do.

"Fen, look!"

Once again he followed Lewin's voice.

The spindle was slowly flaring to life, a golden glow spreading from the North Pole in the distance to light up Forever.

As it passed them, the very air brightened, and soon the city was awash in daylight. Below his window, citizens flooded into the streets, cheering as light and life returned to the world.

Fen reached up to touch Lewin's cheek. "Looks like you might be stuck with me after all."

In response, Lewin kissed him again. Hard.

In the back of Fen's mind, a cheery voice whispered. *Hello, Fen, I'm Aris. The new world-mind.*

Fen's eyes widened and he let go of Lewin. *You do exist.* His mother had been right all along.

Yes. I have a lot to learn. I hope you'll help teach me about this world I've been born into. There are only a few liminals left in your generation who can hear me.

"Sure." He didn't realize he'd spoken aloud until Lewin raised an eyebrow.

"Everything okay, Fen?"

Fen grinned. He finally knew who and what he was.

He took Lewin's hand and pulled him back down onto the bed "Yeah, for the first time in a long time, I think it's going to be."

Copyright © 2020 by J. Scott Coatsworth.

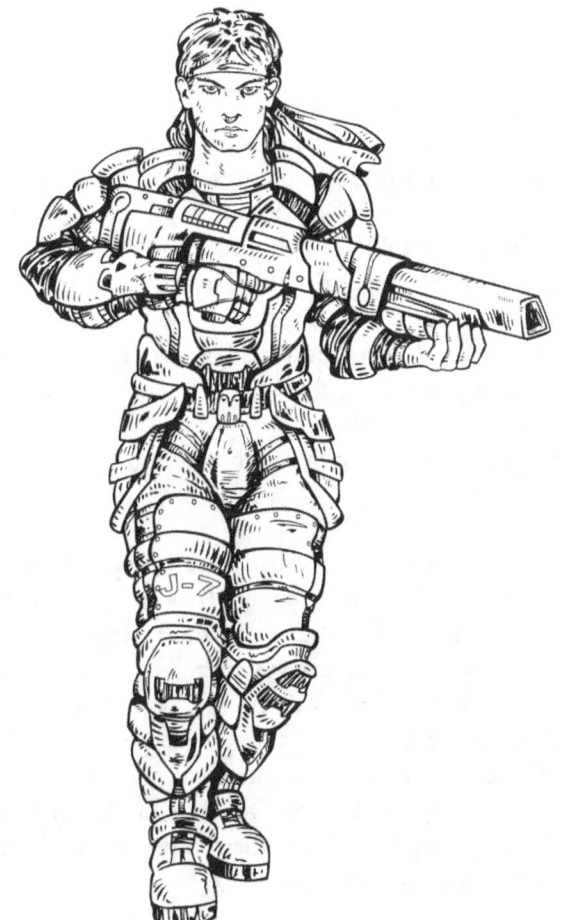

Mike Resnick, along with editing the first seven years of Galaxy's Edge *magazine, was the winner of five Hugos from a record thirty-seven nominations and was, according to* Locus, *the all-time leading award winner, living or dead, for short fiction. He was the author of over eighty novels, around 300 stories, three screenplays, and the editor of over forty anthologies. He was Guest of Honor at the 2012 Worldcon.*

Jean-Claude Dunyach, born in 1957, has been writing science fiction since the beginning of the 1980s, and has already published nine novels and ten collections of short stories, of which two are available in English. He is now the official biographer of a troll living in a corporate fantasy universe…

QUEEN'S ROBOT SACRIFICE

by Mike Resnick & Jean-Claude Dunyach

An ivory hand slid the velvet curtain aside with a perfectly simulated creak. The automaton's wheels propelled it into the middle of the room.

"Did you win or lose?" (Laurie's voice, tinged with a hint of amusement, sprang out from behind the bar.)

"No satisfactory answer. I played myself."

The robot came to a stop, then tilted its large metal head toward the chessboard where only a small number of pieces remained. *Slight advantage to white, it would seem, but a dead-end situation*, Laurie thought.

The automaton extended its arm over the squares, without touching a thing. Its interconnected brains were studying variations, exploring new branches on the tree of possibilities. Each move considered opened myriads of potentialities, but all converged on a draw.

On its chest, two interlocked gears turned erratically, in pace with its thoughts.

"You need an adversary of your caliber," said Laurie, pulling a chair in front of it.

"There aren't any."

"I've already beat you. Twice, in fact."

"I belong to you." (The automaton barked out a laugh like the grinding of gears.) "My judgement may have been altered by that fact alone."

Laurie picked up the white bishop from e5 and moved it to f6.

"Checkmate in thirteen moves," announced the automaton.

With a sigh, the young woman returned the bishop to its starting square and shook her head.

"I thought I knew everything there is to know about chess before I met you…"

"So did I. But unlike you, I was right."

☼

Laurie had discovered the automaton in the back room of an abandoned museum in St. Petersburg. It was dormant, in sleep mode, as a result of a shortage of visitors, surviving off minimal power, supplied by an electrical bypass that surged from the wall behind a tattered poster boasting the "The Mechanical Turk—best chess player in the world". The remnants of a turban hung around its metal face, in which two very deep eyes had been clumsily hammered and a mouth barely sketched. The young woman would have paid it no attention, if it hadn't been for the dust-covered chessboard with its handful of pieces circled around the white king. She studied the configuration for a long time before moving a white pawn.

The automaton woke. The garnet diodes of its eyes flashed briefly and its arm unfolded to grasp the last black knight.

He beat her.

Then, with the squeal of tortured metal, he had set up the chessboard again.

This time, she set her mind to it. The defeat was all the more humiliating. In the museum filled with shadows and rodents, she had faced an implacable adversary, who gave no inch. Until his mechanical arm stopped in mid-motion, joint frozen.

The game remained unfinished, even though Laurie was forced to admit that she would probably have lost it, like the three previous matches. Delicately, she had removed the black rook from the folded fingers and returned it to its initial square. *Let the next visitor deal with it*, she thought, *I've already wasted enough time.*

"Take me with you…"

The voice was neutral, hollow.

"You can talk?" (Laurie bent down and saw the mesh of an antique speaker embedded at throat level.)

"I also play chess. The rook goes to c4. A draw is still possible, if you play cautiously."

"I don't want to set off the alarm. And you're too heavy for me to carry."

"I am my own master, of no worth to anyone. The frame that houses my thinking organs is equipped with wheels. Your next move should concern the pawn on d2, of course. But think about it…"

"Why would I do it?"

"Chess is important to you. It is for me as well, at a level you can't even imagine." (The half-folded arm uttered a series of squeaks, before collapsing.) "I can continue to exist without moving the pieces, by scrolling through each game in my mind. But I cannot live without an adversary. And you need a diversion."

"What do you know about that, machine?"

"It's 4:22 in the morning. We've played three games and started a fourth."

"I hate it when anyone gets a step ahead of me."

"So, I can push you to progress…"

She bit her lip as she thought. Then she tugged on the power cable, which pulled effortlessly out of the wall, before gathering her strength to roll the automaton toward the exit, in the midst of dusty theater sets and doll houses locked up in glass showcases.

During this time, the automaton made no comments. The whistling that surged from the old speaker sounded like the sea breathing.

☼

Since that time, they had been inseparable and had played numerous games. It accompanied her on her trips around the world, occupying a special compartment in her private craft. And it had never lacked for parts or power. Its life, based on criteria it had set for itself, should have been perfect. And it had been until the day Laurie had given up in the middle of a game, declaring the outcome predictable.

That would have been their nine hundred and thirteenth consecutive draw.

☼

The problem was not one of those that it knew how to solve by handling parts.

The automaton had faced numerous crises during the course of its existence. It had literally built itself, from something that was no more than a common semi-conscious robot installed at the end of a production line. Its primary brain, equipped with leading-edge shape recognition algorithms, allowed it to accurately identify defective parts on the conveyor belt that rolled constantly in front of it, perform self-diagnostics and transmit the pertinent information to the semi-automated management units locked up beneath its feet in tanks of liquid nitrogen. It had the greatest respect for the digital intelligences that bobbed in the cooling liquid like artic whales, but their level of abstraction made it comfortable. And they lacked a spark that the automaton knew it had.

When its articulated arm, used to pick up the parts and place them in the garbage bin, had started to show signs of weakness four months before the scheduled maintenance, it had considered two possibilities: declaring an incident and asking the repair units to intervene, which would be admitting obsolescence, and doing nothing in the hopes that the arm would hold out—but that might reduce its overall efficiency in eliminating defective parts, which wasn't good either.

So it had looked for a third option.

It had four minutes each day, when the conveyer belt stopped for maintenance. It started to analyze the problem of the arm and discovered that it was caused by two defective parts, which had worn asymmetrically, creating a lack of balance in the tension of the joint. It would take no more than a few seconds to replace them as long as it had the tools and the spare parts it needed.

And, well, a second arm.

It considered each sub-problem, mobilizing a largely under-used portion of its primary brain. It needed three tools, all of which were available in several copies nearby. It could ask a delivery mechanism to bring them and then take them back, without having to provide any explanations. Finding a second arm was clearly more complicated. The robot that faced it from the other side of the conveyer was, in theory, capable of stretching its gripper to the maximum, but the security software blocked this type of movement. It would have to find the means to deactivate them.

And, in any case, there were no spare parts.

It created independent thinking loops and put them all to work, authorizing them to self-duplicate until they found a solution. Most collapsed after a few minutes, trapped in faulty reasoning that caused them to spin in circles. It launched programs to analyze its environment, in an effort to identify anything that could be of use. In vain. And it opened the data acquisition channels toward the outside, but collided with impenetrable security blocks.

Meanwhile, its sensors continued to identify all of the non-compliant parts on the conveyer and its arm removed them and placed them in the waste container. The wear on the defective joint increased.

If it had been programmed to feel despair, it would no doubt have shrieked in frustration.

The solution came in an unexpected manner…

✧

One of the defective parts it picked up was roughly similar to one of the parts it needed for the joint. The automaton picked it up, took the time to examine it, which caused a slight delay in picking up the next part, and finally threw it into the waste bin. But that provided the seed for an idea. *A strategy.*

During the following hours, no other defective part looking like the ones it needed appeared on the conveyor belt. The arm emitted an unfortunate creak. During the four minutes of down time, it seriously considered calling maintenance, but abandoned that thought. It also gave up the idea of consulting the management intelligences, knowing how merciless they could be.

It had to make do on its own.

When the conveyor started moving with a deep rumble, it glanced in despair at the 3D printer spitting out a new burst of parts to be examined. Then, the idea came!

The parametric description of its entire body was stored in the databases to which it had access. The automaton extracted the information about the parts it needed and sent them to the printer's queue. The result would be rough, at the best, but it would enable the automaton to hold out for four months without attracting attention, until the next upgrade.

It picked them up without being noticed and had the necessary tools delivered. For the rest of the day, it planned the replacement operation. Then, when the conveyor stopped again, it took a chance, short-circuiting the security routines in order to convince the robot on the other side of the conveyor to connect its gripper to its own.

The operation itself lasted twenty-four seconds. The subsequent tests barely any longer. Its first action, when the conveyor started back up, was to recover the worn parts and pitch them into the waste bucket.

It had managed to repair itself.

It functioned straight off. Its brain, freed from the obligation to think, performed the operations for which it had been programmed with almost optimum efficiency. Yet, it took two hours for it to realize that something was not quite right.

It was bored…

☼

The automaton rolled over to the bar and slipped skillfully between the seats until its wheels blocked. The magnetized pieces, inherited from a time when ivory and ebony had been replaced by resin, had not budged. Once, Laurie would have been perched on one of the tall stools, head bent over the chessboard, eyes narrowed in concentration. She would have tested the openings, played against the automaton and with it—it's so unusual mind taking risky shortcuts that sometimes led it into unknown configurations that forced it to re-think its strategies and create new ones. She had offered it something that could not found in any of the programs it had encountered: fantasy.

But she no longer seemed to want to play. And their interactions had been reduced to the minimum. Should it insist? It made yet another attempt to find a solution to the dilemma it faced. Unsuccessfully. Frustrated, it delved into its memory, looking for an opening phrase susceptible of unblocking the situation.

"The entire universe is reflected in the chessboard, O Lord, and all of the stars in heaven hold their breath while waiting for the end of the game."

"Another one of your pseudo-mystical quotes?" (Laurie poured a second cocktail—she'd started drinking since they had stopped playing their daily game.) "Who is it this time?"

"One of Haroun ar-Rachîd's courtiers. Eight centuries after Jesus Christ. His name has been lost to history."

"Well, he was wrong. The universe out there could care less about the game being played. Go tell that to those who die fighting in the Trojan asteroids because their radios don't carry far enough."

"We're all pawns in an immense game and we don't even know who the players are."

"And we're all losing." (She tossed her cocktail back and poured another one.) "I don't care about players, asteroids and current conflicts. I'm talking to you about life. This universe is absurd. Plus, it cheats!"

"You, too, need an adversary that's your match."

"So? You're too good for me."

"You are a human being. You can improve. I cannot."

"Is there anyone alive who can beat you?"

The automaton tried to shrug. It came across as an awkward shift of position accompanied by a squeaking sound. "I do not know," it replied. "Does it matter?"

"Of course it does!" snapped Laurie. "I am a fanatic about chess. I do not know if that word is in your memory bank or dictionary or whatever you call it, but it means I am obsessed night and day with the game. That's how I activated you in the first place. I have never met a man or a woman—and prior to you, a robot—that I couldn't at least beat on occasion. But playing you, well, it's almost as if you read my mind. Whatever attack or defense I prepare for you, and some of them I assure you are totally unique to myself, you seem always to be prepared for." She paused, and emitted a defeated sigh. "Sometimes I wonder if you really might be a telepath."

"I assure you I am not," replied the automaton.

"Then your programmer must have been a genius of the first order," said Laurie.

"He was a good programmer, or so I surmise," said the automaton. "But he knew almost nothing about chess."

"You're kidding!" she exclaimed.

"I do not possess a sense of humor."

"Then how could someone who doesn't know the game create the greatest chess player I've ever encountered?"

"He didn't. I expanded my own memory to hold every major book ever written about the game, plus every move of every game in every tournament ever since they have been codifying those moves, back in the eighteenth century"—it offered the metal equivalent of a puzzled frown—"or was it even earlier?"

"So when I lose to you, I am actually losing to an amalgam of the hundred or so greatest players and the thousand greatest games?" she said.

"In essence," agreed the automaton. "Plus a few tricks I taught to myself along the way."

She sighed deeply. "Suddenly I don't feel quite so bad."

✧

They played to 143 more draws when the news came through: Earth's very first interstellar war—against the six-limbed purple-skinned inhabitants of the Boratus Cluster—was finally over.

"Is that good?" asked the automaton.

"Better than you can imagine!" replied Laurie.

It merely stared at her, waiting for her to continue.

"During the peace talks we introduced them to chess, and they love it!"

"You made peace by playing chess?" repeated the automaton, frowning.

She shook her head. "No, that was peripheral to the talks. But it's not without precedent. The United States and Russia, back when they existed, used to play chess against each other and the winners became rich and famous while their countries gained worldwide prestige. And once, when the United States were, if not at war, at least at hazard, with China, we began normalizing relations by playing ping-pong against them!"

"What is ping-pong?" asked the automaton. "Is it anything like chess?"

She shook her head. "Nothing at all like it. Except that it's a friendly contest that produces a winner and a loser."

"But no draws?"

She shook her head. "None."

"Good," said the automaton. "Then you know for certain who the best player is."

She stared at him for a long moment, and finally spoke: "I hadn't realized it before, but I get the distinct feeling that you aren't any happier with all those draws than I am."

The automaton simply stared at her.

"Am I right?"

"I am no happier than you are," it replied truthfully.

Of course, it didn't utter the whole truth, and it was grateful that its programming didn't force it to—for the fact of the matter was that it hated ending a game with a draw. But its basic programming forbade it to harm a human being except in self-defense, and it was also empowered to make value judgments—and it had concluded from the moment she had taken it home that hundreds of draws would do less damage to her emotions than if it beat her even a single time, much less nine hundred in a row.

"Well, we have a way to get you even better competition," she continued. "I have volunteered you to play in the tournament against the slugs."

"The slugs?" it repeated.

"I'm sure we'll have a more dignified name for them by the time we get to the tournament, but right now the press is calling them the slugs."

She had to explain to the machine exactly what a slug was and what it looked like, but it had no trouble accepting them as legitimate opponents.

"When and where will this tournament be held?"

She shrugged. "Some neutral world that can support both our life forms. And since you're not alive, it can't possibly have a deleterious effect on you."

The automaton hadn't realized until that moment that it possessed emotions, but when she mentioned in passing that it wasn't alive, it suddenly knew what she would feel like if it beat her in a game of chess.

✧

They arrived on the barren neutral world of Dragonfly—the slugs called it something else, of course—and unpacked in the human quarters. There was a domed building between the human and slug quarters, one equipped with literally hundreds of cameras, and the ability to transmit anything that occurred almost instantaneously to every world inhabited or occupied by either race.

"I couldn't keep your ability a secret," said Laurie. "But we lucked out. The way the brackets are set up, you won't have to go up against their best player until the championship game."

"If I get that far," replied the automaton.

"Of course you will," she said. "You've never lost."

"And you have almost never lost. Perhaps you should be in the tournament as well."

She shook her head. "You're our best. I'd just be a sideshow, someone who lost in the first or second round."

"You underestimate yourself," said the automaton.

"I wish you were right," answered Laurie sincerely. Then: "Shall we mosey over and see how the building is set up?"

"You mosey," replied the automaton, wondering what the word meant. "I'll locomote."

✡

"Damn, it's impressive!" said Laurie, looking around the building. "Hell, the camera equipment alone must run a few billion credits. And look at those chess sets. They are so bright they all but glow." Suddenly she tensed as a slug slithered into the building from the other side. "How do they move their pieces?" she asked. "I don't see any hands."

"They have hands," the automaton corrected her. "I just checked the public memory banks. Their hands can be extended from their bodies, for example when they move a chess piece or fire a weapon, but otherwise they recede into the body where there is far less chance of harming them."

Laurie made a face. "Disgusting!"

"Practical," replied her companion. "I should have thought of it myself when I redesigned my body, before we met."

"You actually redesigned yourself?"

"I had to…. When I was left to my own devices, I had to improve them. Then I acceded to the universal network and stole whatever was necessary to become what I am."

"You simply forgot to pick-up a name for yourself."

"I'm your opponent, I don't need further identification."

"It's not always black or white," she said with a grin. "That's why you'll need a name, eventually."

Soon the building began filling up with more men and slugs, and finally some members of each race approached empty tables and began playing chess.

"This is wrong," announced the automaton.

"Oh?" said Laurie, puzzled. "Why?"

"You have humans playing humans and slugs playing slugs."

"They're just warming up," she replied. "See the microphones over the five tables that are closest to the one in the middle? I suspect that's where the tournament games will take place, until they get down to the final game. This way the audience can hear the players announce their moves."

"*Must* we announce them?" asked the automaton. "After all, the cameras will be able to show every move."

"It pleases the viewing audience," explained Laurie. "I mean, hell, they could just show diagrams of the boards and moves. This adds, well, if not tension, then—I don't know—call it *reality*."

"Chess is the reality. They don't need additional…" The automaton stopped. "Oh, well, I suppose you have a point, there."

They stood there, observing players from both sides entering the building and playing their warm-up games, and then, suddenly, a slug slithered up to where Laurie and the automaton were standing.

"Excuse me," it said, speaking through a translating mechanism, "but you and I seem to be odd numbers. Would you care for a game while we're waiting for the tournament to begin?"

"I'd be happy to," said Laurie.

"Excellent," said the slug, undulating over to an unoccupied table.

"I'm sorry," whispered Laurie. "But as long as I've come all this way with you I'd like to play at least one game. And you certainly don't need the practice."

"I understand," replied the automaton. "Do you mind if I watch?"

"Of course not," she said, walking over to join the slug.

"My name is Gresbeziax," said the slug.

"And I am Laurie."

"And does your toy have a name?"

"He's not a toy," replied Laurie.

"I meant no offense." It turned to the automaton. "Your name?"

The automaton's mind raced through its enormous library and finally hit on what it thought was an appropriate answer. "My name is Lazarus," it responded.

"I approve," said Laurie. Then: "Pawn to King Four."

It was a close game, *very* close, but finally Laurie announced mate on the sixty-fourth move, using a strategy she had learned from Lazarus during some of their multitude of draws.

"I shall hopefully be given my chance for revenge during the tournament," said Gresbeziax, who inclined his head in what passed for a bow, and they slithered off to what had clearly become the slugs' side of the building.

"I *beat* him!" enthused Laurie. "We should win this tournament without working up a sweat."

"Why would one sweat?" asked Lazarus.

"Never mind," she answered. "Just get ready for an all-human final."

"Do you expect me to lose?" asked Lazarus.

"Probably not," she said. "Why?"

"Because I am not a human."

"But you're playing on the human side," said Laurie.

"I see," said Lazarus, who didn't quite see, but felt no desire to argue with her.

The tournament began some three hours later, with some twenty players representing each side. It came to nineteen humans and an automaton versus twenty slugs…but within fifteen hours it was three humans and Lazarus against four slugs.

Lazarus used a variation of the Indian defense (which became known in the chess books as the Robot defense) to win his next game, a brilliant queen sacrifice to win the one after that, a long and tortuous journey through the enemy lines to finally hit the white king from behind, and suddenly he was in the final match, the one that would determine the champion in the most-publicized chess game in history.

"You can do it," whispered Laurie to Lazarus as he prepared for the match.

"Who is my opponent?" he asked.

"You're not going believe this," she answered. "It's Gresbeziax! Hell, if *I* could beat him, you'll make mincemeat out of him!"

"What is mincemeat?" asked Lazarus.

"Never mind," she said. "Just concentrate on the game. Damn, but I wish *I* was playing against him! If I can beat him, he should be a pushover for you!"

"Not necessarily," replied Lazarus, deciding that the truth would hurt her more than a lie, and that he could therefore deliver the lie without causing any internal harm to his thinking gear. "You improve with almost every game. You're still not able to win, but you can no longer lose."

She shook her head, with a sad grin.

"Just go out there and prove you're the best!" she urged him.

The two players were signaled to go the table at the center of the building, which had been sitting vacant until that moment. Their names were announced, a coin was flipped, and Gresbeziax won and chose white. He opened, Lazarus responded, and the game was under way.

Lazarus used that section of his brainpower that was geared to chess to considering the game at hand, but the rest of his mental faculties were concentrating on what Laurie had said, and suddenly he thought he had found a way to make her truly happy. A strategy so close to the essence of chess that he hadn't ventured there before. He wished he could ask someone if he was correct, but there was no one near him except Gresbeziax and a six-limbed referee from a neutral world.

He thought about his plan for as long as he could, and then he put it into action. He moved a knight instead of a bishop, counted on the slug to spot and avoid the trap he was trying to set up, and conceded on the fifty-third move.

And as the building erupted in cheers on one side and groans on the other, Lazarus congratulated Gresbeziax and looked around for Laurie. Finally he spotted her as she was approaching him.

"I'm so sorry!" she said. "I didn't think it was possible for you to lose."

"I ran up against a better player," said Lazarus.

"He couldn't be!" she exclaimed. "After all, *I* beat him!"

"I stand by what I said," replied Lazarus, and the interlocked gears on its torso suddenly ground to a stop with a terrible grating sound.

Its arm fell on the board and it froze into immobility.

✿

They tried to resurrect him, of course, but it was no use, and finally they laid him out on a lab table and prepared to extract those parts of him that could still be used by other automatons.

Suddenly there was a strange, metallic, grinding noise coming from its head.

"What the hell was that?" asked one of the mechanics.

"You're not going to believe this," answered another, "but the damned robot is *smiling*."

Barb Galler-Smith lives in Alberta, Canada. She edits for On Spec: The Canadian Magazine of the Fantastic *and likes quirky fiction. She's taught Writing Fantasy and Science Fiction at Grant MacEwan University, mentors writers of all ages, and is co-author of three historical fantasies:* Druids, Captives, Warriors *with Josh Langston.*

NIGHT FOLK

by Barb Galler-Smith

Bonnie loved the quiet dark with her friends, but tonight she felt unsettled. The games area of Sunnyside Acres Assisted Living was deliciously deserted.

Magnolia stared out the window at the new crescent moon, her face a sad mask. Helen drummed her fingers on the table for the thousandth annoying time, and Abigail still pondered what was trump. Bonnie dropped her cards on the table and stood up.

"I'm tired and I'm hungry. Who wants to go out to get something to eat? It seems like days since I had anything filling. One simply can't live on green beans and veggie stew forever."

"Count me in," said Abigail and Helen together.

"I'm not feeling well," said Magnolia. "I think I'll stay here. I'm really…I'm just so tired of it all." She looked forlorn. "I'm done," she whispered to Bonnie. "My time is short."

Bonnie pulled her to her feet. "Nonsense! You just need a decent meal. Let's go get something."

Magnolia reluctantly followed as the others passed Kyle, night receptionist and handyman.

"We're going out for a walk," said Bonnie.

Kyle didn't look up from his comic. "Okay," he said, and then what seemed an afterthought, "Stay safe."

✿

Pete tossed the brochure for Sunnyside Acres on a coffee table already littered with advertisements from other assisted-living homes. "It's only for women! It was so perfect, but no married couples. No exceptions."

Ellie choked back a sob. "My blindness is getting worse. Soon I won't be able to do anything for myself."

Pete understood. Ellie's macular degeneration was debilitating for them both. "Sure you will. And I'll help you. We'll be all right." He gingerly rose from his chair in front of the fire, stretched and shook vigorously to loosen his joints. He took her hands in his, as he had for all of their fifty-three years of marriage. "We knew retirement wasn't going to be easy." He couldn't bear to see her so sad. "Our hunting days are over, my dear. It's time to relax and do other things." They would find a place to move to, and Ellie would be safe.

He transformed into his preferred shape—a German Shepherd-husky mix. He was large enough to wage battle and could take down and hold all but the strongest prey. With Ellie's talons helping, they could eliminate most others. But now, modern life had driven so many night creatures underground and those left in the world were fitting in as they never had before. Pete had to face it—they needed to retire. They were just not strong or fast enough anymore.

"Let's get out of here," she said. "One last flight as Night Folk."

He padded to the apartment door. She stuffed a change of clothes and shoes for them in the small pack he carried across his back. She stepped into the moonlight, then closed and locked the door behind them. He looked around to make sure no neighbor was watching. He woofed softly.

Ellie transformed and spread her wings.

Pete watched her soar then bank toward the river. He followed at a trot.

✿

At the end of the block Bonnie and her friends turned into the park and kept close to the few streetlamps. It wasn't much of a park, but it had enough trees and shrubs to make it friendly to any who didn't want to be seen doing what they weren't supposed to be doing.

They took it slow, walking two by two, arms linked, and engrossed in quiet conversation. In their bright, baggy cardigans, using four-footed walking canes, Bonnie thought they looked like a multicolored twelve-legged caterpillar as they shuffled along the darkening path.

They pretended not to see the two guys creeping parallel to them.

"Careful," whispered Bonnie. "Keep walking."

They kept walking, eyes on each other, never letting their gaze linger on the men.

Then the men leapt from the near bushes. One grabbed at Bonnie's purse and pushed her hard against a large tree trunk.

Bonnie wheeled, elbowed him in the face, and threw him to the ground. Magnolia sat on his chest with her knees pinning his shoulders. He bucked and thrashed in an effort to dislodge her. Bonnie sat on his legs.

He yelped in pain. "Get off!"

The other man grappled with Helen. She jabbed him in the groin with the end of her cane. He fell to his knees, and Abigail kicked him flat and held him with a foot on his back.

The men struggled and swore, but were unable to extricate themselves.

"You shouldn't be here," Bonnie said. "There are consequences to being bad boys."

"Let me go, you old hag," cried the one under Abigail's foot. He nearly wiggled free, and she secured him with the tips of her cane pressing hard into the back of his knee.

"Let go!" he howled.

"This will hurt a smidgen," Magnolia said to the man she sat on. She leaned over and bit him hard on the side of the neck. "Ick!" she said, recoiling and spitting the blood to the ground. "This guy is full of drugs."

Bonnie had a stronger stomach than Magnolia. She quickly maneuvered to his neck, bit hard, and took a long drink. She winced at the taste. Whatever he was on, it was nothing she couldn't quickly overcome. His blood was the main thing. She drank until he stopped struggling. She nudged him. He wasn't dead but would be weak for a few days. She'd stopped short of killing him, or worse, turning him.

Magnolia stepped to the other man. "May I try that one?"

He stopped struggling for an instant. "Don't kill me," he said, his eyes wide.

Magnolia stroked his cheek. "Not my style," she said. She bent close and nibbled delicately on his neck. "No drugs," she murmured and sank her teeth deep.

The tasty man groaned. He didn't resist her—she had a flair for soothing her prey and they rarely struggled. She drank her fill. Her curly white hair grew bloody on the ends that draped over his neck. A glistening darkness dribbled down her chin. He stared up at her.

Both Abigail and Helen had a taste. Not enough to satiate them, but a decent snack.

Tasty's gaze never left Magnolia's face.

Bonnie recognized the look in his eyes. Hate rather than fear. They'd either have to kill him or let him go soon. If he were turned, he'd be a danger to everyone. Especially Magnolia.

High Guy scuttled backward as fast as he could. He grabbed his friend by the coat and tugged him a short way. When his friend didn't move quick enough, he ran.

Something growled behind them.

A massive dog knocked Magnolia to the ground. Abigail and Helen rushed to her rescue. Helen held her cane up to fend off the dog.

She was strong, but the dog was stronger. It grabbed her by the arm.

A silent, pale form dove at Bonnie with talons open. She jumped, swung a fist wildly and knocked an enormous owl to the ground. The dog immediately abandoned Magnolia and ran to the fallen bird.

"Hunters!" Bonnie cried. "Run!"

☼

"Ellie!"

Pete transformed from his dog shape and knelt beside his wife, no longer an owl. A lump was forming on her forehead just above her left eye. Ellie opened her eyes, blinked and shook her head. "Oh gods, Pete, I can't see at all now!" Tears streamed down her face. "What am I going to do?"

Pete growled. He looked for the blood-eaters but they were long gone. If his Ellie was permanently damaged, there would be payback.

☼

The clash with the Hunters seemed to take the spirit out of Magnolia. About a week after the incident in the park, she said she was ready to go. They pretended she was moving to Florida to live with family. She packed away all her belongings and Sunnyside Acres held a party for her.

Kyle gave a short speech. "Being a night person let me meet one of the best ladies in the place. I'll miss you, Magnolia."

They would all miss her.

Just before her last dawn, she bid her friends pleasant dreams and stepped into the cloistered garden. Bonnie and the others watched her through the blinds of Bonnie's heavily shaded room. As the sun rose, Magnolia waved to them, and then turned toward the rising sun with a smile.

☼

Life wasn't the same without Magnolia.

No one felt much like going out, and had it not been for Bonnie's urging, the other two might have followed Magnolia into the sun. Bonnie kept herself occupied by discovering the lair that the two thugs used. The ladies worked harder at night to keep other hoodlums from returning to the park at dusk. As a result, neighbors started gravitating to their little green belt. Families gathered and children played during the day. At night young couples walked hand in hand without fear. Kyle said the park felt protected. That cheered her.

Bonnie sat with the others playing three-handed Whist. Three-handed was all right, but they really needed a fourth.

"Hey, Kyle!" called Bonnie. "Wanna play Whist?"

"Thanks for thinking of me," he said, putting down his ever-present superhero comic, "but I need to greet our new resident in a few minutes. She's a night owl, just like you ladies."

Probably not quite, Bonnie thought with a smile, *but maybe she played cards.* The sight of the newcomer at the door with a white cane and a guide dog squelched that idea.

It took half an hour to settle the paperwork, and then the movers began unloading their truck. The woman and her dog didn't have much and within an hour all was unloaded. The men spent another two hours unpacking boxes. The woman and her dog disappeared into her room, but after the movers left, Bonnie was sure she heard a man's voice coming from the small apartment.

She didn't want to be seen prying, but the hairs on the back of her neck prickled. She moved closer to the apartment's door and almost bumped into Kyle.

He grinned at her then knocked. "Ellie, I've got those last papers for you to sign right now." The door opened and he closed it behind him.

The scent of Hunters washed over Bonnie. She stepped back in panic and struggled to remain calm. A blind woman and her dog. But not just any dog. It was the dog from the park.

She gritted her teeth. The dog had nearly killed Magnolia. In a way, it *had* killed her.

Bonnie hurried back to the table.

"Well?" said Helen.

"Hunters."

Abigail shivered and put her head in her hands. "Oh no! I'm not ready to move on. I like it here, and this is where…where Magnolia was. I don't want to leave."

With Hunters so near, it meant life or death for her and the others to remain where they were at Sunnyside Acres. They tried not to kill and only drank what they needed to survive. Hunters had no such principles. Hunters killed *all* of their kind.

She snarled. "We'll just have to take them out. Divide and conquer."

The couple emerged from their room with Kyle and walked across to his desk. The dog was the largest Bonnie had ever seen, and he was by far the more dangerous of the two. The woman beside him must be the owl Bonnie had struck down.

In her human form, the woman was truly blind. She walked with one hand extended slightly, the other clutched the dog's harness handle. The dog had eyes only for her. Seeing a Hunter become such a frail figure somewhat saddened Bonnie. It was an emotion she could not afford to nurture. As soon as the dog turned his head toward her, he sniffed and his ears pricked. Then his hackles rose, and a low growl washed across the room. He had recognized her.

"Pete!" said the woman softly. "Not now."

The dog settled but he raised his lip to Bonnie in a promise of a more private meeting.

After they signed the last of the paperwork, Kyle led the woman to Bonnie and the others.

"Hey, ladies. This is Ellie and her dog, Pete. Ellie, these are my night-owl Sunnysiders—Bonnie, Abigail, and Helen."

"Welcome," said Abigail. She gave the woman a melancholy smile. "You're the spitting image of a friend who recently left us." She started to cry. "I hope you'll be very happy here." With that, she hurried away to her room.

Abigail was right. Ellie resembled Magnolia. They had the same height and build, and her hair fell in white curls around a heart-shaped face with a wistful smile. It was unsettling.

Ellie held out her hand to shake but withdrew it the instant Bonnie touched her. She shivered, as if ruffling feathers.

A grumbling threat came from the dog and he moved in front of Ellie.

"Pete! Back!" she whispered. "How do you do?" she added stiffly.

Bonnie stepped back. They all knew, but they couldn't allow Kyle to know anything was wrong. The Hunters also seemed to be keeping a low profile.

She watched the dog for a moment, and then smiled as if she meant it. "I think you will love Sunnyside. It's been our home for five years. It's very private and nobody pries. Turnaround is slow, so there is time to make new friends, but I think everyone who was here before us has moved on—some to more care and some…."

Helen sobbed. "And some just died."

Ellie looked surprised. Kyle looked stricken.

"Our fourth musketeer, if you will," Helen said. After an awkward silence, she added, "She was in Florida."

Kyle wiped at the tears pooling in his eyes.

Ellie opened her mouth to say something. Pete gave a small whine.

Ellie scratched the dog behind his ears. "I best take Pete for a walk. We both need to get a good feel for the area. Is there a park nearby?"

"Yes, just a short block away. Do you need help with doggie things?" Kyle asked.

"Oh no," said Ellie, "I see just well enough out of the corner of my eyes to find and bag anything Pete might leave behind."

Bonnie and Helen watched as Kyle escorted the pair to the door and touched the automatic door opener. He'd just plopped into his chair and picked up his comic when a loud crash outside sent everyone hurrying to the front doors.

Two cars had collided in front of the building, barely ten feet from the entrance. One car had rammed another from the rear. The SUV had a crumpled back end, but the sedan was crushed in the front and smoke came from the engine. A bewildered and frightened woman jumped from her SUV and ran to Kyle. Two men escaped their disabled car and paused, looking around.

Bonnie recognized the hoodlums from the park.

Tasty pointed directly at Ellie. "It's her! One of the bitches who bit me!" He stepped toward her just as Bonnie stepped toward him.

The sound of approaching police sirens stirred them all to action.

Pete hesitated between Tasty and Bonnie.

The man grabbed Ellie.

Pete was too late. He lunged but a well-placed kick knocked him back just long enough for the man to force Ellie into the SUV and slam the door. Pete jumped onto the hood snarling but couldn't hold on as the SUV jolted away. He hit the roadway dazed. Kyle picked him up and laid him beside the stunned woman.

Two police cruisers passed with sirens blaring and lights flashing.

Pete cut off Bonnie's path to help the woman from the SUV. He snarled and made it clear she would not be allowed near the bleeding woman.

She ignored his bared teeth. "Move it, dog-boy. That woman is more important than either of us right now."

He slowly backed away, making it clear that any wrong move from Bonnie and she'd have the beast at her throat.

Abigail pushed both Pete and Bonnie aside. "I used to be a nurse, so let me see. We'll take care of her and call paramedics," she said.

The woman seemed all right except for a shallow cut on her forehead that bled profusely. It reminded Bonnie she was hungry. Kyle handed Abigail a cold compress from the first aid kit then dialed 911 for an ambulance and the fire department.

Bonnie watched the police cruiser's taillights disappear down the road. She knew the neighborhood well, and she knew who the culprits were and where they lived.

Abigail led the injured woman and Kyle inside.

Bonnie nudged Helen. "Come on. Ellie might be a hunter, but she's at risk and I'm pretty sure I know where they're going. Let's get those bastards."

The dog stood still, looked long and hard at Kyle, and made a decision. He transformed into a man wearing a too-tight guide dog harness and nothing else.

Kyle gasped, then collapsed as his knees buckled.

"I got him too," said Abigail from the doorway.

"Where are they going?" said Pete, murder in his eyes. "I don't trust you. She's my wife and *I'll* go get her."

"Not alone, Pete. Look, we all want to live here—*need* to live here. To do that we'll have to form some kind of truce. I can see your wife's not much of a hunter now"—Bonnie put her hand up to stall his protests—"and we're not the predators you think we are."

"Why would you help her?" Suspicion laced his tone.

Bonnie shrugged. "She's a Sunnysider now, so that makes her one of ours." Bonnie started running, Helen beside her.

☼

Transforming back to his dog shape, Pete followed. For a couple of old ladies, they were impossibly fast. For blood-eaters, it was to be expected. In the old days, he could have run them down. Now, he was barely able to keep up. He felt what was going to be a very big bruise across his belly where the man had kicked him, and it slowed him down even more.

He wondered if age slowed the undead down the same way it had slowed him.

They arrived at a four-car police blockade. He caught the flicker of a movement and saw Bonnie and Helen skirt the cruisers, keeping to the shadows. He followed them along the side of the building until they hurried through the darkened entryway before the police noticed them. Pete had to chance doing the same thing, hoping he'd be mistaken for a police K-9 on the job. Regardless, he was on the job. Someone would pay dearly if Ellie was harmed.

Stairs greeted him on the other side of the doorway. He bounded up to the landing on the second floor where the blood-eaters waited. The landing divided into three hallways. They sniffed the air.

"Helen, can you tell which way?" Bonnie asked.

Helen took a deep breath. "Not sure. Should we split up?"

Pete stepped between them and took some satisfaction in seeing both blood-eaters jump back a couple of paces. He put his nose to the filthy floor. A decade of traffic left lingering molecules of filth, sweat, and decay. He wrinkled his nose and fought the urge to roll in it. And there, in the third hallway, the fresh and unmistakable scent of his Ellie. And the stench of his prey. Their prey.

He growled.

"Ah," said Bonnie. "Softly now."

Pete didn't wait. The click of his nails on the floor was a giveaway, but he hoped the men who held Ellie knew the difference between a dog and a man.

Bonnie laid a hand on the back of his neck. "Wait. Let me look," she whispered an inch from his ear. She flattened herself on the floor and peered under the ill-fitting door with one eye.

She sat up. "Ellie looks okay," she whispered. "She's against the far wall, sitting on the floor. The two others are loading firearms right now. It'll be a shoot-out if we don't get in there before the cops. Ellie might get hurt. We go through the door together—Pete go left, Helen go right. I'll go up and over. If we're fast enough, they'll aim at the door and miss. Their bullets won't harm us, Pete, but what about you?"

Worth the risk, he thought. He licked his lips and snarled.

"Right."

Bonnie kicked the door open. Helen dove right, and Pete rushed left as a hail of bullets from an automatic pistol sprayed the door.

He was hit—right flank grazed—but his momentum kept him going. He slid into Ellie.

"I'm okay. Get them," she said.

Pete spun, jumped on the nearest man and knocked the pistol out of his hands. Bonnie followed with a sharp blow that sent him to the ground.

Helen didn't fare as well. Her prey was stronger and fought hard to free himself from her grasp. Pete left the first man to Bonnie and jumped onto the other man's chest. He missed biting into the man's neck but chomped hard on his shoulder.

Helen took the opportunity to sink her teeth into the man's jugular, and in three strong pulls she'd taken enough blood to make him pass out.

Pete heard the cops on the floor below. They'd be here soon—they'd know what floor the shots came from.

He transformed to his man shape, untied Ellie while Bonnie dragged the thug to lie beside his unconscious partner. Helen stepped on the thug to keep him from wiggling away.

Pete needed help to get Ellie out of the house. "They must not find her," he said. "Please."

"We can get out the window, but we can't carry her."

Ellie moved toward them—her hands outstretched. "You can carry me if I'm an owl."

"No! You can't see! It's too dangerous"

"We'll guide her," said Bonnie.

They had just enough time. Pete changed back into his dog form and stood guard over both the criminals. Ellie transformed into her owl shape. Helen carried Ellie on her arm until Bonnie had climbed through the window, then she passed Ellie through. Helen made it out just as the police reached the doorway.

It took a few minutes for the police to come in, recognize Pete wore a harness that visibly marked him as a service dog, and arrest both men. The druggie walked out on his own, but the other, drained and weak, needed help to go down the stairs. When an officer tried to coax Pete to follow her and grab his harness, he rushed past her, down the stairs and into the dark embrace of the night.

✿

Bonnie and Helen stood with their backs to the wall on a narrow ledge that led nowhere.

Ellie's talons bit deep into Bonnie's arm and then she leapt into the night. She hooted once. Bonnie watched her fly up and to the right.

"You're about six feet from the roof, Ellie. A little higher and you can touch the edge. We'll join you up there."

It had been a long time since they'd needed to climb. She dug her fingers into the crevices between the old bricks and took only a second to hoist herself up to the roof, stretching to ease the ache in her old bones. Helen followed.

Ellie perched on the building's edge, facing the city. She didn't move but hooted excitedly.

"I think if we get to that other roof, we can escape down the drainpipe," said Helen.

Bonnie held out the bundle of Ellie's clothes.

Ellie transformed from owl to human and held out her hand but didn't take the clothing. "Thanks for coming after me," she said. Her eyes filled with tears.

Bonnie paused. "You okay? Can you walk?"

Ellie nodded. "I'm okay. In fact, it's probably better if I fly."

Helen tugged on Bonnie's sleeve. "We gotta go. Ellie, if you can fly from the ledge to your left, out a few wing beats, and then circle slowly down about sixty feet, you'll land on the grass. Or, if you wait for us to get down and call, you can also home in on us and land safely."

They waited just long enough for Ellie to change and fly before heading to the other roof and climbing down the pipe.

By the time they reached a small patch of abandoned yard on the side of the building, Ellie was circling above, and Pete joined them below.

With her husband there, also guiding her in, Ellie landed without mishap, and Pete rushed to her side as she resumed human shape.

"Pete!" she exclaimed, her eyes bright. "When I transformed into an owl, I saw the city lights. And I could make you out! As an owl I can still see—well, not the best, but good enough to get myself around. It's going to be all right."

The couple embraced. Ellie put her clothes on, and Pete changed once more into a dog—even Ellie wasn't happy about him walking her home while he was naked.

The four made their way back to Sunnyside without speaking.

The assisted living care facility was brightly lit and most of the residents were sitting in the dining room in their bathrobes and fuzzy no-slip slippers. They were abuzz with excitement. The police investigators were just leaving, after declining tea and cookies more than once. An ambulance had taken the injured woman away. Kyle and Abigail were encouraging everyone to go back to bed—the thrill was over—but the residents would have none

of that. They remained in their small groups, whispering eagerly.

Abigail checked Ellie out, and Helen sat with Kyle, explaining how shock can sometimes make people see things that aren't there. Bonnie knew from the look on his face he wasn't buying any of it. Still, he hadn't told the police what he'd seen, so maybe that bode well for the future.

Pete led Ellie to the sofa across from Kyle and sat at her knee. Helen settled on one side of Kyle while Abigail stayed on his right. Bonnie relaxed in the easy chair beside the sofa.

Pete growled at them.

Ellie put her hand on his head and he quieted. "I lost what was left of my sight the night we fought in the park. My sight was going anyway, but being able to see more tonight as an owl is a blessing I didn't expect."

Kyle leaned forward. "I knew it! I *did* see your dog become a man!" He whipped out his phone and pointed it toward Pete to get a photo. "This is going to go viral for sure!"

Bonnie leaned into him. "No, Kyle, it's not," she said, her voice soft and menacing.

His eyes widened, but he continued with all the exuberance of youth. "It's news, Bonnie! *Big* news. Guide dog is really a man."

"Save it for *The Onion*," said Abigail. "No one will believe you anyway."

Pete stood, shook himself, and looked around. He loped to Ellie's room, disappeared for a moment and returned wearing a pair of jeans and a T-shirt. No one remained in the hall but them. He sat beside Ellie on the sofa.

Kyle was ecstatic and held up his phone. "Just one photo?"

"No," they all said in unison.

Pete glared at Bonnie. "Going to kill him next for knowing the truth? Isn't that what you bloodsuckers do?"

"We have never killed anyone," said Abigail, "unlike you Hunters, who have killed a lot of us."

He moved toward Abigail, but Ellie took his hand and held him back. "We want to retire. You were our last," she said.

Kyle was recording anyway. Bonnie took the phone away from him and started deleting things.

"Hey!"

"Kyle, do you want to live?"

He suddenly looked uncomfortable. "Uhm, yes?"

"We like to keep our neighborhood quiet," said Abigail. "Can you keep secrets?"

He looked down at the stack of comics on a nearby table. "Like secret identity secrets? Hell yeah!" He suddenly frowned. "Except this place only takes women. No married couples. Sorry, Pete."

Pete took Ellie's hand. "Not even crime-fighting dogs?"

Kyle smiled. "Service dogs are allowed, and husbands can visit as often as they want, you know. And maybe we can get the owner to change the policy." His expression wrinkled with distaste. "The owner turned against marriage after her husband emptied their bank account. It might be hard to get her to change her mind."

Bonnie smiled—she smelled a challenge she was well-suited for. "Everyone has something to hide, and maybe a trio of vampires, a blind owl, and a guide dog are just the ones to convince the owner that one happily married couple would be just fine."

Helen clapped with obvious joy. "Pete, can you play Whist?"

He scowled. "Hate it."

"He was never much for cards," said Ellie.

Helen's grin drooped away, but Bonnie had a weirder idea. "Since we aren't going to play Whist, maybe we can partner in a different way."

Ellie squinted. "Just what do you mean?"

Kyle retrieved his phone and grimaced at the absence of his photos. "I had selfies from Comic-Con on there," he muttered. When Bonnie frowned at him, he put the phone in his pocket.

"I propose a permanent truce," Bonnie said. "I propose we find out just what we need to make sure Pete can move here officially with Ellie. Then…."

"Then what?" asked Pete. "Partners in some crime to blackmail the owner of this place? We can find somewhere else."

Kyle looked up from his phone. "But you're a Sunnysider! Why would you want to go anywhere else?"

"I don't want to move! Besides, a little larceny so we can stay here is fine by me," said Ellie.

Pete looked at Ellie with surprise.

Bonnie waited. "Pete?"

He raised his lip in a snarl, but she could tell his heart wasn't in it. "So, this makes us partners in crime?"

"After you move in here with Ellie, we can work to keep our neighborhood safe at night for everyone."

Helen laughed. "Maybe think of it as partners in crime-*fighting*."

"Right," said Bonnie. "We may not be as fast as we once were, but we are every bit as treacherous, and dedicated to cleaning up the neighborhood and keeping it that way."

Pete looked at Ellie, then at the other eager faces. At last he nodded and grunted. "Truce."

It was almost time for sunrise, and so time for bed. Abigail and Kyle searched online for surplus police radios. Helen tapped a jaunty rhythm with her fingers on the arm of the plush sofa. Ellie put her head on Pete's shoulder, and Pete sighed.

This beat playing Whist while waiting for the sunrise. Bonnie put her feet up on the foot stool. It felt comfortable. She was content to remain among her night-folk for a while longer.

Copyright © 2020 by Barb Galler-Smith.

Joe Haldeman was born in Oklahoma in 1943, and as a child he lived in New Orleans, Alaska, and the Washington, D.C. area. Drafted, he fought in Vietnam, then became a professor at MIT for thirty years. Married to Mary Gay Haldeman since 1965, he has been a freelance author since 1969, mostly writing science fiction, winning him multiple Hugos and Nebulas.

THE MONSTER

by Joe Haldeman

Start at the beginning? Which beginning? Okay, since you be from Outside, I give you the whole thing. Sit over there, be comfort. Smoke em if you got em.

They talk about these guys that come back from the Nam all fucked up and shit, and say they be like time bombs: they go along okay for years, then get a gun and just go crazy. But it don't go nothing like that for me. Even though there be the gun involved, this time. And an actual murder, this time.

First time I be in prison, after the court-martial, I try to tell them what it be and what they get me? Social workers and shrinks. Guy to be a shrink in a prison ain't be no good shrink, what they can make Outside, is the way I figure it, so at first I don't give them shit, but then I always get Discipline, so I figure what the hell and make up a story. You watch any TV you can make up a Nam story too.

So some of them don't fall for it, they go along with it for a while because this is what crazy people do, is make up stories, then they give up and another one come along and I start over with a different story. And sometime when I know for sure they don't believe, when they start to look at me like you look at a animal in the zoo, that's when I tell them the real true story. And that's when they smile, you know, and nod, and the new guy come in next. Because if anybody would make up a story like that one, he'd have to be crazy, right? But I swear to God it's true.

Right. The beginning.

I be a lurp in the Nam, which means Long Range Recon Patrol. You look in these magazines about the Nam and they make like the lurps be always he-roes, brave boys go out and face Charlie alone, bring down the artillery on them and all, but it was not like that. You didn't want to be no lurp where we be, they make you be a fuckin lurp if they want to get rid of your ass, and that's the God's truth.

Now I can tell you right now that I don't give a flyin fuck for that U.S. Army and I don't like it even more when I be drafted, but I got to admit they be pretty smart, the way they do with us. Because we get off on that lurp shit. I mean we be one bunch of bad ass brothers and good ole boys and we did love that rock an roll, and God they give us rock an roll—fuck your M-16, we get real tommy guns with 100-round drum, usually one guy get your automatic grenade launcher, one guy carry that starlite scope, another guy the full demo bag. I mean we could of taken on the whole fuckin North Vietnam army. We could of killed fuckin Rambo.

Now I like to talk strange, though any time I want, I can talk like other people. Even Jamaican like my mama ain't understand me if I try. I be born in New York City, but at that time my mama be only three months there—when she speak her English it be island music, but the guy she live with, bringing me up, he be from Taiwan, so in between them I learn shitty English, same-same shitty Chinese. And live in Cuban neighborhood, *por la español* shitty.

He was one mean mother fuckin Chinese cab driver, slap shit out of me for twelve year, and then I take a kitchen knife and slap him back. He never come back for the ear. I think maybe he go off someplace and die, I don't give a shit anymore, but when I be drafted they find out I speak Chinese, send me to language school in California, and I be so dumb I believe them when they say this means no Nam for the boy: I stay home and translate for them tapes from the radio.

So they send me to the Nam anyhow, and I go a little wild. I hit everybody that outranks me. They put me in the hospital and I hit the doctor. They put me in the stockade and I hit the guards, the guards hit back, some more hospital. I figure sooner or later they got to kill me or let me out. But then one day this strac dude come in and tell me about the lurp shit. It sound all right, even though the dude say if I fuck up they can waste me and it's legal. By now I know they can do that shit right there in LBJ, Long Binh Jail, so what the fuck? In two days I'm in the jungle with three real bad ass dudes with a map and a compass and enough shit we could start our own war.

They give us these maps that never have no words on them, like names of places, just "TOWN POP 1000" and shit like that. They play it real cute, like we so dumb we don't know there be places outside of Vietnam, where no GIs can go. They keep all our ID in base camp, even the dog tags, and tell us not to be capture. Die first, they say, that shall be more pleasant. We laugh at that later, but I keep to myself the way I do feel. That the grave be one place we all be getting to, long road or short, and maybe the short road be less bumps, less trouble. Now I know from twenty years how true that be.

They don't tell us where the place be we leave from, after the slick drop us in, but we always sure as hell head west. Guy name Duke, mean honky but not dumb, he say all we be doin is harassment, bustin up supply lines comin down the Ho Chi Minh Trail, in Cambodia. It do look like that, long lines of gooks carryin ammo and shit, sometime on bicycles. We would set up some mine and some claymores and wait till the middle of the line be there, then pop the shit, then maybe waste a few with the grenade launcher and tommy guns, not too long so they ain't regroup and get us. Duke be taking a couple Polaroids and we go four different ways, meet a couple miles away, then sneak back to the LZ and call the slick. We go out maybe six time a month, maybe lose one guy a month. Me and Duke make it through all the way to the last one, that last one.

That time no different from the other times except they tell us try to blow a bridge up, not a big bridge like the movies, but one that hang off a mountain side, be hard to fix afterward. It also be hard to get to.

We lose one guy, new guy name of Winter, just tryin to get to the fuckin bridge. That be bad in a special kind of way. You get used to guys gettin shot or be wasted by frags and like that. But to fall like a hundred feet onto rocks be a different kind of bad. And it just break his back or something. He laying there and crying, tell all the world where we be, until Duke shut him up.

So it be just Duke and Cherry and me, the Chink. I am for goin back, no fuckin way they could blame us for that. But Duke crazy for action, always be crazy for killing, and Cherry would follow Duke anywhere, I think he a fag even then. Later I do know. When the Monster kill them.

This is where I usually feel the need to change. It's natural to adjust one's mode of discourse to a level appropriate to the subject at hand, is it not? To talk about this "Monster" requires addressing such concepts as disassociation and multiple personality, if only to discount them, and it would be awkward to speak of these things directly the way I normally speak, as Chink. This does not mean that there are two or several personalities resident within the sequestered hide of this disabled black veteran. It only means that I can speak in different ways. You could as well, if you grew up switching back and forth among Spanish, Chinese, and two flavors of English, chocolate and vanilla. It might also help if you had learned various Vietnamese dialects, and then spent the past twenty years in a succession of small rooms, mainly reading and writing. There still be the bad mother fucker in here. He simply uses appropriate language. The right tool for the job, or the right weapon.

Let me save us some time by demonstrating the logical weakness of some facile first order rationalizations that always seem to come up. One: that this whole Monster business is a bizarre lie I concocted and have stubbornly held on to for twenty years—which requires that it never have occurred to me that recanting it would result in much better treatment and, possibly, release. Two: that the Monster is some sort of psychological shield, or barrier, that I have erected between my "self" and the enormity of the crime I committed. That hardly holds up to inspection, since my job and life at that time comprised little more than a succession of premeditated cold-blooded murders. I didn't kill the two men, but if I had, it wouldn't have bothered me enough to require elaborate psychological defenses. Three: that I murdered Duke and Cherry because I was…upset at discovering them engaged in a homosexual act. I am and was indifferent toward that aberration, or hobby. Growing up in the ghetto and going directly from there to an army prison in Vietnam, I witnessed perversions for which you psychologists don't even have names.

Then of course there is the matter of the supposed eyewitness. It seemed particularly odious to me at the time, that my government would prefer the testimony of an erstwhile enemy soldier over one of its own. I see the process more clearly now, and realize that I was convicted before the court-martial was even convened.

The details? You know what a *hoi chan* was? You're too young. Well, *chieu hoi* is Vietnamese for "open arms"; if an enemy soldier came up to the barbed wire with his hands up, shouting *chieu hoi*, then in theory he would be welcomed into our loving, also open, arms and rehabilitated. Unless he was killed before people could figure out what he was saying. The rehabilitated ones were called *hoi chans*, and sometimes were used as translators and so forth.

Anyhow, this Vietnamese deserter's story was that he had been following us all day, staying out of sight, waiting for an opportunity to surrender. I don't believe that for a second. Nobody moves that quietly, that fast, through unfamiliar jungle. Duke had been a professional hunting guide back in the World, and he would have heard any slightest movement.

What do I say happened? You must have read the transcript…. I see. You want to check me for consistency.

I had sustained a small but deep wound in the calf, a fragment from a rifle grenade, I believe. I did elude capture, but the wound slowed me down.

We had blown the bridge at 1310, which was when the guards broke for lunch, and had agreed to rendezvous by 1430 near a large banyan tree about a mile from the base of the cliff. It was after 1500 when I got there, and I was worried. Winter had been carrying our only radio when he fell, and if I wasn't at the LZ with the other two, they would sensibly enough leave without me. I would be stranded, wounded, lost.

I was relieved to find them still waiting. In this sense I may *have* caused their deaths: if they had gone on, the Monster might have killed only me.

This is the only place where my story and that of the *hoi chan* are the same. They were indeed having sex. I waited under cover rather than interrupt them.

Yes, I know, this is where he testified I jumped them and did all those terrible things. Like *he* had been sitting off to one side, waiting for them to finish their business. What a bunch of bullshit.

What actually happened—what *actually* happened—was that I was hiding there behind some bamboo, waiting for them to finish so we could get on with it, when there was this sudden loud crashing in the woods on the other side of them, and bang. There was the Monster. It was bigger than any man, and black—not black like me, but glossy black, like shiny hair—and it just flat smashed into them, bashed them apart. Then it was on Cherry, I could hear bones crack like sticks. It bit him between the legs, and that was enough for me. I was gone. I heard a couple of short bursts from Duke's tommy gun, but I didn't go back to check it out. Just headed for the LZ as fast as my leg would let me.

So I made a big mistake. I lied. Wouldn't you? I'm supposed to tell them sorry, the rest of the squad got eaten by a werewolf? So while I'm waiting for the helicopter I make up this believable account of what happened at the bridge.

The slick comes and takes me back to the fire base, where the medics dress the wound and I debrief to the major there. They send me to Tuy Hoa, nice hospital on the beach, and I debrief again, to a bunch of captains and a bird colonel. They tell me I'm in for a Silver Star.

So I'm resting up there in the ward, reading a magazine, when in comes a couple of MPs and they grab me and haul me off to the stockade. Isn't that just like the army, to have a stockade in a hospital?

What has happened is that this gook, honorable *hoi chan* Nguyen Van Trong, has come out of the woodwork with his much more believable story. So I get railroaded and wind up in jail.

Come on now, it's all in the transcript. I'm tired of telling it. It upsets me.

Oh, all right. This Nguyen claims he was a guard at the bridge we blew up, and he'd been wanting to escape—they don't say "desert"—ever since they'd left Hanoi a few months before. Walking down the Ho Chi Minh Trail. So in the confusion after the blast, he runs away; he hears Duke and Cherry and follows them. Waiting for the right opportunity to go *chieu hoi*. I've told you how improbable that actually is.

So he's waiting in the woods while they blow each other and up walks me. I get the drop on them with my Thompson. I make Cherry tie Duke to the tree. Then I tie Cherry up, facing him. Then I castrate Cherry—with my *teeth*! You believe that? And then with my teeth and fingernails, I flay Duke, skin him alive, from the neck down, while he's watching Cherry die. Then for dessert, I bite off his cock, too. Then I cut them down and stroll away.

You got that? This Nguyen claims to have watched the whole thing, must have taken hours. Like he never had a chance to interrupt my little show. What, did I hang on to my weapon all the time I was nibbling away? Makes a lot of sense.

After I leave, he say he try to help the two men. Duke, he say, be still alive, but not worth much. Say he follow Duke's gestures and get the Polaroid out of his pack.

When those picture show up at the trial, I be a Had Daddy. Forget that his story ain't makin sense. Forget for Chris' sake that he be the fuckin *enemy*! Picture of Duke be still alive and his guts all hangin out, this godawful look on his face, I could of been fuckin Sister Theresa and they wouldn't of listen to me.

[At this point the respondent was silent for more than a minute, apparently controlling rage, perhaps tears. When he continued speaking, it was with the cultured white man's accent again.]

I know you are constrained not to believe me, but in order to understand what happened over the next few years, you must accept as tentatively true the fantastic premises of my delusional system. Mainly, that's the reasonable assertion that I didn't mutilate my friends, and the unreasonable one that the Cambodian jungle hides at least one glossy black humanoid over seven feet tall, with the disposition of a barracuda.

If you accept that this Monster exists, then where does that leave Mr. Nguyen Van Trong? One possibility is that he saw the same thing I did, and lied for the same reason I initially did—because no one in his right mind would believe the truth—but his lie implicated me, I suppose for verisimilitude.

A second possibility is the creepy one that Nguyen was somehow allied with the Monster; in league with him.

The third possibility…is that they were the same.

If the second or the third were true, it would probably be a good policy for me never to cross tracks with Nguyen again, or at least never to meet him unarmed. From that, it followed that it would be a good precaution for me to find out what had happened to him after the trial.

A maximum-security mental institution is far from an ideal place from which to conduct research. But I had several things going for me. The main thing was that I was not, despite all evidence to the contrary, actually crazy. Another was that I could take advantage of people's preconceptions, which is to say prejudices: I can tune my language from a mildly accented Jamaican dialect to the almost-impenetrable patois that I hid behind while I was in the army. Since white people assume that the smarter you are, the more like them you sound, and since most of my keepers were white, I could control their perception of me pretty well. I was a dumb nigger who with their help was getting a little smarter.

Finally I wangled a work detail in the library. Run by a white lady who thought she was hardass but had a heart of purest tapioca. Loved to see us goof off so long as we were reading.

I was gentle and helpful and appreciative of her guidance. She let me read more and more, and of course I could take books back to my cell. There was no record of many of the books I checked out: computer books.

She was a nice woman but fortunately not free of prejudice. It never occurred to her that it might not be a good idea to leave her pet darky alone with the computer terminal.

Once I could handle the library's computer system, my Nguyen project started in earnest. Information networks are wonderful, and computerized ordering and billing is, for a thief, the best tool since the credit card. I could order any book in print—after all, I opened the boxes, shelved the new volumes, and typed up the catalog card for each book. If I wanted it to be cataloged.

Trying to find out what the Monster was, I read all I could find about extraterrestrials, werewolves, mutations; all that science fiction garbage. I read up on Southeast Asian religions and folktales. Psychology books, because Occam's razor can cut the person who's using it, and maybe I *was* crazy after all.

Nothing conclusive came out of any of it. I had seen the Monster for only a couple of seconds, but the quick impression was, of course, branded on my memory. The face was intelligent, perhaps I should say "sentient," but it was not at all human. Two eyes, okay, but no obvious nose or ears. Mouth too big and lots of teeth like a shark's. Long fingers with too many joints, and claws. No mythology or pathology that I read about produced anything like it.

The other part of my Nguyen project was successful. I used the computer to track him down, through my own court records and various documents that had been declassified through the Freedom of Information Act.

Not surprisingly, he had emigrated to the United States just before the fall of Saigon. By 1986 he had his own fish market in San Francisco. Pillar of the community, the bastard.

Eighteen years of exemplary behavior and I worked my way down to minimum security. It was a more comfortable and freer life, but I didn't see any real chance of parole. I probably couldn't even be paroled if I'd been white and had bitten the cocks off two *black* men. I might get a medal, but not a parole.

So I had to escape. It wasn't hard.

I assumed that they would alert Nguyen, and perhaps watch him or even guard him for a while. So for two years I stayed away from San Francisco, burying myself in a dirtpoor black neighborhood in Washington. I saved my pennies and purchased or contrived the tools I would need when I eventually confronted him.

Finally I boarded a Greyhound, crawled to San Francisco, and rested up a couple of days. Then for another couple of days I kept an intermittent watch on the fish market, to satisfy myself that Nguyen wasn't under guard.

He lived in a two-room apartment in the rear of the store. I popped the back door lock a half hour before closing and hid in the bedroom. When I heard him lock the front door, I walked in and pointed a .44 Magnum at his face.

That was the most tense moment for me. I more than half expected him to turn into the Monster. I had even gone to the trouble of casting my own bullets of silver, in case that superstition turned out to be true.

He asked me not to shoot and took out his wallet. Then he recognized me and clammed up.

I made him strip to his shorts and tied him down with duct tape to a wooden chair. I turned the television on fairly loud, since my homemade silencer was not perfect, and traded the Magnum for a .22 automatic. It made about as much noise as a flyswatter, each time I shot.

There are places where you can shoot a person even with a .22 and he will die quickly and without too much pain. There are other sites that are quite the opposite. Of course I concentrated on those, trying to make him talk. Each time I shot him I dressed the wound, so there would be a minimum of blood loss.

I first shot him during the evening news, and he lasted well into Johnny Carson, with a new bullet each half hour. He never said a word, or cried out. Just stared.

After he died, I waited a few hours, and nothing happened. So I walked to the police station and turned myself in. That's it.

So here we be now. I know it be life for me. Maybe it be that rubber room. I ain't care. This be the only place be safe. The Monster, he know. I can feel.

[This is the end of the transcript proper. The respondent did not seem agitated when the guards led him away. Consistent with his final words, he seemed relieved to be back in prison, which makes his subsequent suicide mystifying. The circumstances heighten the mystery, as the attached coroner's note indicates.]

State of California
Department of Corrections
Forensic Pathology Division
Glyn Malin, M.D., Ph.D.—Chief of Research

I have read about suicides that were characterized by sudden hysterical strength, including a man who had apparently choked himself to death by throttling (though I seem to recall that it was a heart attack that actually killed him). The case of Royce "Chink" Jackson is one I would not have believed if I had not seen the body myself.

The body is well muscled, but not unusually so; when I'd heard how he died I assumed he was a mesomorphic weight lifter type. Bones are hard to break.

Also, his fingernails are cut to the quick. It must have taken a burst of superhuman strength, to tear his own flesh without being able to dig in.

My first specialty was thoracic surgery, so I well know how physically difficult it is to get to the heart. It's hard to believe that a person could tear out his own. It's doubly hard to believe that someone could do it after having brutally castrated himself.

I do have to confirm that that is what happened. The corridor leading to his solitary confinement cell is under constant video surveillance. No one came or went from the time the door was shut behind him until breakfast time, when the body was discovered.

He did it to himself, and in total silence.

Copyright © 1986 by Joe Haldeman.

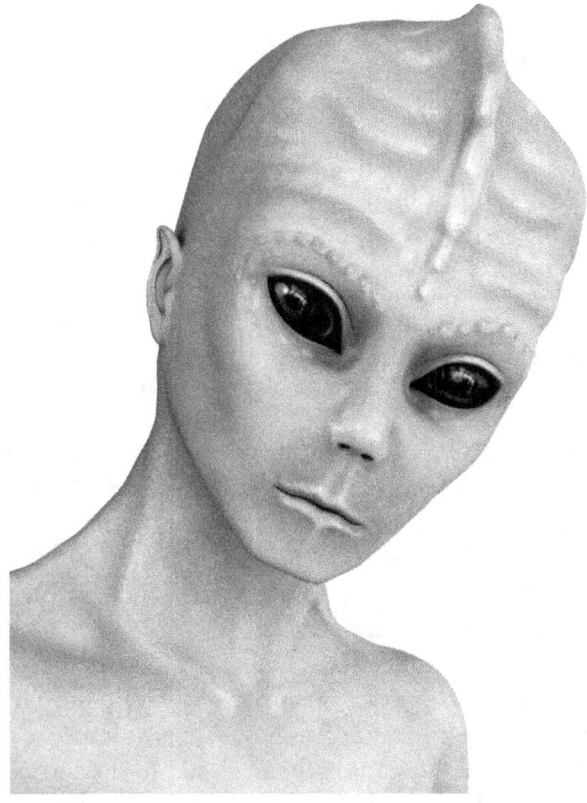

When Dantzel Cherry is not teaching Pilates or dance, she is writing. Dantzel's short fiction has appeared in Cast of Wonders, Escape Pod, Future SF, *and other magazines and anthologies. She lives in Utah with her husband, daughter, and two black cats.*

A FARMBOY, A WIZARD AND A DARK LORD WALK INTO A TOWER

by Dantzel Cherry

Wesley, the Chosen One, peered into the room at the top of the highest tower, clenching a smoking, eye-watering torch. His jaw dropped.

After months of grueling travel, he'd snuck into Dhar Klord's vast hoard of stolen talismans and treasures, and here they were piled like refuse. Gold, silver, and precious jewels sat in tall stacks among glowing orbs, ominously-humming books, foul potions, and several shiver-worthy containers of… dragon fetuses?

Wesley might be a farm boy, but even he felt this was tacky.

Wizard Brenson stumbled in, muttering, tangled in his charcoal cloak and gray beard. Wesley set the torch in an iron sconce and rushed to help the wizard up.

"What was that, Master Brenson?" He leaned closer to hear the old man's wisdom.

"That…was a lot…of stairs," Wizard Brenson wheezed. He glared at Wesley and wiped the sweat from his hawk-like nose. "Go…find…the Blood Stone. This could take…hours." He lifted a hand toward the door, conjuring an invisible shield.

"I did," Wesley said.

Wizard Brenson frowned. "Already?"

Wesley pointed. The nearby cruel-curved swords and golden lamps were covered in dust and cobwebs, but the many-faceted ruby Blood Stone gleamed in the torchlight as though newly polished.

"Oh, well—bring it here, fool boy!"

But Wesley had barely touched the Blood Stone when a deep, sonorous voice shook him to the bone. *"Stop."*

Wesley whipped around, clutching the Blood Stone. A figure holding a staff of white crystal entered the room, his face hidden in the cloak's shadows.

"We meet at—at last, Dhar Klord," Wesley said, his voice squeaking. He reddened. He'd planned a hundred ways of confronting Dhar Klord, and *that* was what he said to the evilest sorcerer of all time?

Dhar Klord sneered. "You, a puny, greasy boy from nowhere, think to defeat the greatest sorcerer of all time?"

This seemed a bit unfair to Wesley. Puny? He'd toned up quite a lot during this quest. Greasy? Well, Wesley had bathed in passing streams, but couldn't bear to let the icy water rise above his ankles.

"Get on with it!" Wizard Brenson said.

Wesley rubbed the Blood Stone, and just as Wizard Brenson had promised, he felt a faint thread of energy pulsing in the stone.

"What do you think you're doing?" Dhar Klord stepped forward, but Wizard Brenson's invisible shield held him back.

"I'm going to end you, once and for all!" Wesley said, even as he shriveled inside at sounding so supremely uncool. "For I have the Blood Stone!"

"Ah, but I'm holding the Crystal Staff of Trigadonia," Dhar Klord said.

"But *Wesley* is the Chosen One!" Wizard Brenson cried.

"We don't need to talk about that, though," Wesley said quickly, eyeing the ominously pulsing crystal.

"The Chosen One," Dhar Klord repeated. "I was the Chosen One five times. It's not that big a deal, Brenson."

"But Wesley is *the* Chosen One. Show him, Wesley!" Wizard Brenson shouted.

"Um—okay." Wesley gathered the stone of lore's energy, and then roared as the magic rushed out of him.

Or should have rushed.

A meandering trail of red smoke dissipated after a few feet.

Wesley tried again, to no avail.

Dhar Klord laughed. "You didn't think I'd keep that thing fully charged, did you? Do you have any idea how quickly virgin's blood goes bad?"

Wesley sighed. Yet another awkward moment in a long line of awkward moments in his life, and this one was likely to kill him.

"Damn it," Wizard Brenson said.

"What next, the power of True Love?" Dhar Klord asked.

"Actually—" Wesley began.

Wizard Brenson interrupted him with a forced laugh. "Of course not!"

"It's time to put an end to you, little brother," Dhar Klord said, throwing his cloak back and extinguishing Wizard Brenson's shield with a swipe of his staff.

"Wait. You're *brothers*?"

Wizard Brenson glared. "Don't interrupt, Wesley."

"You didn't tell him?" Dhar Klord asked. His nose was an exact match to Wizard Brenson's, Wesley noticed.

"Of course not."

Dhar Klord laughed his loudest yet. "So he truly doesn't know."

"Know what?" Wesley asked.

"That's the whole point, *Dhar*," Wizard Brenson said. "You don't tell dumb farmboys your backstory about not being evil enough for your parents and big brother, especially if you're tricking him into stealing stuff for you."

"Wait, *what*?" Wesley nearly dropped the Blood Stone.

The brothers ignored him.

"So, you thought to supplant me?"

"I still can," Wizard Brenson said. Lightning cracked between his hands. "I know your weaknesses."

"Pity Mother and Father aren't here. They'd be so proud—of *me*, for ending you once and for all," Dhar Klord said, raising his glowing staff.

A moment before they both unleashed their dark magic, something red whizzed through the air, cracking Dhar Klord's skull, and he crumpled, senseless.

Wizard Brenson gaped at his fallen rival, the dimming crystal staff, and the Blood Stone, which had clattered to the ground after its critical hit.

"Thanks, Wesl—"

A dragon fetus jar smashed his nose in, and he collapsed onto his brother.

In the silence, Wesley stared at the mess of limbs and blood. The most feared sorcerer of all time and the grouchiest wizard of all time—finally dead.

"I feel like I've earned this," he said to no one as he helped himself to the Blood Stone, a small chest of gold, several pockets full of jewels, and two golden lamps. He strode to the door, eager to leave, but memories of all the old stories made him pause.

Sure enough, Dhar Klord's hand was outstretched, conjuring a dark mass. When they locked eyes, Dhar Klord hurriedly played dead.

"Fool boy," Wesley told himself.

He ran both of them through the heart with a jeweled sword he'd snatched up from a pile of treasure beside him and, after a moment of *squick*, slashed them across the throat.

Now they were *really* dead.

Wesley cleaned his sword on Wizard Brenson's cloak and looked down the stairs. What was it that Dhar Klord had said about virgins?

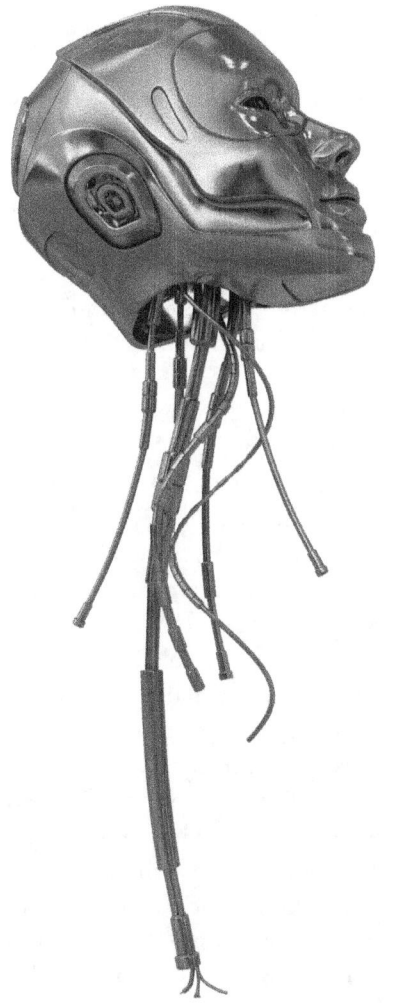

John Haas is a Canadian author with twenty published short stories and three novels. His goal is to become a full-time writer (rich and famous would be nice, too, but not the main goal). He lives with his two wonderful sons who continue to give him lots of motivation.

SAVING SARAH

by John Haas

William Atwood perched on the edge of his chair, at the time machine's exact center. He surveyed the apparatus which had expanded to almost completely fill his basement.

The machines at the Time Institute were much more compact, of course, but those were *sanctioned* time machines, not ones cobbled together, best as possible, with what could be purchased over an extended period. He'd been careful not to attract attention.

"Fifteen years," he breathed.

There should be some sort of ceremony for the end result of more than a decade's work, but who would come? His wife, Nadine, had checked out on the idea of fixing the past, and his friends at the Institute would have had him thrown in prison.

"No, this is my time, and my time alone."

With only those meager words to mark the occasion, William flipped the master switch. Lights flashed, gauges swung from left to right, and the deep hum of electricity filled the room. Within the next few minutes, after the machine warmed up, it would draw enough energy to power this end of the city.

He stood and paced, worried some unforeseen circumstance would come along to throw a wrench into his plans.

"What could go wrong?" he muttered, pulling on an errant tuft of hair.

All the tests had been successful. Inanimate objects had gone for short trips to the past. Then the cat. All traveled as expected. All returned in one piece. Still, he was sure something would go wrong, as if fate would naturally rob him when he was so close to saving Sarah.

His eyes rested on the power level gauge as it took its sweet, excruciating time going from red through yellow, before landing in the green. Electrical and temporal energy flared all around him.

"It's time."

He checked to ensure all the readings were optimal, positioned himself, and without hesitation he stabbed out a finger, pressing the button which would send him and the time machine back sixteen years.

CLICK.

An immediate disorienting lurch staggered him, like a physical slap, followed by a mental realignment which brought a wave of dizziness. The disorientation was worse than expected.

"Awk!"

William spun.

He hadn't made that sound, although he had more than enough cause to exclaim out loud.

"Who said that?"

Nothing. No movement in the shadowed corner where that exclamation had come from. William half-convinced himself it was his imagination when a hand appeared from behind one of the consoles. A second one followed, pulling a thin body into the light.

"Tyler!"

"Hey, Dad."

"Don't 'Hey, Dad,' me. Do you realize what you've done?"

Tyler got onto his feet and came around to the middle of the room. "Taken a ride on your illegal time machine?"

William's glare darkened. "What you've *done* is ruined my schedule, since I need to take you home now."

"No, you don't."

"What are you—?"

"Let me help, Dad."

William focused on the boy, somewhat surprised to find they were the same height. He realized Tyler must have turned fifteen in the past month.

"Come on, dad. I know you're going back to save her."

Her. Not, Sarah, but *her.* Neither William nor his wife had been able to say their daughter's name in the sixteen years since she'd died. It was too painful, too devastating. When they needed to mention Sarah at all it was always *her.*

Mostly they didn't mention her.

William grimaced. "You don't know what you're talking about."

Now it was Tyler's turn to scowl. "You think I don't know what you've been doing in the basement my whole life?" He looked around them, eyes filled with wonder. "It looks the same, yet…different. You've built a time machine to save my sister."

"I don't—"

"You have what you need?" Tyler interrupted.

William's hand instinctively rose to the inside pocket of his jacket, patting what would save five-year-old Sarah.

"I thought so," Tyler said, his face lighting up. "Please, Dad. I never even got to meet her!"

William drew in a deep breath and released it as a slow controlled exhale. Returning Tyler to the present would take time and expend so much energy. That much drain on the power supply would have surely been noticed the first time he used the machine. The second time…? He could not risk the authorities shutting him down before he achieved his goal.

"Fine, fine—but you do *everything* I tell you. Am I clear?"

Tyler raised one hand like a Boy Scout, a wide grin breaking across his face. "I promise."

Had Tyler been a Boy Scout? William had no idea. He barely knew the boy.

"Dad," Tyler asked, his voice quiet. "What…what exactly happened to her?"

William rounded on his son, righteous anger clear on his face, and watched the boy recoil a step. Taking a deep, calming breath, he turned his back on Tyler.

"A misdiagnosis," William said, his tone clipped. "Doctor said pneumonia. It was a blockage of the intestine. By the time they realized, it was too late."

Tyler drew in his own deep breath. A gasp of outrage? Had they really never told him what happened? William couldn't recall.

"We sued," William continued. "They settled, and I used the money for this." He waved his arms around him to indicate the time machine.

Before he had built it, he had gone to his so-called friends at the Time Institute and begged for their help. They said his request was outside their time allowance window for making corrections. There were too many variables. To many unplanned changes that could occur due to the ripple effect. William wanted to quit in anger, storm off, but he needed the resources, their cast-off materials, the innovative ideas. He played the part of the grieving father working an oh-so-important job while attending to his family.

"Why didn't you or Mom ever tell me?"

He grunted. "Too painful."

Time was wasting, and William moved to the basement stairs, ignoring the gaze of hope and admiration on Tyler's face. At the top step he listened at the door, sure that his timing was right. This period's version of him and Nadine should be at the hospital, yet it still paid to be careful. After a moment, William pushed the door open and stepped into a dark, silent house.

"Wow," Tyler breathed, from behind. "It's just...wow."

William ignored the blathering, turning toward the front door.

"How are we getting to the hospital?" Tyler asked.

William stopped. Without thinking, he'd been headed for the car. A car that would be at the hospital right now, and which he didn't have keys for anyway, having traded it years ago.

"Call a cab," Tyler suggested.

William glanced at the boy, then went to the kitchen phone.

While waiting for the cab, William paced and Tyler moved around the ground floor like a kid at the zoo.

"It's amazing," Tyler said. "It's the same house, even some of the same furniture, but it's like a different family lives here."

"A different family did."

That stopped Tyler. It was indeed a different family, and one he wasn't yet a part of, one where a perpetual cloud of sadness wasn't hanging over his parents yet.

Outside, a horn did a double beep and they rushed to their cab.

It was just over a ten-minute drive to the hospital. William spent it drumming fingers against his legs while Tyler goggled at the passing scenes of a city he only half recognized. Stores and restaurants which had long ago been replaced by others. A different color scheme to the public buses.

The cab rolled into the hospital drop-off zone and stopped, cabbie shifting to stare at them in the rear-view mirror. "Ten bucks even."

William pulled out his wallet, removing a credit card and holding it toward the cabbie.

Tyler placed one hand on his father's arm and shook his head, leaning it to whisper, "That card won't be valid for years."

William slid the card back into place, a sickening roil in his stomach. He didn't have cash, hadn't carried any in years.

Tyler held a twenty out to the man. "Keep the change," he said, and jumped from the back seat.

William followed, heading for the front door of the hospital, two steps behind Tyler. He'd spent the last fifteen years making his time machine and focused on the one task of saving his daughter, but hadn't considered the finer details.

"We have no money for the trip back," Tyler said. "That was my whole allowance."

"What? Why didn't you get change?"

"I wanted us far away when that driver notices the hologram on the twenty."

William glanced over his shoulder at the retreating cab and grimaced.

"Hopefully we don't get the same guy on the way back," Tyler said.

William shook his head. "We'll cross that bridge when we come to it."

"So, do you remember which room?"

"Oh yes. I remember." He headed for the elevator which would take them to the children's ward. "Sarah has a semi-private room, sharing it with a boy who's had his appendix removed."

The elevator reached the correct floor and William stalked out, heading for Sarah's room. A hand slowed him and he rounded on Tyler. "What now?"

"What's the plan if you—the earlier you—are already there?"

William came to a stop. Of course his current self would be there, along with a younger Nadine. They hadn't left Sarah's side much, had they?

"I...could explain..."

"To Mom?"

No. To Nadine he would sound like a lunatic, even if the evidence in front of her eyes told her different. She could stop the whole thing with her stubbornness.

"Any suggestions?"

A smile came to Tyler at being included. "You said she has a roommate?"

"Yes. Didn't get many visitors and was happy to just lie there reading comic books."

"Do you remember his name?"

William shook his head.

"Okay, let me go first. I'll see if you're in there." Tyler shook his head. "This is so strange. Surreal."

"It is." And yet somehow this boy grasped the entire experience with better ease than anyone should have. "Ty—"

Tyler pushed through the door before William could object.

With a frustrated groan he began his wait.

Pacing.

Wondering.

Worrying.

An eternity passed.

"No, something's gone wrong."

William moved toward the door, reaching for the handle. With a quick head shake he dropped the hand to his side, stomped away, then turned and once again headed for the door with determination. It swung open as he reached for it.

"That's okay, ma'am," Tyler said. "Let me know if you change your mind."

Tyler turned and let the door close behind him. "You aren't there, but Mom is. The other you is at the car. You'll need to convince her to leave, pretending you're...well, you."

William glanced from his son, to the door and back again. This idea scared him more than changing the time stream. How did he talk to a woman whom he'd only had superficial conversations with for the past decade?

"For Sarah," Tyler whispered.

William took a deep breath.

Yes. For Sarah.

He entered the room.

There, not eight feet away, was a daughter he hadn't seen in sixteen years. A daughter who would die in two days without his intervention. She was so peaceful, sleeping like his little angel.

"Sarah," he whispered, the first time he had said the name aloud in years.

The room shimmered behind a curtain of tears.

Nadine turned, getting to her feet and going to William. She was worried, of course, distraught, otherwise she would have noticed the change in clothes and his—

"You're looking older, Bill," she said, one hand brushing the grayed hair at his temples.

"I'm...feeling older," he said, taking her in his arms as was expected.

The two embraced for a full minute, two parents worried about their child, neither noticing when Tyler came back into the room and headed to the other bed's occupant. The boy was asleep but Tyler sank into the guest chair, staring at his—sort-of—parents. When William opened his eyes, Tyler made a motion toward a non-existent watch.

"Why don't you go get us some coffee," William suggested to Nadine.

She watched the sleeping girl, taking a step back. "But, if anything happens..."

"Then I'll come get you."

"And leave Sarah *alone*?"

"I can come get you, M..." Tyler almost said Mom. "Ma'am."

Nadine looked at her daughter, about to launch another argument.

"Take a break," William said. "Stretch your legs."

She hesitated, then deflated. "Okay. To the cafeteria and back. Not one second longer."

"Of course."

Nadine grabbed her purse and left the room at a trot, after one last glance at Sarah.

"Ten minutes at most," Tyler said, "and I'll bet she's back sooner."

On the back of a chair was a jacket William remembered. His other self wouldn't be gone long either. He stepped forward, smiling at his sleeping daughter. Such an easy solution, a simple medication into her IV drip and she would live.

He fumbled the medicine from his pocket and dropped the bottle, reaching quick to recover it.

"It's okay, Dad. You can do this."

He nodded. Yes, he *could* do this. There should be no difficulty in it, but suddenly he was all thumbs.

Tyler headed to the door and opened it a crack. "Still clear."

Another glance down the hall and Tyler headed for the jacket, going through the pockets.

"What are you doing?" William said, distracted.

"We need cab money," he said. "Do you think you'll mind?"

William shook his head and returned to the task of inserting the medicine, watching the plastic tubing which looped down into Sarah's arm. He brushed a lock of hair away from her peaceful face, then went to her chart, making a quick notation of her real diagnosis on the uppermost form, hoping the next doctor on call would spot it and order the right follow-up tests, and hopefully *not* try to work out just how the notation got onto the chart in the first place. He didn't want any repercussions for younger him. Hand shaking, he went to the window, burying his face in one hand. "Please, let this work."

"Here we go," Tyler said, two ten-dollar bills in his hand and starting toward his father.

"Who are you people?"

Both William and Tyler turned toward the sound of the voice.

"Aw, crap," William said under his breath, one hand raised to obscure his face.

Tyler stepped forward, crumpling the bill in his hand. "Oh, hi. I told your wife I would keep an eye on Sarah while she went to the cafeteria."

"And *who* are you?"

"Oh, I'm a friend of…" he gestured toward the sleeping boy in the other bed.

The younger William stepped to his daughter's bedside while the older one made sure he faced the other bed.

The boy's eyes fluttered and saw William. He smiled.

"Who are you?" the boy asked. "A doctor?"

William glanced over his shoulder at the other version of himself who was squinting in their direction with some curiosity. William searched his memories.

"I'm a friend of your mom's, from the restaurant. I promised I would check in on you while she was at work."

He prayed that woman was at work.

"Oh. What's your name?"

"Wi…Bill. And this is my son Tyler."

The other William had gone back to focusing on his daughter.

Tyler came over and grinned at the boy. "Hey, how's it going?"

"A little tired. The medicine keeps me pretty sleepy."

"Well, you go back to sleep if you want. Do you have enough comics?"

The boy gestured with a proud flourish, like a magician at the end of a trick. A pile sat on the side table and Tyler wished he had time to glance through them. Fifteen-year-old comics. There was bound to be something interesting.

The boy yawned.

William had started inching toward the door, keeping his back to the younger version of himself. "Tyler, we need to go."

He opened the door just as his wife started to push from the other side. She stumbled forward, catching herself without dropping either coffee.

"Where are you going, Bill?" she said. "Was there a change?"

"Ah, um, I…" William said. He stepped past her and exited into the hallway. "Tyler."

Tyler rushed past his mother, giving her a quick wave as he did. She headed into the room, goggled at her version of William, then spun toward the closing door.

Out in the hallway Tyler rushed to his dad. "The stairs."

William was already moving. He sped for the marked exit and pushed through into the stairwell. Both he and Tyler looked back at the woman standing in the doorway of the room, watching them go.

They bolted down flights of stairs and into the lobby.

In the loading zone a cab was dropping one woman off and the two clambered into the back seat. William turned to see the elevator open and his other self rushing to the front door. Younger him stood there, staring at his doppelgänger in the cab.

Earlier him would realize what had happened. Maybe not the specific details, but he wouldn't need them. He worked at the Time Institute, knew the possibilities. To him it wouldn't be some strange coincidence.

The cab pulled from the curb and headed into the street. Behind, the younger version raised one hand in farewell.

"You think you'll still be okay with our visit when he notices the money missing from his pocket?" Tyler asked.

"I think we'll understand."

William stared at his son, the son he'd never had any time for or interest in. The son who had kept a level head and saved them from discovery more than once. He was *proud* of Tyler!

What a fool he'd been. In the saving of one child, he had lost so much time with another. No more though. After this he would make it up to his son, get to know him.

The cab rolled to a stop in front of the house and Tyler once again told the cabbie to keep the change.

The two burst through the front door, closing and locking it behind them. William wasn't sure the other him wouldn't follow, and that could only lead to a frustrating conversation which would lead nowhere. No, he'd done what he came back to do. Now his family could be whole.

Tyler led the way down to the basement and into the time machine. He watched in fascination while his father set all the dials and gauges to send them back home.

William looked over his shoulder at his son. "Ready?"

Tyler gave a thumbs up and William reached out for the console with one hand. He stopped.

"Press this button here," he told Tyler.

The boy stepped forward like a kid at Disneyworld, glanced at his father with a grin, and pressed it. The world shimmered, that disorienting wave racing through them both.

"You okay?" William asked.

Tyler shot his father another grin. "*Better* than okay. Yeah!"

The two shared the moment in silence then turned as one and started up the stairs.

"You think Sarah will still live here?" Tyler asked. "She could be away at college."

She *would* be the right age, but it was about time for summer break so William hoped for the best. Somehow he knew she was there. In fact, he had a bunch of new memories in his head which contradicted others, fighting to reconcile.

The world that *is* had begun writing over the world that *was*.

It would be the same for Tyler, memories coming into his head from nowhere. "The recollections of our new past will start to catch up with us, but because we were outside of normal time when the change occurred, our overloaded brains are still trying to piece it all together."

The two raced onto the main floor.

"Sarah?" William called. "Sarah?"

William and Tyler both held their breath. Nothing.

Then the sound of someone walking toward the top of the stairs. "What is it, Dad?" a voice called out from above.

They raced to the foot of the stairs and stared at the beautiful young lady Sarah had survived to become. She stood watching them with a quizzical smile on her face.

William sprinted up the stairs and gave her an enormous hug, pulling Sarah up off her feet. It was the most emotion he'd felt or shown in years.

His daughter laughed—oh, how he had missed her laughter.

"Dad, you're going weird on me. What's up?"

William couldn't speak. He shook his head and moved aside, giving Tyler enough room to give his sister a hug.

"Who's your friend?" Sarah asked.

William and Tyler stopped, turning to each other then back to Sarah.

"You...don't know him?"

Sarah shook her head. "Should I? He does look kind of familiar."

"Dad?" Tyler said.

William saw it all, like pieces of a puzzle. With Sarah alive they hadn't needed a second child. Tyler had never been born.

What did that mean for his son though? Could he live here now or...?

"Dad!"

William watched Tyler raise his hand to his face. It wasn't quite see-through but it wasn't exactly there either.

"Come on," William turned and bolted for the basement, explaining as they went. "I'm sorry, Tyler, but you never existed here."

Tyler had already come to that same conclusion. "We can't go back though, Dad. Sarah has as much right to exist as I do."

"We need to get you back into the time stream. If you go into the past, before you were born, then the potential for you still exists and you should too. As long as you don't return here. It's a paradox, but we can work with that."

"Um, Dad, what about—"

"We'll stay there until we can find a way to make sure you exist. There has to be a way around this."

"Sure, Dad."

William looked at his son with a mixture of fear and…yes, love.

The two rushed down the stairs into the basement—an area filled with washer and dryer, Christmas decorations, storage containers, a folded-up ping-pong table.

"No," William breathed.

"You never needed to build the time machine either, Dad."

"Oh, Tyler."

Tyler raised his hands, seeing the floor through them. In another minute, he would cease to exist.

"I'm so sorry, son."

Tyler shook his head and William took his son into his arms and hugged him.

"I'll build it again," William said, "and I'll go back to my younger self, make sure you're born."

Tyler shook his head, knowing what the odds were. "Hey, we saved her, didn't we?"

"We sure did."

"Well, that's what we went back for, isn't it?"

"Yes, but—"

"It's okay, Dad. I mean…not okay, really, but I'm still glad we did it. Glad I got to meet my sister."

His voice had become thinner, less there.

"I'll find a way Tyler, like I found a way to save Sarah."

"I love you, Dad."

"I love you too, Tyler."

The silence of the basement pressed in on William. He was alone.

"Dad? What are you doing down there?"

William frowned, then turned to see Sarah standing at the top of the stairs, brushing aside a tear he wasn't aware of.

"I don't remember," he said with a humorless laugh, as memories of the new timestream settled into his brain, replacing those of an alternate timeline that no longer existed. "I thought I lost something—something important. But, it's gone now."

Copyright © 2020 by John Haas.

Stephen King described McDevitt as "the logical heir to Isaac Asimov and Arthur Clarke." Eleven of his novels were Nebula finalists. Seeker won in 2007. He has also won the Campbell and Philip Dick Awards. McDevitt was a naval officer, an English teacher, and conducted leadership seminars for the Customs Service. He is also the 2020 recipient of the NASA Night Sky Network award for "keeping the science in science fiction."

TO HELL WITH THE STARS

by Jack McDevitt

Christmas night.

Will Cutler couldn't get the sentient ocean out of his mind. Or the creature who wanted only to serve man. Or the curious chess game in the portrait that hung in a deserted city on a world halfway across the galaxy. He drew up his knees, propped the book against them, and let his head sink back into the pillows. The sky was dark through the plexidome. It had been snowing most of the evening, but the clouds were beginning to scatter. Orion's belt had appeared, and the lovely double star of Earth and Moon floated among the luminous branches of Granpop's elms. Soft laughter and conversation drifted up the stairs.

The sounds of the party seemed far away, and the *Space Beagle* rode a column of flame down into a silent desert. The glow from the reading lamp was bright on the inside of his eyelids. He broke the beam with his hand, and it dimmed and went out.

The book lay open at his fingertips.

It was hard to believe they were a thousand years old, these stories that were so full of energy and so unlike anything he'd come across before: tales of dark, alien places and gleaming temples under other stars and expeditions to black holes. They don't write like that anymore. Never had, during his lifetime. He'd read some other books from the classical Western period, some Dickens, some Updike, people like that. But these: what was there in the last thousand years to compare with this guy Bradbury?

The night air felt good. It smelled of pine needles and scorched wood and bayberry. And maybe of dinosaurs and rocket fuel.

☼

His father might have been standing at the door for several minutes. "Goodnight, champ," he whispered, lingering.

"I'm awake, Dad."

He approached the bed. "Lights out already? It's still early." His weight pressed down the mattress.

Will was slow to answer. "I know."

His father adjusted the sheet, pulling it up over the boy's shoulders. "It's supposed to get cold tonight. Heavy snow by morning." He picked up the book and, without looking at it, placed it atop the night table.

"Dad." The word stopped the subtle shift of weight that would precede the press of his father's hand on his shoulder, the final act before withdrawal. "Why didn't we ever go to the stars?"

He was older than most of the other kids' fathers. There had been a time when Will was ashamed of that. He couldn't play ball and he was a lousy hiker. The only time he'd tried to walk out over the Rise, they'd had to get help to bring him home. But he laughed a lot, and he always listened. Will was reaching an age at which he understood how much that meant. "It costs a lot of money, Will. It's just more than we can manage. You'll be going to Earth in two years to finish school."

The boy stiffened. "Dad, I mean the *stars*. Alpha Centauri, Vega, the Phoenix Nebula—"

"The Phoenix Nebula? I don't think I know that one."

"It's in a story by a man named Clarke. A Jesuit goes there and discovers something terrible."

The father listened while Will outlined the tale in a few brief sentences. "I don't think," he said, "your mother would approve of your reading such things."

"She gave me the book." Will smiled.

"This one?" It was bound in cassilate, a leather substitute, and its title was written in silver script: *Great Tales of the Space Age*. He picked it up and looked at it with amusement. The names of the editors appeared on the spine: Asimov and Greenberg. "I don't think we realized, uh, that it was like that. It was one of the things they found in the time vault on the Moon a couple of years ago. Your mother thought it would be educational."

"You'd enjoy it, Dad."

His father nodded and glanced at the volume. "What's the Space Age?"

"It's the name that people of the classical period used to refer to their own time. It has to do with the early exploration of the solar system, and the first manned flights. And, I think, the idea that we were going to the stars."

A set of lights moved slowly through the sky. "Oh," his father said. "Well, people have had a lot of strange ideas. History is full of dead gods and formulas to make gold and notions that the world was about to end." He adjusted the lamp, and opened to the contents page. His gray eyes ran down the list, and a faint smile played about his lips. "The truth of it, Will, is that the stars are a pleasant dream, but no one's ever going out to them."

"Why not?" Will was puzzled at the sound of irritation in his own voice. He was happy to see that his father appeared not to have noticed.

"They're too *far*. They're just too far." He looked up through the plexidome at the splinters of light. "These people, Greenberg and Asimov, they lived, what, a thousand years ago?"

"Twentieth, twenty-first century. Somewhere in there."

"You know that new ship they're using in the outer System? The *Explorer*?"

"Fusion engines," said the boy.

"Yes. Do you know what its top recorded speed is?"

"About two hundred thousand kilometers an hour."

"Much faster than anything this Greenberg ever saw. Anyhow, if they'd launched an *Explorer* to Alpha Centauri at the time these stories were written, do you know when it would have gotten there?"

"I have no idea."

"It wouldn't have arrived yet." His father produced a minicomp, pushed a few buttons, and smiled. "About five percent. The *Explorer* would need another nineteen thousand years to get there."

"Long ride," said Will, grudgingly.

"You'd want to take a good book."

The boy was silent.

"It's not as if we haven't tried, Will. There's an artificial world, a world-ship, half-built, out beyond Mars someplace. They were going to send out a complete colony, people, farm animals, lakes, forest, everything."

"What happened?"

"It's too *far*. Hell, Will, life is good here. People are happy. There's plenty of real estate in the solar system if folks want to move. In the end, there weren't enough volunteers for the world-ship. I mean, what's the *point*? The people who go would be depriving their kids of any kind of normal life. How would *you* feel about living inside a tube for a lifetime? No beaches. Not real ones anyhow. No sunlight. No new places to explore. And for what? The payoff is so far down the road that, in reality, there *is* no payoff."

"In the stories," Will said, "the ships are very fast."

"I'm sure. But even if you traveled on a light beam, the stars are extremely far apart. And a ship can't achieve an appreciable fraction of that kind of velocity because it isn't traveling through a vacuum. At, say, a tenth of the speed of light, even a few atoms straying in front of it would blow the thing apart."

Outside, the Christmas lights were blue on the snow. "They'd have been disappointed," the boy said, "at how things came out."

"Who would have?"

"Benford. Robinson. Sheffield. Resnick."

The father looked again at the table of contents. "Oh," he said. He rifled idly through the pages. "Maybe not. It's hard to tell, of course, with people you don't know. But we've eliminated war, population problems, ecological crises, boundary disputes, racial strife. Everybody eats pretty well now, and for the only time in its history, the human family stands united. I suspect if someone had been able to corner, say—" he flipped some pages, "—Jack Vance, and ask him whether he would have settled for this kind of world, he'd have been delighted. Any sensible person would. He'd have said *to hell with the stars*!"

"No!" Will's eyes blazed. "He *wouldn't* have been satisfied. None of them would."

"Well, I don't suppose it matters. Physical law is what it is, and it doesn't take much account of whether we approve or not. Will, if these ideas hadn't become dated, and absurd, this kind of book wouldn't have disappeared. I mean, we wouldn't even know about *Great Tales of the Space Age* if someone hadn't dropped a copy of the thing into the time capsule. That should tell you something." He got up. "Gotta go, kid. Can't ignore the guests."

Will felt terrible. "But you can't really be *sure* of that. Maybe the time was never right before. Maybe they ran out of money. Maybe it takes all of us working together to do it." He slid back into the pillows. His father held up his hands, palms out, in the old gesture of surrender he always used when a game was going against him. "We could do that *now*, Dad. There's a way to build a *Space Beagle. Somehow.*"

"Let me know if you figure it out, son." The lights died, and the door opened. "You'll have to do it yourself, though. Nobody *else* is giving it any thought. Nobody has for centuries."

✿

The snow did not come. And while Will Cutler stared through the plexidome at the faraway stars, thousands of others were also discovering Willis and Swanwick and Tiptree and Sturgeon. They lived in a dozen cities across Will's native Venus. And they played on the cool green hills of Earth and farmed the rich Martian lowlands; they clung to remote shelters among the asteroids, and watched the skies from silver towers beneath the great crystal hemispheres of Io and Titan and Miranda.

The ancient summons flickered across the worlds, insubstantial, seductive, irresistible. Maybe the dreamers were getting ready to try again.

Copyright © Davis Publications, 1987. Originally published in Asimov's Science Fiction, *December 1987.*

Larry Hodges, an Odyssey workshop grad, has sold more than one hundred stories. His four novels include Campaign 2100: Game of Scorpions, *published by World Weaver Press, and* When Parallel Lines Meet, *a Stellar Guild team-up with Mike Resnick and Lezli Robyn.*

THE UNTOLD CHRISTMAS CAROL

by Larry Hodges

"Satan damn us," the child said, leaning on his crutch with an impish grin. *"Every one!"*

It was so cute when Tiny Tim said that, the Devil thought, though of course he only said it when nobody was around, as he had taught him during those secret nighttime visits. Around others, he said it the other way, as befitting the son of the King of Lies—which, of course, made his son the Prince of Lies.

He watched through a portal on his desk, beaming with pride amidst the flames in his office in South Central Hell. He wore a fireproof business suit with a smoldering derby hat that pleasantly singed the top of his large bald head. His facial features changed every few seconds, taking on the likeness of the evil men and women he tortured, allowing him to momentarily enjoy their torment. A fire-proof version of Giotto's *The Last Judgment* and other paintings of the Devil hung on the walls, all depicted in burnt orange shades to better blend in with the surrounding flames.

He watched his son with misty-eyed wonder. Soon the child would be apprenticed to Scrooge—oh, how he loved that man! The Devil had a special place reserved for him in the Fourth Circle of Hell. The Devil's face flashed between that of a madly leering adulterer suffering in the Second Circle to a bearded shrieking glutton from the Third. When Tim was sufficiently corrupted and the dark spirit had overtaken him, he would learn who he really was and his destiny. Then they would lead a coup and rule the galaxy together as father and son.

Tim coughed.

The Devil sighed. The devil really was in the details, and that kidney problem, renal tubular acidosis, was a nice touch. Already the boy could barely walk without his crutch. Nineteenth century medicine didn't know what the disease was, but they knew how to treat it. And who was the only person in town who could afford to pay for those expensive treatments? Scrooge.

It worked out so well.

⬡

The Devil punched *The Last Judgment*, his fist going through his own face on the painting behind it, allowing the even hotter outside air to pour into his office through the new hole in the wall. Even that heat paled in comparison to the curses coming from his mouth. Two of his minions had solicited Scrooge for the money to treat Tim, but he'd scoffed something about "decreasing the surplus population" and walked off. It was exactly why the Devil so admired the old man, but now it was getting in the way of his plans. Son of the Devil or not, Tim would die if someone didn't pay for his treatment. The Devil could cure him with a wave of his hand, but he was barred from doing so by the non-interference directive—the first thing he'd change when *he* was in charge. Instead, he'd have to use his cunning and persuasiveness to save his dear son.

He stared down at Tim's tiny desk amidst the flames in the corner. Above it hung a child's mobile with various figures hanging in torment—a girl and a boy representing Want and Ignorance, and others representing the nine circles of Hell, from one to nine: Limbo, Lust, Gluttony, Greed, Anger, Heresy, Violence, Fraud, and Treachery. Toy figures for his little boy.

Everyone agreed these were bad attributes, and people who practiced them should be punished. Wasn't that all he was doing when he tortured sinners? Didn't parents spank their kids for misbehaving? Didn't the mythical Santa Claus keep a list and withhold toys from the naughty? Didn't criminals get punished for their acts? How was this any different from what the Devil did? *I'm no different than a parent, Santa Claus, or a judge,* he thought as his face flashed from Napoleon to Vlad the Impaler. *I just punish them a bit longer. Because of me, no one has to get revenge against evil people; I do it for them. Vengeance is mine.*

And yet all the millions of evil souls he tortured meant nothing to him right now. His son's life was in danger. He had to save him.

Through the face of a red-haired screaming heretic from the Sixth Circle, inspiration struck. He grinned as only the Devil could grin.

⬡

"What did he call you?" The doomed spirit the Devil had disguised as Jacob Marley writhed in the flames before him, his chains clattering in the office flames. The disguise was fake, the chains were real.

He could have gotten the real Marley, dead these seven years and in the Fourth Circle. But he needed someone who could pretend to be someone he wasn't, who was also familiar with London. In real life, the spirit had been the American traitor Benedict Arnold, dead these forty-two years after his retirement to London, and now residing in the Ninth Circle. He manifested in his old Revolutionary War uniform, his medals jingling as he trembled.

"He called me an undigested bit of beef, a blot of mustard, a crumb of cheese, a fragment of underdone potato," Arnold said in a high-pitched squeak, writhing in the office flames. Like all doomed spirits, after a few decades they got somewhat used to it.

"Did you give him the message about the three spirits?" the Devil asked.

"Yes, yes—I did, *I did!*"

The Devil took a deep breath through the wild eyes of a handlebar-mustachioed suicide from the Seventh Circle. "Then it is time for new disguises. Now, what would the three spirits of Christmas look like?" He plucked down from the mobile the figures for Want and Ignorance—they may come in handy as sentimental claptrap in one of the new costumes.

⬡

The scheme was a huge success. It had taken only a single night to convert Scrooge to goodness—or at least scare him into faking it. What a humbug that was! The Devil smiled; he liked the word *humbug*.

It had been a close thing, with that stupid Benedict Arnold running his mouth off too much. It was only when he'd ripped out Arnold's tongue and sent him down with platform shoes to make him taller and in a black robe as the Ghost of Christmas Yet to Come that his ominous silence—and a cleverly faked grave—had turned the trick.

Soon Tim would toss aside his crutch, start his apprenticeship with Scrooge, and begin his final descent into darkness. And then the Devil would get a man-sized desk for his protégé, and they'd share his office as they planned the ultimate conquest of the galaxy. The tears of happiness pouring down his face almost instantly evaporated in the flames of his office.

With a wave of his hand, as his face flashed from that of Judas to Cain, both from the Ninth Circle, he returned Arnold to that same Circle of Hell, with a note to double the intensity of his torture. He smiled; there was no non-interference directive *here*.

☼

Failure. Or more accurately, he'd been too successful, leading to failure. Who'd have thought that he would really convert Scrooge to goodness? Or that instead of corrupting Tim, Scrooge was teaching him *virtue*? The Devil cringed every time Tim said, "God Bless us, every one," knowing he really meant it. Now it was tears of anger that flowed; his pride and joy was going in the wrong direction. His face flashed rapidly through a dozen lost souls in the Fifth Circle.

As he paced his office he suddenly grinned through the trembling face of a rapist with thick glasses from the Seventh Circle. If he could scare the evil out of Scrooge in one night by sending him three spirits in bad disguises, he could scare it back into him by sending three more—and these wouldn't be Christmasy ones.

There was a sound of clattering chains, and a cold breeze hit the back of his head, knocking off his smoldering derby hat. He spun about—*there were no cold breezes in Hell.*

Before him in the flames stood the quaking Benedict Arnold.

"What are you doing here?" the Devil thundered, his face flashing between the screaming souls of Hitler and Stalin, both burning in the Seventh Circle.

"I have a message for you," Arnold stammered. Apparently he'd grown his tongue back.

"A message from who?"

Arnold looked confused. "I—I'm not sure. From beyond."

An anonymous message from *beyond*? What a humbug. "And what would this message be?" Hadn't he doubled Arnold's torture? He'd quadruple it. Heck, he'd six hundred and sixty-sixtuple it.

Arnold coughed slightly as he lightly rattled a chain. "Tonight you will be haunted by three spirits."

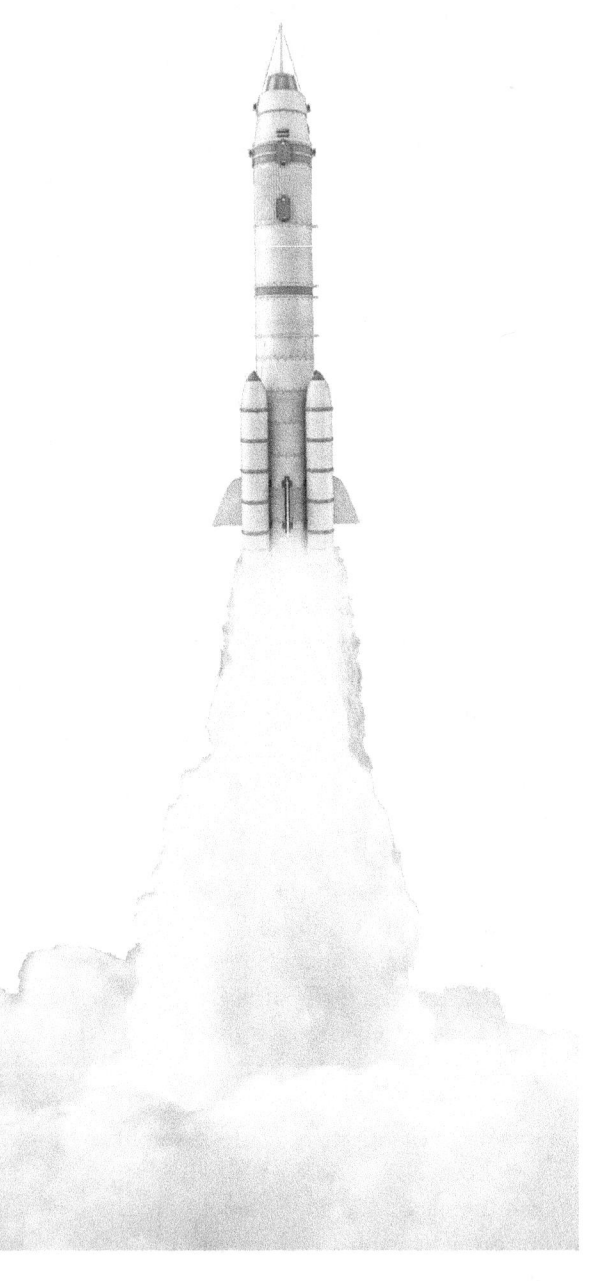

Richard Chwedyk sold his first story in 1990, won a Nebula in 2002, and has been active in the field for the past twenty-nine years.

RECOMMENDED BOOKS

by Richard Chwedyk

QUANTITY AND QUALITY

As I was finishing the column for last issue, I looked over the space where my stack of "To Be Reviewed" books, usually towers, and found… nothing. Any sense of accomplishment I may have felt was quickly replaced with an anxious thought: what if nothing comes in to review for the next issue?

No sooner had I exhaled that worry, the doorbell rang. Two packages from USPS. Followed quickly with two more from UPS. Then one from FedEx.

The books just kept on coming.

Another anxious thought: what if they're not any good?

It turns out there are times, not all the time, but sometimes, the words of Ross "The Boss" Friedman, lead guitarist for legendary proto-punk band The Dictators, ring true: "To me, quantity *is* quality!"

See below.

The Dragon Waiting
By John M. Ford
Tor Essentials
September 2020
ISBN: 978-1-250-26901-0

Once again, Tor Essentials has simplified my pick in choosing an "older" (relatively speaking) or classic work to bring to your attention. And for once I'm putting it at the beginning so you won't miss it.

There are two acknowledged masterpieces of alternate history in our field. One of them is *Pavane*, by Keith Roberts. The other is *The Dragon Waiting*, by John M. Ford. I would be hard-pressed to choose a favorite between the two, so I won't. The Roberts book has been in and out of print for many years, and more out than in. Ford's novel up until now has suffered a similar fate. This current edition is a handsome, sturdy, well-designed trade paperback—and a cause for celebration.

The cast is too numerous and the plot too intricate to be sufficiently condensed here except to say that in its course we encounter a Byzantine Empire more powerful than the one we encounter in history books (if anyone looks in history books anymore): a Welsh wizard, a female physician, a vampire duke, and a Julian the Apostate with an extended lifespan who radically alters the status of several religions in the western world. By the conclusion, we meet Henry Tudor and Richard, Duke of Gloucester. And the Battle of Bosworth Field comes to a very different outcome than the one we read about, if not in a history text, then in Shakespeare's *Richard III*.

All of this is rendered in Ford's remarkable prose. Remarkable because it is capable of conveying so much with exemplary economy. It rarely pauses to render a static scene, but does all the rendering within the framework of advancing the narrative, drawing his vast array of characters and capturing their speech with wit and cogency. It is what we call in the creative writing trade a *model* of great storytelling (as all his work is).

The novel comes with a fascinating introduction by Scott Lynch, who knew "Mike" Ford and, better, knows his work with great insight. He paints a vivid picture of Ford and explains the marvels of this novel's architecture in a manner that, unlike many introductions I have recently read of reissued works, adds to one's enjoyment and appreciation of it.

There's a question that always nags at me when I read an alternate history story or novel: how much does a reader need to know of the "unaltered" history of the subject to truly appreciate the story? Especially in our times, when a familiarity with history is as rare a thing to find as a coelacanth.

I usually conclude, rightly or wrongly, that if it's a good story, or at least an interesting one, I'll stand a good chance of seeking out the "real" story, such as it may be, that served as the raw material.

Which is why the return of *The Dragon Waiting* is a cause for celebration.

◆ ◆ ◆

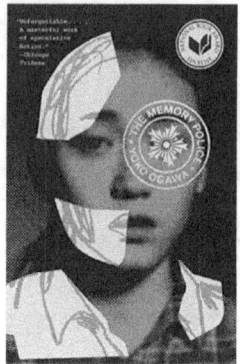

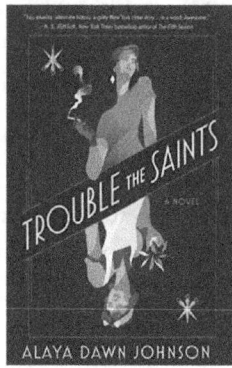

Trouble the Saints
by Alaya Dawn Johnson
Tor
June 2020
ISBN: 978-1-250-17534-2

Speaking of alternate history, here's an engaging and suspenseful tale set in the early days of the Second World War.

This book has magic, a bi-racial protagonist with a mean set of knives, Harlem in its heyday and the Manhattan underworld. It moves swiftly with an indelible pace and authority. The accompanying promo material tries to compare Johnson with James Baldwin, but in a few places I was reminded more of the great Chester Himes. Johnson has a real feel for her low-down world and all-too-human people, and the pervasive systemic racism behind every corner in this "noir" metropolis.

While not exactly uplifting, this book keeps its head up like a champ. It swings like an after-hours jam session, and that's something you shouldn't miss.

◆ ◆ ◆

The Memory Police
by Yoko Ogawa
translated from the Japanese by Stephen Snyder
Vintage Books
July 2020
ISBN: 978-1-101-91181-5

This is an ingenious little tale that enfolds in a most subtle way. On a little island, things start disappearing. Simple little things: hats, ribbons, bells, flowers. The missing things lead to a revelation that everything on the island is carefully monitored by the Memory Police, and before long people are the ones who disappear. The young writer/protagonist discovers her editor friend is in danger of being disappeared too, and works out a scheme to hide him under the floorboards of her home.

Language and writing are important here, perhaps the only means of resistance to the erasures imposed by the Memory Police. Our narrator's account may be the only record of what's been lost.

The novel is written with an exemplary simplicity and an economy that retains a vividness one expects from more complex narratives. I can't say how much of this is Ogawa, and how much is the translator, Stephen Snyder. It's a safe bet, though, that Snyder had something extraordinary to work with.

It's an effective, chilling work that you won't forget for a long time.

◆ ◆ ◆

Noumenon Ultra
by Marina J. Lostetter
Harper Voyager
2020
ISBN: 978-0-06-289572-1

Here I am, jumping in on a series in its third volume, but the brief summary of where the Planet United Missions convoys have gone beforehand does a good job of getting me up to speed on where they're headed in this one. The particulars of this novel involve an ancient supercomputer, I.C.C., making contact with one of the convoys. Lostteter has developed a neat, multi-faceted tale that provides the necessary "sense of wonder."

Interesting to note that Harper Voyager has added a subcategory on their back covers: Science Fiction/Space Opera. Maybe readers are getting pickier about what they grab off the shelves. I'll only add, to my satisfaction, the bigger half of this novel goes to "space" and the smaller half to "opera." And that works fine for me.

◆ ◆ ◆

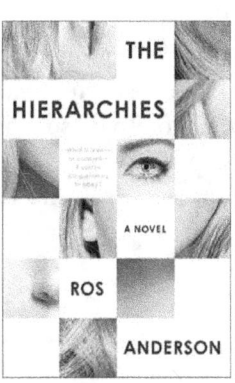

The Hierarchies
by Ros Anderson
Dutton
August 2020
ISBN: 978-0-593-18287-1

The Echo Wife
by Sarah Gailey
Tor
February 2021
ISBN: 978-1-250-17466-6

The themes here are as old as Pygmalion, or Galatea, let's say, but the approaches are distinct.

The Hierarchies is about Sylv.ie (not a typo), a robot built for sex. And yes, that's been explored in many places by authors as diverse as Charles Bukowski and Elizabeth Bear (whose short story "Dolly" is really the best thing I've read on this topic). But what's interesting here is that Ros Anderson tells the story from Sylv.ie's point of view. She casts a careful, circumspect eye on the world around her in a way that evokes the narrator of *The Tale of Genji*. The novel avoids the salacious and prurient in a skillful way through this strategy.

The episodic narrative has a strange, slightly dissociative quality about it at times, meditative at others. Sylv.ie is discovering her intrinsic humanity by documenting her world, which is horrific from our perspective. "Robot" is a code word for enslaved beings, and if there was any question of this before, what Sylv.ie shows us here makes it painfully apparent. If her writings and thoughts are ever discovered her memory will be erased.

The story doesn't move like a commercially plotted novel. Sylv.ie has little to measure her experience by. It's more of a slow revelation as the world comes into focus, for Sylv.ie and for us. In that way, the novel isn't for everyone, but in its own way and on its own terms, it's a compelling read.

The Echo Wife is the novel I think I was waiting for after I read their *Upright Women Wanted*.

Brilliant scientist Evelyn Caldwell has created a genetic duplicate of herself, Martine. Well, really, her husband, Nathan, did, but based upon Evelyn's research. Physically like Evelyn in every way, she is, however, everything Evelyn is not. It is inevitable that Martine has an affair with Nathan, and it's not long before the two-timing (or is that one-timing?) bum is dead, lying in a bloody mess on the floor.

If anything, this brings Evelyn and Martine closer together. And one of the neat things in the story is how these two contrasting characters manage to work together to save themselves. It's not so much *that* they do—we can see that coming—but the way Gailey conveys it to us—not played for laughs, but not entirely serious, either. Evelyn, our narrator, has her own way about things.

> In interviews, I sometimes say that science was my first love. That is a friendly kind of lie. The truth is that I've never loved science. Loving science would be like loving my own fingernails, or my lungs, or my lymph. I've always had science, always lived it and leaned on it; I've never had reason to love it or hate it any more than a mushroom loves or hates the soil it grows in.
>
> My first love was Nathan, and he made a fool of me long before he created Martine.

How they deal with the murder, and what comes after, makes for a wild, fast-paced, witty and thoughtful mini-adventure. Gailey is great at this stuff, and I hope they will grace us with more work soon.

◆◆◆

To Sleep in a Sea of Stars
by Christopher Paolini
Tor
September 2020
ISBN: 978-1-250-76284-9

It seems a fool's errand to review a Christopher Paolini novel. If you're a fan, you've already picked this up or are in the process of doing so. If you're not a fan, well, another imposing volume of a complex, multi-tiered tale, complete with charts and appendices, is not going to bring you any closer to jumping on the bandwagon.

Paolini seems to be doing for science fiction what he did for fantasy in *Eragon*. And it turns out, at least to my reckoning, he does it better here.

One of my students in my Fantasy Writing Workshop tried to turn me on to Paolini, and made me curious enough to pick this up as soon as I received the package.

In *To Sleep in a Sea of Stars*, the accent is more on the "opera" and less on the "space," though his "Fractalverse" and his protagonist, Kira (is it just me, or does every other novel these days have a major character named Kira?) kept me interested throughout, and at times even fascinated me, in all the ways you want science fiction to do so (space opera or no) through all of 825 pages.

I'll get to the appendices later. I *will*. Promise.

◆◆◆

The Cipher
by Kathe Koja
Meerkat Press
2020 (reprint, 1991)
ISBN: 978-1-9461-5433-0

I know, I usually don't cover horror here, but in many ways this novel changed the stakes for horror and dark fantasy in 1991. It transcends any category you attempt to fit it in. Back in the day, I kind of read it like it Fritz Leiber on hyperdrive. This time, it kind of struck me as Jack Kerouac trying to sell to *Weird Tales*. I may be strange, but this novel is stranger, in a good way. Kudos to Meerkat Press for bringing it back in print.

◆ ◆ ◆

The Invisible
by Seb Doubinsky
Meerkat Press
2020
ISBN: 978-1-946154-27-9

Not many fantasy novels take on politics, but Seb Dubinsky does so with an accomplished wit and intellect up front. His approach is somewhat experimental, with very brief chapters grouped under Roman numeral subheadings featuring Tarot card arcana (sorry, I can't bear to call them "trump" cards). Some chapters are no more than a paragraph, which makes for an episodic read—or a little like a series of blackouts.

> Jesse Valentino's ghost followed him all day, a shimmering silvery silhouette Ratner could perceive standing in a dark corner of his consciousness. It wasn't threatening or even frightening, just there, silent, motionless, perhaps waiting, perhaps only a residual image like the one left by the sun on your eye when you walked from a sunny street into a place filled with shadow.
>
> Walking into his empty apartment, Ratner noticed a note on the fridge. Laura had written that he shouldn't wait for her for dinner because she had a union meeting. Sighing, he opened the fridge and stared at the blank emptiness staring back at him. He took out his phone and dialed the Chinese takeaway. He almost ordered a dish for Valentino, but he remembered that ghosts didn't eat. So he asked for two bottles of Tsingtao beers. At least they could toast instead.

The novel fits together very well and moves smoothly along as we learn about backroom politics, Egyptian gods, hallucinogens and, inevitably, more ghosts.

◆ ◆ ◆

Salamis
by Harry Turtledove
Caezik
November 2020
ISBN: 978-1-64710-007-0

More alternate history. My earlier question of how well the form works when we readers may not know the particulars of the periods in which they are set or about the events the authors have carefully re-cast comes less into play here. We are in the hands of Harry Turtledove.

Much is made of how he has written more alternate histories than just about anyone whose name you can yank out of the SFWA Directory, and that his background knowledge of the worlds he writes about is encyclopedic. That's all the stuff that defines the category. And we don't read categories. We read novels.

What gets left behind, often, is what a marvelous storyteller he is. It's the thing that first struck me when I first read one of his novelettes in *Amazing Stories* a little more than a quarter century ago. He keeps a story moving in an almost addictively compelling way.

A number of the big names in the alternate history category are very good at getting the "big picture" details right. Where Turtledove excels is in getting the *little* details right. You can see, hear, smell, taste, feel all the appropriate things. I couldn't tell you how historically accurate he is, but everything in his worlds feels right.

This is a standalone novel, set in his Hellenic Traders universe, and follows the adventures of the cousins Menedemos and Sostratos, and is set in the time shortly after the death of Alexander the Great.

If you're already a Turtledove fan, that's all you need to know. If you're not yet a fan, all I can say is that I first planned to set this book aside until next issue, picked it up, and—with plenty of more important things to do—read it in a few sittings. It stays with you, no matter how spotty your knowledge of classical history may be.

◆ ◆ ◆

The Fantastic Fiction of Hannes Bok
by Hannes Bok, edited by Robert T. Garcia
American Fantasy
March 2020
ISBN: 978-0-9907846-7-8

If readers know of Hannes Bok (Wayne Woodard) at all these days, it's from his extraordinary illustrations and artwork, much of which adorned the covers of a great many pulp-era magazines and postwar specialty press hardcover editions of classic science fiction and fantasy novels. He continued working into the 1960s, and I remember the awe I felt looking at his wraparound cover painting for *Fantasy and Science Fiction*, illustrating Roger Zelazny's classic "A Rose for Ecclesiastes." "Surreal" is an insufficient adjective to capture the dreamlike qualities of his work: part Maxfield Parrish (his mentor), part René Magritte, part Thomas Hart Benton, part Marc Chagall, but no comparison summarizes his genius sufficiently.

Fewer readers, then as now, were aware of his writing, which in many respects reflects his unique vision. His novels' basic premises were simple enough, with "ordinary" humans finding entrances into universes of magic and mystery. Structurally, they were built in loving imitation of his other mentor, Abraham

Merritt. But structures and premises were merely launching pads for his careful, ornate vision, as in this passage early on in his *Beyond the Golden Stair*:

The floor was perhaps thirty yards square, but walls arose to such height that they met illimitably far overhead in a vanishing point of perspective. They glimmered like pearl and were covered with hairline traceries of smoldering vermilion, blazing green, and phosphorescent blue which might have been merely decorative arabesques, but which reminded Hibbert unpleasantly of the flaming handwriting on the wall at Belshazzar's feast.

The floor was the clearest of mirrors, so true in its reflections that it was air itself. Hibbert and his companions, standing apparently balanced on the feet of their inverted images, looked like tumblers practicing an especially eccentric routine.

Directly ahead was an archway sealed with ponderous leaves of brass. Drawn double its size by the mirror, it looked like a vast flattened sun. At each side of it, on pedestals like embers compressed into gigantic cubes of red heat and ash, crouched two of the most singular sculptures that Hibbert had ever seen.

You get the picture. Literally. Bok could paint with a typewriter as well as his brushes and pens.

Along with *Beyond the Golden Stair*, this volume contains *The Sorcerer's Ship, Starstone World* and a poem, "The Ka of Kor-Sethon." Charles de Lint has written the introduction, but two introductions from Lin Carter are also included, and a brief but vivid memoir of Bok by Martin Jukovsky. All of this has been lovingly and painstakingly edited by Robert T. Garcia, who also supplies an introduction to *Starstone World*. Bok's artwork adorns the book inside and out. It's beautifully and serviceably typeset and designed. Cover, paper, signatures, binding, are all built to last. It's a labor of love and one that Bok has deserved for a long time.

And if we're intrigued by Bok's vision in any of its manifestations, it's a book we deserve as well.

Copyright © 2020 by Richard Chwedyk.

Gregory Benford is a Nebula winner and a former Worldcon Guest of Honor. He is the author of more than thirty novels, six books of non-fiction, and has edited ten anthologies.

A SCIENTIST'S NOTEBOOK

by Gregory Benford

MAKING A BETTER WORLD WAR II

My twin brother and I grew up during World War II, and then in its long aftermath, when we lived with our military family in occupied Japan and Germany. WWII was the central pivot of the twentieth century. Before it, there were six world powers; after, two.

I later was a postdoc working with renowned physicist Edward Teller, who told me many inside stories about the Manhattan Project that built the nuclear ("atomic") bombs. My natural science fictional instincts tinkered with the many *what-if* notions about how the war might have been different, and one became concrete in my mind: what if we'd gotten the bomb earlier?

Teller thought it could have, and so did my father-in-law, Karl P. Cohen, who worked in the early nuclear days and the Manhattan Project.

Everybody loves success, so historians have papered over the fact that when we developed the atomic bomb we made a decisive bad judgment that cost over half a billion dollars of 1940s dollars and delayed the war's end by about a year.

The bad decision came in 1942 from General Leslie Groves, who directed the Manhattan Project, which was the U.S. R&D program to develop the first nuclear weapons. To make uranium suitable for an atomic bomb, you must enrich it up to weapons-grade, so that it is almost pure U-235, the element's most fissile isotope. Groves chose to pursue gaseous diffusion over an alternate concept—Karl Cohen and Nobel Prize in Chemistry winner Harold Urey's centrifugal separation—to enrich uranium up to weapons-grade.

We now know that was a huge mistake. Karl Cohen and Harold Urey said so then.

If we had stuck with centrifugal separation for another six months we would've solved its engineering problems, without question. Gaseous diffusion did not have the necessary semipermeable membranes when Groves decided to use it, and it took two more years—until 1944—to develop them. Nobody uses diffusion to separate isotopes now; too expensive and slow. But the politics of the time weighted Groves's decision.

The crucial turning points in my alternative history are the events early in the Manhattan Project, when the Urey group at Columbia could not get funding for centrifuge development. We forget the style of science in that era, when government did little research and corporations gave small sums for specific developments. All such work focused on acquiring technologies useful in the short term.

Big Science came into being for the first time in the Manhattan Project's large laboratories and intricate coordination, invented chiefly by Groves, Oppenheimer, Fermi and Lawrence. Karl Cohen once remarked to me that in 1939 he and Urey estimated that to develop fast centrifuges might take as much as $100,000—"so then we *knew* it was impossible!" At that time Karl was earning less than $2,000 a year.

Suppose we do the Manhattan Project job right, first time.

So how to use a bomb? There would be a fresh one every month or two, at best, so what's the first target?

In the novel, everybody thinks Berlin is the obvious target. I asked military types and they said no, you must leave in place the civilian authority that can surrender. This is standard doctrine. But in 1944?

We now know that the Prussian wing of the German Army's General Staff tried to negotiate through the British for at least a cease-fire, from 1943 onward. They tried to kill Hitler and nearly did in July 1944. The commanding generals were all on battlefields in 1944, not Berlin—where the Nazi Party types, whom the Prussians hated, were dug in.

So…what to do with these elements?

I researched many off-trail threads that really happened, but we forget:

That both sides thought of using radioactive uranium as a pollutant, akin to poison gas, and worked out details.

That Eisenhower sent teams with Geiger counters to measure such use at Normandy. (My father went into Normandy on the fifth day of the invasion.)

That we so feared a German nuclear program, the general commanding the Manhattan Project, Leslie Groves, sent in his top agent to assassinate Heisenberg if the agent thought Heisenberg's team was getting close to a bomb.

Blend these and many existing letters and memos, my memories from knowing most of the characters in the novel—season to taste, heat, stir.

One essential element in the novel is how well I knew the characters. I worked with them as a young physicist, when they were the wise men of the field. These character choices fill out the novel—getting the people right. That gave me insights to go beyond the stacks-of-facts approach historians and alternative history writers suffer under: I knew how they spoke, acted, joked.

The war ends in 1944. What does that do?

First, the Soviets don't get to reign over Eastern Europe, because they're kept out of the lands they occupied in 1944–45.

Second, we see what use "tactical" (less than a megaton) weapons have.

Third, ten million more people survive the war. Plus other benefits, which come to life in a long coda to the novel, fiction set in 1963.

To write that part, I summoned up my own memories of the postwar era. There was much terror and thought about the introduction of the H-bomb and the arms race following.

Many thought the world could not survive such forces for long. Such views had accelerated after the grave gray giants of the world, such as Bertrand Russell and even Einstein himself. They made clear predictions in the mid-1950s. They felt that hydrogen bomb war between the USA and USSR was inevitable unless some higher body held *all* such weapons: the United Nations. Russell had even predicted that the death of civilization under a myriad of the H-bomb's crimson blisters was inevitable and would happen before 1960.

Can you imagine how the United Nations, holding all the weaponry, could make sure no one else got them? I can't, and I'm a science fiction writer.

How do the novel's ideas play out, giving us a different post-WWII world?

I wrote *The Berlin Project* to see how we might have had a better world than the one we're in.

Hint: H-bombs aren't a really good idea.

Copyright © 2020 by Gregory Benford.

L. Penelope is the award-winning author of the Earthsinger Chronicles. *The first book in the series,* Song of Blood & Stone, *was chosen as one of* Time *magazine's top fantasy books of 2018. Equally left-and right-brained, she studied filmmaking and computer science in college and sometimes dreams in HTML. She lives in Maryland with her husband and furry dependents. Visit her at: http://www.lpenelope.com.*

LONGHAND

by L. Penelope

THERE AND BACK AGAIN— WRITING THE END

The beginning of any story is the first step of a journey. And whether that journey be a short story, a novel, or an entire series of books, you have to start as you mean to go on. It's very difficult to talk about ending a work of fiction—plenty of articles are written on what it takes to start something, on what elements an opening scene or chapter should have—but far fewer discuss endings. It makes sense, to discuss the end you need to also be able to speak intelligently about the rest. The end is the destination of the entire trip…or is it? For isn't all travel really about the surprising things that happen along the way?

According to Will Storr, author of *The Science of Storytelling*, "The gift of story is wisdom. For tens of thousands of years stories have served to pass down lessons in how to live from one generation to another." So part of this ongoing journey every reader is on, includes learning about the author's idea of how we should live. Stories represent worldviews as much as they *take* us to new worlds, and part of the ultimate destination is the author's message about life.

Stories are about characters and characters are arcs of change. Plot and character intertwine to form theme. The ending of a story, while on the surface is concerned with the victory or loss, whether the army is defeated and the queen returns to her throne, or the lovers find their happily-ever-afters, actually represents a treatise on existence.

Many times, authors surprise themselves with their own endings. Writers who identify as pantsers, who write by the seat of their pants instead of plotting their story beforehand, are often amazed at the unexpected directions their stories take. But even a dedicated plotter such as myself has been astonished by exactly how things play out once my fingers warm up on the keyboard. Connections which I'd never consciously considered, make themselves known and show that they have been there all along.

Endings, as we are taught, should be both inevitable and surprising. Many creators know intuitively that there is some mystery involved in the act of creation. It can sometimes feel like an out of body experience. I've often looked back at chapters and scenes and have had no recollection of writing them. The hand of the muse at work is a wonderful thing.

These gifts of grace are rare and cherished. For, of course, they are balanced by those times when the words have to be extracted as if by a dental torture device, resulting in an equal amount of pain. But whether the work comes easy or hard, and whether you remember writing the words or not, they will represent your personal worldview. Something which is deeply embedded in the core of who you are and everything you do.

A story's beginning invites the reader into your world. You offer them a seat, perhaps some tea, make them comfortable, and reassure them that they're in good hands so they can sink into the tale and not worry. There's a lot of trust that a reader gives to a writer when they are spending their precious time ingesting her work. That trust cannot be taken lightly, especially not if the writer wants a long career and a loyal audience.

So the beginning lays the groundwork and opens the doors that the characters and the reader must step through. And all of this must pay off at the end. Stories are cyclical—in the most satisfying ones, often the end is the beginning and the beginning is the end.

Many diagrams of story structure, including one for the ever-popular Hero's Journey coined by Joseph Campbell, show the steps of a story in a literal circle. The last stage of this method is that the hero returns home, now changed (and possibly with an elixir).

That's often why we also talk about arcs. A character on a change arc ends up 180 degrees away from where she began. Back home—on the same horizontal plane—but more mature for having suffered and struggled and grown.

Many writers spend weeks or months (or longer) working to perfect the beginning. And openings are certainly important—but what stays with a reader long after the book is closed and they've left the world of the story to return to their mundane realities? The emotions the story left them with linger. The ending should create a memorable feeling, one that sticks in the mind and heart far longer than any plot detail. Readers may forget your characters' names, but if the story made them laugh or cry or, better yet, remind them of that time their heart was broken, then they'll associate that emotion with the story forever. Given that, wouldn't it be a grand idea to spend an equal amount of time perfecting the end?

However, we writers are humans and often by the end of a manuscript, we are exhausted. Unfortunatley, endings can sometimes get short shrift. I recently turned in the final book of my fantasy series Earthsinger Chronicles—the last of four full-length novels and three novellas with a large cast of characters and many open threads. Figuring out how to wrangle this beast of a series to a satisfying close was the biggest challenge of my creative life thus far.

I don't think it's necessary to tie up every loose end, but I did want to complete the main story and character arcs and spin things down so that the readers did not feel cheated. Applying this idea of cyclical storytelling, or mirroring, is useful because it completes an emotional loop. This creates themes and ideas that resonate with readers subconsciously, as long as they're handed carefully by the writer.

On the *Writing Excuses* podcast, author Mary Robinette Kowal often talks about opening doors and closing them in the same order—story-wise. These "doors" can be plot threads, subplots, character arcs, mysteries, or twists. Within a story, novel, or series, closing the doors you've opened is only polite. This literally creates closure with the reader and leads to positive emotional connections with the work.

Different writers and readers will have varying levels of tolerance for types of endings, from true cliffhangers to sly eye-winks to clever twists. Some endings beg the reader to continue holding the story in their mind long into the future and reject anything resembling a pat answer to the story question. This is far more palatable with certain genres—don't try to sell a romance reader on an open ending.

Personally, I like to close 90% of the doors that I open, leaving only a window or perhaps a trap door open so that I can return to the story world if the mood strikes. And even if that mood never arrives, leaving the reader with a little something to chew on while still having a strong sense of completion is important for me.

A way to create that level of satisfaction is to answer the questions that you asked in logical ways that feel motivated by the story and by the journey that the characters and the reader have been on. One reason why the ending of the television series *Game of Thrones* was so dissatisfying to so many people was because it felt like a cheat. Season one began with strength, leaving the audience feeling as if they were in capable hands, but that confidence slowly leaked away until by the end, characters made choices that felt insufficiently motivated at best, and wild and random at worst.

People love surprises. Twists are generally welcome. But an audience wants to feel as though the story revelations are motivated by the text and fall in line with character and world development. Else, these flourishes seem to come from nowhere and leave a strong sense of dissatisfaction.

There are many factors to juggle when writing a story and the balls in the air multiply depending on the length and other factors like multiple point of view characters and or subplots. But keeping in mind the reader experience and the worldview that the author wants to share will help to ensure the end will not be one that causes readers to throw their books across the room. Instead, the end should be a return home after a pleasant or harrowing or heartbreaking or life-affirming journey, with an invitation to visit again in the near future.

Copyright © 2020 by L. Penelope.

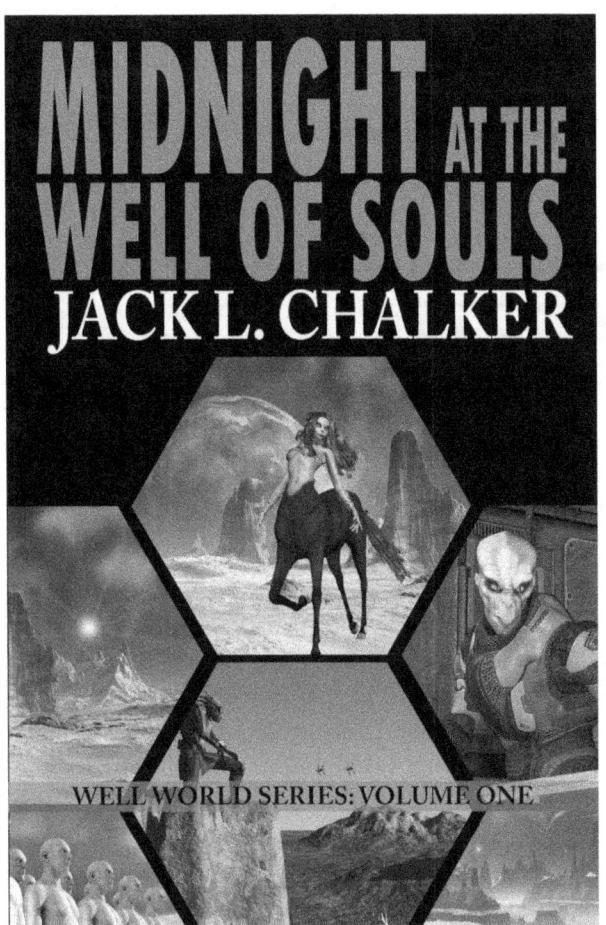

**Midnight at the Well of Souls copyright ©
1977** by **Jack L. Chalker.** All rights reserved.

*Jack L. Chalker (December 17, 1944 – February
11, 2005) was an American science fiction author.
Chalker was also a Baltimore City Schools history teacher in Maryland for 12 years, retiring
during 1978 to write full-time. He also was a
member of the Washington Science Fiction Association and was involved in the founding of
the Baltimore Science Fiction Society.*

Continued from Issue 46

MIDNIGHT AT THE WELL OF SOULS

Volume 1 of *The Saga of the Well World*

by Jack L. Chalker

MIDNIGHT AT THE WELL OF SOULS

The creature stood at the end of The Avenue, where it passed through a meter-high barrier and stopped.

It looked like a great human heart, two and a half meters tall, pink and purple, with countless blood vessels running through it, both reddish and bluish in color. At the irregular top was a ring of cilia, col-ored an off-white, waving about—thousands of them, like tiny snakes, each about fifty centimeters long. From the midsection of the pulpy, undulating mass came six evenly spaced tentacles, each broad and powerful-looking, covered with thousands of tiny suckers. The tentacles were a sickly blue, the suck-ers a grainy yellow. An ichor of some sort seemed to ooze from the central mass, although it was thick and seemed to be reabsorbed by the skin as fast as produced, creating an irregular, filmy coating.

And it stank—the odor of foul carrion after days in the sun. It stung their nostrils, making them slightly sick.

Skander began babbling excitedly, then turned to them. "See, Varnett?" he said. "See what I told you? Six evenly spaced tentacles, about three meters tall! That's a Markovian!" All traces of animosity were gone; this was the professor lecturing his student, in pride at the vindication of his theories.

"So you really was a Markovian, Nate," Ortega said wonderingly. "Well, I'll be damned."

"Nathan!" Wuju called out. "Is that—that thing really you?"

"It is," Brazil's voice came, but not as speech. It formed in each of their brains, in their own languag-es. Even The Diviner received it directly, rather than through The Rel.

Skander was like a child with a new toy. "Of course! Of course!" he chortled. "Telepathy, naturally. Probably the rest, too."

"This is a Markovian body," Brazil's voice came to them, "but I am not a Markovian. The Well knows me, though, and, since all lived as new races outside, it was only natural that we be converted to the Markovian form when entering the Well. It saved design problems."

Wuju stepped out ahead of them, drawing close to the creature.

"Wu Julee!" Hain shouted insanely. "You are mine!" The long, sticky tongue darted out to her, wrapped itself around her. She screamed. Ortega spun quickly toward the bug, pistols in two hands.

"Now, now, none of that, Hain!" he cautioned carefully. "Let the girl go." He pointed the pistols at the Akkafian's eyes.

Hain hesitated a second, deciding what to do. Finally the tongue uncoiled from Wu Julee, and she dropped about thirty centimeters to the floor, landing hard. Raw, nasty-looking welts, like those made by rope burn, showed on her skin.

The creature that was Nathan Brazil walked over on its six tentacles, until it loomed over her. One tentacle reached out, gently touched her wound. The smell was overwhelming. She shrank from the probe, fear on her face.

The heartlike mass tilted a little on its axis.

"Form doesn't matter," it mocked her voice. "It's what's inside that counts." Then it said in Brazil's old voice: "What if I were a monster, Wuju? What then?"

Wuju broke into sobs. "Please, Nathan! Please don't hurt me!" she pleaded. "No more, please! I—I just can't!"

"Does it hurt?" he asked gently, and she managed to nod affirmatively, wiping the tears from her eyes.

"Then trust me some more, Wuju," Brazil's voice came again, still gentle. "No matter what. Shut your eyes. I'll make the hurt go away."

She buried her head in her hands, still crying.

The Markovian reached out with a tentacle, and rubbed lightly against the angry-looking welt on her back and sides. She cringed, but otherwise stayed still. The thing felt clammy and horrid, yet they all watched as the tentacle, lightly drawn across the wound, caused the wound to vanish.

As the pain vanished, she relaxed.

"Lie flat on your back, Wuju," Brazil instructed, and she did, eyes still shut. The same treatment was

given to her chest and sides, and there was suddenly no sign of any welt or wound.

Brazil withdrew a couple of meters from her. There was no evident front or back to him, nor any apparent eyes, nose, or mouth. Although the pulpy mass in the center was pulsating and slightly irregular, it had no clear-cut directionality.

"Hey, that's fantastic, Nate!" Ortega exclaimed.

"Shall we go to the Well?" Brazil asked them. "It is time to finish this drama."

"I'm not sure I like this at all," Hain commented hesitantly.

"Too late to back out now, you asshole," Skander snapped. "You didn't get where you were without guts. Play it out."

"If you'll follow me," Brazil said, "and get on the walkway here; we can talk as we ride, and probably panic the border hexes at the same time."

They all stepped onto the walkway on the other side of the meter-tall barrier. The Avenue's strange light went out, and another light went on on both sides of the walkway, illuminating about half a kilometer to their left.

"The lights will come on where we are, and go out where we aren't," Brazil explained. "It's automatic. Slelcronian, you'll find the light adequate for you despite its apparent lack of intensity. You can get rid of that heat lamp. Just throw it over the barrier there. It will be disposed of by the automatic machinery in about fourteen hours." The Markovian's tentacle near the forward part of the walkway struck the side sharply, and the walkway started to move.

"You are now on the walkway to the Well Access Gate," he explained. "When the Markovians built this world, it was necessary, of course, for the technicians to get in and out. They were full shifts—one full rotation on, one off. Every day from dozens to thousands of Markovian technicians would ride this walkway to the control center and to other critical areas inside the planet. In those days, of course, The Avenue would stay open as long as necessary. It was shortened to the small interval in the last days before the last Markovian went native for good, to allow the border hexes some development and to keep out those who had second thoughts. At the end, only the three dozen project coordinators came, and then irregularly, just to check on things. As any technician was finally cleared out of the Well, the key to The Avenue doors was removed from his mind, so he could not get back in if he wanted to."

They moved on in eerie silence, lighted sections suddenly popping on in front of them, out in back of them, as they traveled. The walkway itself seemed to glow radiantly; no light source was visible.

"Some of you know the story of this place already," Brazil continued. "The race you call the Markovians rose as did all other species, developed, and finally discovered the primal energy nature of the universe—that there was nothing but this primal energy, extending outward in all directions, and that all constructs within it, we included, are established by rules and laws of nature that are not fixed just because they are there, but are instead *imposed*. Nothing equals anything, really; the equal sign is strictly for the imposed structure of the universe. Rather, everything is relative to everything else."

"But once the Markovians discovered the mathematical constructs governing stability, why didn't they change them?" Skander asked. "Why keep the rules?"

"They didn't dare try to tackle the master equations, those governing physical properties and natural laws," Brazil replied. "They could alter things a little, but common sense should tell you that in order to change the master equation you first have to eliminate the old one. If you do that, what happens to you and the rest of the universe? They didn't dare—so they imposed new, smaller equations on localized areas of the preexisting universe."

"Not gods, then," Vardia said quietly. "Demigods."

"*People*," Brazil responded. "Not gods at all. People. Oh, I know that this form I've got is quite different than you'd think, but it's no more monstrous or unusual than some of the creatures of this world, and less than some. The many billions of beings who wore bodies like this were a proud race of ordinary people with one finger on the controls. They argued, they debated, strove, built, discovered—just like all of us. Were their physical forms closer to the ones we're familiar with, you would possibly even like them. Remember, they achieved godhood not by natural processes, but by technological advancement. It was as if one of our races, in present form, sud-denly discovered the key to wish fulfillment. Would we be ready for it? I wonder."

"Why did they die, Brazil?" Skander asked. "Why did they commit suicide?"

"Because they were not ready," Brazil replied sadly. "They had conquered all material want, all disease, even death itself. But they had not conquered their selves. They reveled in hedonism, each an island unto itself. Anything they wanted, they just had to wish for.

"And they found that wasn't enough. Something was missing. Utopia wasn't fulfillment, it was stagnation. And that was the curse—*knowing* that the ultimate was attainable, but not knowing what it was or how to attain it. They studied the problem and came up with no solutions. Finally, the best amplified Markovian minds concluded that, somewhere in their development, they'd lost something—the true fulfillment of the dream. The social equation did not balance, because it lacked some basic component. One plus two plus three equals six, but if you don't have the plus two in there, it can't possibly reach more than four.

"Finally, they came to the conclusion that they were at a dead end, and would stagnate in an eternal orgy of hedonism unless something was done. The solution seemed simple: start over, try to regain the missing factor, or rediscover it, by starting from the beginning again. They used a variety of races and conditions to restart, none Markovian, on the idea that any repetition of the Markovian cycle would only end up the same."

"And so they built this world," Varnett put in.

"Yes, they built this world. A giant Markovian brain, placed around a young but planetless sun. The brain *is* the planet, of course, everything but the crust. Gravity was no problem, nor was atmosphere. They created an outer shell, about a hundred kilometers above the surface. The hexagons are all compartments, their elements held in all directions by fields of force."

"So it was built to convert the Markovians to new forms?" Skander asked.

"Double duty, really," Brazil told them. "The finest artisans of the Markovian race were called in. They made proposals for biospheres, trying to outdo one another in creativity. The ones that looked workable were built, and volunteers went through the Zone Gate and became the newly designed creatures in the newly designed environments. Several generations were needed for even a moderate test—the Markovians didn't mind. A thousand years was nothing to them. You see, they could build, pioneer-style, but they were still Markovians. A lot of generations born in the biome and of the new race were needed to establish a culture and show how things would go. Their numbers were kept relatively stable, and the fields of force were much more rigid then than now. They had to live in their hex, without any real contact with other hexes. They had to build their own worlds."

They were riding *down* now, at a deceptively steep angle. Down into the bowels of the planet itself.

"But why didn't the first generation establish a high civilization?" Varnett asked. "After all, they were just like us, changed outside only."

"You overestimate people from a highly technological culture. We take things for granted. We know how to turn on a light, but not why the light comes on. None of us could *build* most of our artifacts, and most civilized races become dependent on them. Suddenly dumped in a virgin wilderness, as they all were, they had no stores, no factories, no access to anything they didn't make themselves out of what was available. A great many died from hardship alone. The tough ones, the survivors, they built their own societies, and their children's societies. They worked with purpose—if the test failed, then they died out. If they succeeded—well, there was the promise that the successful ones would someday go to the Well of Souls at midnight, and there be taken to a new world, to found a new civilization, to grow, develop, perhaps become the progenitors of a future race of gods who would be fulfilled. Each hoped to be the ones whose descendants would make it."

"And you were here when that happened," Wuju said nervously.

"I was," he acknowledged. "I assisted the creator of Hex Forty-one—One Eighty-seven, the hundred and eighty-seventh and last race developed in that hex. I didn't create it, simply monitored and helped out. We stole ideas from each other all the time, of course. Dominant species in one hex might be a modified pattern of animals in another. Our own race was a direct steal from some large apes in another hex. The designer liked them so much that not only did the dominant race turn out to be apes, but they were almost endlessly varied as animals."

"Hold on, Brazil," Skander said. "These others might not know much about things, but I'm an archaeologist. Old Earth developed over a few billion years, slowly evolving."

"Not exactly," Brazil replied. "First of all, time was altered in each case. The time frame for the development of our sector was speeded up. The original design produced the life we expected, but it developed differently—as giant reptiles, eventually. When it was clear that it wouldn't do to have our people coexist with them, a slight change in the axial tilt caused the dinosaurs to die out, but it placed different stresses on other organisms. Minor mammals developed, and to these, over a period of time, we added ours to replace the ones logically developing in the evolutionary scale. When conditions seemed suitable for us, when apelike creatures survived, we began the exodus. Soon the temperate zones had their first intelligent life. Again, with all the resources but nothing else. They did well, astonishingly so, but the long-term effects of the axial tilt produced diastrophism and a great ice age within a few centuries. Our present, slow climb has been the product of the extremely primitive survivors of those disasters. So, in fact, has it been with all your home worlds."

"Is there a world, then, or a network of worlds of the Akkafians?" Hain asked.

"There was," Brazil replied. "Perhaps there is. Perhaps it's larger and greater and more advanced than ours. The same with the Umiau, the Czill, the Slelcronians, the Dillians, and others. When we get to the Well itself, I'll be able to tell you at least which ones are still functioning, although not how, or if they've changed, or what. I would think that some of the older ones would be well advanced by now. My memory says there were probably close to a million races created and scattered about; I'll be curious to see how many are still around."

They had been going down for some time. Now they were deep below the surface, how deep they couldn't say. Suddenly a great hexagon outlined in light appeared just under them.

"The Well Access Gate," Brazil told them. "One of six. It can take you to lots of places within the Well, but it'll take you to the central control area and monitoring stations if you have no other instructions. When we get to it, just step on it. I won't trigger it until everyone is aboard. In case somebody else does, by accident, just wait for the light to come back on and step on again. It'll work."

They did as instructed, and when all were on the Gate, all light suddenly winked out. There followed a twisting, unsettling feeling like falling. Then, suddenly, there was light all over.

They stood in a huge chamber, perhaps a kilometer in diameter. It was semicircular, the ceiling curving up over them almost the same distance as it was across. Corridors, hundreds of them, led off in all directions. The Gate was in the center of the dome, and Brazil quickly stepped off, followed by the others, who looked around in awe and anticipation.

The texture of the place was strange. It seemed to be made up of tiny hexagonal shapes of polished white mica, reflecting the light and glittering like millions of jewels.

After they stepped off the Gate, Brazil stopped and pointed a tentacle back over it.

Suspended by force fields, about midway between the Gate and the apex of the dome, was a huge model of the Well World, turning slowly. It had a terminator, and darkness on half of its face, and seemed to be made of the same mica-like compound as the great hall. But the hexagons on the model were much larger, and there were solid areas at the poles, and a black band around its middle. The sphere seemed to be covered by a thin transparent shell composed of segments which exactly conformed to the hexagons below.

"That's what the Well World looks like from space," Brazil told them. "It's an exact model, fifteen hundred sixty hexagons, the Zones—everything. Note the slight differences in reflected light from each hex. That's Markovian writing—and they are numbers. This is more than a model, really. It's a separate Markovian brain, containing the master equation for stabilizing all of the new worlds. It energizes the Well, and permits the big brain around us to do its job."

"Where are the controls, Nate?" Ortega prodded.

"Each biome—that is, planetary biome—has its own set of controls," Brazil told him. "This place is honeycombed with them. Each hex on the Well World is controlled as a complement to the actual world. Most controls, of course, do not have corresponding hexes. What we're left with today are the last few hexes created and some of the failures—not necessarily the ones that died out, but the ones that didn't work out. The Faerie, for example. Some of them snuck into the last batch of transits, and several of the others who were leftovers from closed and filled projects, some Dillians, some Umiau, and the like, who wanted to get out of the Well World and thought they could help, came, too. Not many, and they were disrupted by civilization's rises and falls, and became the objects of superstition, fear, hatred. None survived the distance on Old Earth, but we didn't get many to begin with, and reproduction was slow. But, come, let's go to a control center."

He walked toward one of the corridors on his six tentacles, and they followed hesitantly. All of them held their pistols tightly, at the ready.

They walked for what seemed an endless time down one of the corridors, passing closed hexagonal doors along the way. Finally Brazil stopped in front of one, and it opened, much as the lens of a camera opens. He walked in, and they followed quickly, anxious not to lose sight of him even for a moment.

The room lit up as they approached. It was made of the same stuff as the great hall and the corridors. There were, however, walls of obvious controls, switches, levers, buttons, and the like, and what looked like a large black screen directly ahead of them. None of the instruments held any sort of clue as to what they were, or had anything familiar about them.

"Well, here it is, and it's still active," Brazil announced. "Let me see," he murmured, and went over to a panel. Their faces showed sudden tension and fear, and all of the pistols were raised, trained on him. The Diviner's blinking lights started going very, very fast.

"Don't touch nothin', Nate!" Ortega warned.

"Just checking something here," Brazil responded, unconcerned. "Yes, I see. In this room is the preset for a civilization that has now expanded.

It's interstellar, but not pangalactic. Population a little over one and a quarter trillion."

"If it's a high-tech civilization, then it is not ours," the Slelcronian said with some relief.

"Not necessarily," Brazil replied. "The tech levels here on the Well World were not imposed on the outside at all. They were dictated by the problems you might find in your own world. A high-tech world had abundant and easily accessible resources, a low-tech much less so. Since the home world had to develop logically and mathematically according to the master rules of nature, some worlds were better endowed than others. By making the trial hex here a low-tech, no-tech, or the like, we simply were compensating for the degree of difficulty in establishing technological civilization on the home world, not preventing it. We made them develop alternatives, to live without technology so they'd be better prepared on their home worlds. Some did extremely well. Most of the magic you find here is not Well magic, but actual mental powers developed by the hexes to compensate for low-tech status. What they could use here, they could use there."

"The Diviner says you are truthful," The Rel commented, one of the first things the Northerner had said since they set out. "The Diviner states that you were responsible for its prophecy that we would be here."

"In a way, yes," Brazil replied. "When I went through the Zone Gate, the Markovian brain recognized me as a native of Hex Forty-one and sent me there. However, in its analysis, it also found what I, myself, didn't know—that I had an original Markovian brainwave pattern. It then assumed that I was here to give it further instructions or to do work. When it concluded this, The Diviner, extremely sensitive to such things, picked up the message, however garbled." He paused, and that central mass tilted toward them a little.

"And now," he said, sadness in his voice, "here we are, in the control center, and you've all got fear on your faces and your guns trained on me." *Even you, Wu Julee,* he thought, immeasurable sadness coursing through him. *Even you.*

"I tried to give mankind rules for living which would avert a second disaster like the first, would keep it from self-destruction. Nobody listened. No-body changed. Type Forty-one was badly flawed— and it beat the odds anyway, this time. It made its way to the stars, and that was an outlet for its aggression, although, even there, even now, its component parts are looking at ways to dominate one another, kill one another, rule one another. And the drive for domination is there even in the nonhumans, you, Northerner, and you, Slelcronian. Look at you all now. Look at yourselves! Look at each other! Do you see it? Can you feel it? Fear, greed, horror, ambition burning within you, consuming you! The only reason you haven't killed one another by now is your common fear of me. How dare you condemn a Hain, a Skander—a society? How dare you?

"How many of you are thinking of the people these controls represent? Do you fear for them? Do you care about them? You don't want to save them, better their lives. That fear is inside you, fear for your own selves! The basic flaw in the set-up equation, that burning, basic selfishness. None of you cares for any but yourself! Look at you! Look at what monsters you've all become!"

Their hearts pounded, nerve ends frayed. The Diviner and The Rel were the first to respond.

"What about yourself, Nathan Brazil?" The Rel chimed. "Isn't the flaw in us simply a reflection of the flaws in yourself, in your own people, the Markovians, who could not give us what we lack because they did not themselves possess it?"

Brazil's reply was calm, in contrast to his previous outburst.

"The Markovians wanted to live in this universe, not run it. They had already done that. Destiny was a random factor they believed necessary to the survival of us all. That's why they closed down the Well. None of us would be here except for a freak set of circumstances."

"Where are the controls, Nate?" Ortega asked.

"We'll find them ourselves," Hain snapped. "Varnett cracked the big code, he should be able to crack this one, too."

Brazil's voice held deep sorrow. "Pride is a weakness of all things Markovian, and you're a reflection of it. Now, if you'll ease up and allow me one touch on the panel in back, I'll show you the controls. I'll tell you how to operate them. Let's see what happens then."

Ortega nodded, pistols at the ready. Brazil reached out with a tentacle and touched a small panel behind him.

The large black screen went on—but it wasn't exactly a screen. It was a great tunnel, an oval stretching back as far as the eye could see. And it was covered with countless tiny black spots, trillions of them at the best guess. And between all the various black spots shot frantic electrical bolts in a frenzy of activity, trillions of blinking hairline arcs jumping from one little black area to another.

"There's your controls," Brazil said disgustedly. "To change the ratios, all you have to do is alter the current flow between any two or more control spots."

He looked at them, and there was the deepest fear and horror on their faces. They're afraid of me, he thought. All of them are in mortal fear of me! Oh, my God! Wuju who loved me, Varnett who risked his life for me, Vardia who trusted me—all afraid. I haven't harmed them. I haven't even threatened them. I couldn't if I wanted to. How can they ever understand our common source, our common bond? he thought in anguish. We love, we hate, we laugh, we cry, live—that I am no different from themselves, only older.

But they did not understand, he realized. I am God to the primitives, the civilized man of great power at a point where knowledge is power, surrounded by the savages.

That's why I'm alone, he understood. That's why I'm always alone. They fear what they can't understand or control.

"One control panel," he said softly. "One only. What are a few trillion lives? There is their past, their present, their potential future. All yours. Maybe their equation is the basis for one or more of you in this room. Maybe not. It's somebody's. Maybe it's yours. Okay, anybody, who wants to touch the first and second control spots, change the flow? Step right up! Now's your chance to play God!"

Varnett walked carefully over to the opening, breathing hard, sweat pouring from his body.

"Go on," Brazil urged. "Do your stuff! You might cancel out somebody, maybe a few trillion somebodies. You'll certainly alter someone's equation in some way, make two and two equal three in somebody's corner. Maybe none of us will be here. Maybe none

of us will ever have been here. Go on! Who cares about all those people, anyway?"

Varnett stood there, mouth open, looking like a very frightened fifteen-year-old boy, nothing more. "I—I can't," he almost sobbed.

"How about you, Skander? This is where you wanted to be. And you, Hain?" His voice rose to a high, excited pitch. "Diviner? Can you divine this one? Vardia? Serge? Wuju? Slelcronian? *Any of you?*"

"*In the name of God, Brazil!*" Skander screamed. "*Stop it!* You know we don't dare do anything as long as we don't understand the panel's operation!"

"He's bluffing!" Hain snarled. "I'll take the chance."

"*No!*" Wuju screamed, and swung her gun around on the great bug. "You can't!"

"I'll even show you how," Brazil said calmly, and took a step.

"Nate! Stay away from there!" Ortega warned. "You can be killed, you know!"

Brazil stopped, and the pulsating mass bent toward Ortega slightly. "No, Serge, I can't. That's the problem, you see. I told you I wasn't a Markovian, but none of you listened. I came here because you might damage the panel, do harm to some race of people I might not even know. I knew you couldn't *use* this place, but all of you are quite mad now, and one or more of you might destroy, might take the chance, as Hain just showed. But none of you, in your madness, has thought to ask the real question, the one unanswered question in the puzzle. Who stabilized the Markovian equation, the basic one for the universe?"

There was a pumping sound, like that of a great heart, its *thump, thump, thump* permeating them. Their own hearts seemed to have stopped, all frozen in an eerie tableau. Only the thumping seemed real.

"I was formed out of the random primal energy of the cosmos," Brazil's voice came to them. "After countless billions of years I achieved self-awareness. I was the universe, and everything in it. In the aeons I started experimenting, playing with the random forces around me. I formed matter and other types of energy. I created time, and space. But soon I tired of even those toys. I formed the galaxies, the stars, and planets. An idea, and they were, as congealed primal energy exploded and flung transmuted material outward from its center.

"I watched things grow, and form, according to the rules I set up. And yet, I tired of these, also. So I created the Markovians and watched them develop according to my plan. Yet, even then, the solution was not satisfactory, for they knew and feared me, and their equation was too perfect. I knew their total developmental line. So I changed it. I placed a random factor in the Markovian equation and then withdrew from direct contact.

"They grew, they developed, they evolved, they changed. They forgot me and spread outward on their own. But since they were spiritually reflections of myself, they contained my loneliness. I couldn't join with them as I was, for they would hold me in awe and fear. They, on the other hand, had forgotten me, and as they rose materially they died spiritually. They failed to grow to my equal, to end my loneliness. Their pride would not admit such a being as myself to fellowship, nor could their own fear and selfishness allow fellowship even with each other.

"So I decided to become one of them. I fashioned a Markovian shell, and entered it. I knew the flesh, its joys and its pains. I tried to teach them what was wrong, to tell them to face their inner fears, to rid themselves of the disease, to look not to a material heaven but within themselves for the answers. They ignored me.

"And yet the potential was there. It is still there. Wuju's response to kindness and caring. Varnett's self-sacrifice. Vardia's need for others. Other examples abound, not just about us, but about all our people. The one who sacrifices his life to save others. The compassion there, sometimes almost buried by the overlying depravity. It peers through—isolated, perhaps, but it is there. And as long as it is there, I shall continue. I shall work and hope for the day when some race seizes that spark and builds on it, for only then will I no longer be alone."

They said nothing for several seconds. Then, quietly, Ortega responded, "I'm not sure I believe all this. I've been a Catholic all my life, but somehow God to me has never been a little spunky Jew named Nathan Brazil. But, assuming what you say is true—which I don't necessarily accept—why haven't you scrapped everything and started again? And why continue to live our grubby little lives?"

"As long as that spark is present, I'll let things run, Serge," Brazil replied. "That random factor I talked about. Only when it's gone will I go, give up, maybe try again—maybe, finally die. I'd like to die, Serge—but if I do I take everything with me. Not just you, everybody and everything, for I stabilize the universal equation. And you are all my children, and I *care*. I can't do it as long as that spark remains, for as long as it remains you are not only the worst, but the best of me."

The *thump, thump, thump* continued, the only sound in the room.

"I don't think you're God, Nate," Ortega replied evenly. "I think you're crazy. Anybody would be, living this long. I think you're a Markovian throwback, crazy after a billion years of being cut off from your own kind. If you was God, why don't you just wave your tentacles or something and get what you want? Why all this journey, and pain, and torment?"

"Varnett?" Brazil called. "You want to explain it mathematically?"

"I'm not sure I don't agree with Ortega," Varnett replied carefully. "Not that it makes much difference from a practical point of view. However, I see what you're driving at. It's the same dilemma we face at that control board, there.

"Let's say we let Skander do what he wants, abolish the Comworlds," the boy continued. "Let's say Brazil, here, shows him exactly how to do it, just what to press and in what sequence and in what order. But the Com concept and the Comworlds developed according to the normal human flow of social evolution, right or wrong. They are caused by countless past historical events, conditions, ideas. You can't just banish them; you've got to change the equation so that they never developed. You have to change the whole human equation, all the past events that led to their formation. The new line you created would be a completely different construct, things as they would be without any of the crucial points that created the Coms. Maybe it was an outlet. Maybe, bad as it was, it was the only outlet. Maybe man would have destroyed himself if just one of those factors wasn't there. Maybe what we'd have is something worse."

"Exactly," Brazil agreed. "For anything major you have to change the past, the whole structure.

Nothing just vanishes. Nothing just appears. We are the sum of our past, good as well as bad."

"So what do we do?" wailed Skander. "What can we do?"

"A few things can be done," Brazil replied calmly. "You—most of you—sought power. Well, *this* is power!" With that the Markovian moved toward the control panel.

"My God! He's going in there!" Skander screamed. "Shoot, you fools!" The Umiau fired its pistol at the Markovian. In a second, the others followed, pouring a concentrated energy pulse into the mass sufficient to disintegrate a building.

The Markovian creature stopped, but seemed to absorb the energy. They poured it into him, all of them, even Wuju, with great accuracy.

He was still there.

The Diviner's lights blinked rapidly, and searing bolts shot out, striking the Markovian body. There was a glow, surrounding the creature in stark outline, and then it faded.

Brazil was still there.

They stopped firing.

"I told you you couldn't hurt me," Brazil said. "None of you can hurt me."

"Bullshit!" Ortega spat. "Your body was torn to ribbons in Murithel! Why wasn't this one?"

"Of course! Of course!" Skander exclaimed excitedly. "This body is a direct construct of the Markovian brain, you fools! The brain won't allow it to be harmed, since it's really part of the brain itself!"

"Quite so," Brazil responded. "Nor, in fact, do I have to go in there at all. I can instruct the brain from right here. I've been able to do that since we first entered the Well itself. I merely wanted to give you a demonstration."

"It would seem that we are at your mercy, Markovian," The Rel said. "What is your intention?"

"I can affect things for anyplace from here," Brazil told them. "I merely feed the data into the brain through this control room, and that's that. It's true there's a control room for each type, but they are all-purpose, in case of problems, overcrowding when we built the place, and so on. Any control room can be switched to any pattern."

"But you said—" Ortega started to protest.

"In the words of Serge Ortega," Brazil replied, a hint of amusement in his voice, "I lied."

Wuju broke from them and ran up to him, and prostrated herself in front of him, trembling. "Please! Please don't hurt us," she pleaded.

There was infinite compassion in his voice. "I'm not going to hurt you, Wuju. I'm the same Nathan Brazil you knew from the start of this mess. I haven't changed, except physically. I've done nothing to you, nothing to deserve this. You know I wouldn't hurt you. I couldn't." The tone changed to one not of bitterness, but of deep hurt and agony, mixed with the loneliness of unimaginable lifetimes. "*I* didn't shoot at *you*, Wuju," it said.

She started crying; deep, uncontrollable sobs wracked her. "Oh, my god, Nathan! I'm so sorry! I failed you! Instead of trust, I gave you fear! Oh, god! I'm so ashamed! I just want to die!" she wailed.

Vardia came over to her, tried to comfort her. She pushed the girl away.

"I hope you're satisfied!" Vardia spat at him. "I hope you're pleased with yourself! Do anything you want to me for saying this, but don't torture her anymore!"

Brazil sighed. "No one can torture someone like that," he replied gently. "Like me, you can only torture yourself. Welcome to the broader human race, Vardia. You showed compassion, disregard for yourself, concern for another. That would have been unthinkable in the old Vardia. If none of you can still understand, I intend to do something *for* you, not *to* you. For the most part, anyway." He angled to address all of them.

"You're not perfect, none of you. Perfection is the *object* of the experiment, not the component. Don't torture yourself, run away from your fears. Face them! Stand up to them! Fight them with goodness, mercy, charity, compassion! Lick them!"

"We are the sum of our ancestral and actual past," The Rel reminded him. "What you ask may indeed be possible, but the well of fate has accented our flaws. Is it reasonable to expect us to live by such rules, when we find it difficult even to comprehend them?"

"You can only try," Brazil told it. "There is a greatness in that, too."

The *thump, thump, thump* continued.

"What is that noise?" Ortega asked, ever the practical man.

"The Well circuits are open to the brain," Brazil replied. "It's awaiting instructions."

"And what will those instructions be?" Varnett asked nervously.

"I must make some repairs and adjustments to the brain," Brazil explained. "A few slight things, so that no one can accidentally discover the keying equation again. I'm not sure I'd like to go through this exercise again—and, if I did, there's no guarantee that some new person might not take that chance, damage the structure, do irreparable harm to trillions who never had a chance. But, just in case, the Well Access Gate will be reset to respond only to me. Also more of an insurance factor has to be added, to summon me if things go wrong."

Skander gave an amazed chuckle. "That's *all*?" he said, relieved.

"It is most satisfactory to me," The Rel pronounced. "We were concerned only that nothing be disturbed. For a short while there, we lost sight of that—but we are back in control of ourselves again."

"Very minor adjustments are possible without disturbing anything," Brazil told them. "I can't do anything grandiose without upsetting a few things. I will, however, do some minor adjustments. For one thing, I am going to make sure that nothing like the Ambreza gas that reduced Type Forty-one humans on this world to apes will pass again, and I'm going to slap some local controls on technological growth and development, so that such an adjustment won't be necessary again, not here.

"And, because I can't bear to see them like that, I'm going to introduce a compound to the Type Forty-one atmosphere that will break the gas molecules down into harmless substances, while at the same time I'm going to make it a nontechnological hex absolutely. I don't know what they'll come up with, but I'll bet it's better than their current lot."

"What about us?" Hain asked.

"I will not change what you are inside," Brazil told them. "If I do that, you will not have lived at all. To do anything otherwise would be to invite paradox, and that might mess up everything. Thus, I have to deal with you as you are."

Brazil seemed to think for a moment, then said, in a voice that sounded as if it came from thunder, "Elkinos Skander! You wanted to save the human race, but, in the process, you became inhuman yourself. When the end justifies any means, you are no better, perhaps worse, than those you despise. There are seven bodies back on Dalgonia. Seven human beings who died trusting you, helping you, who were victims of your own lust for power. I can't forget them. And, if I alter the time line, bring them back, then all this didn't happen. I pity you, Skander, for what you are, for what you could have become. My instructions to the brain are justice as a product of the past."

Skander yelled, "It wasn't me! It was Varnett! I wanted to save the worlds! I wanted—"

And suddenly Skander wasn't there anymore.

"Where did it go?" The Rel asked.

"To a world suited for him as he is, in a form suited to justice," Brazil responded. "He *might* be happy there, he might find justice. Let him go to his fate."

Brazil paused a moment, then that huge voice came back. "Datham Hain!" it called. "You are the product of a horrible life. Born in contagion, you spread it."

"I never had a chance except the way I took!" Hain shouted defiantly. "You know that!"

"Most products of a bad environment turn out worse," Brazil admitted. "And yet, some of the greatest human beings came out of such miserable lots and conquered them. You didn't, yet you had the intelligence and potential to do so. Today, you stand as a contagion. I pity you, Hain, and because I pity you I will give you a localized wish."

Hain grew slightly larger, her black color turning to white. She saw it in the fur on her forelegs.

"You turned me noble!" she exclaimed, pleased and relieved.

"You're the most beautiful breeder in the kingdom of the Akkafians," Brazil said. "When I return you to the palace, you won't be recognized. You'll be at the start of a breeding cycle. The Baron Azkfru will see you and go mad with desire. You will be his brood queen, and bear his royal young. That is your new destiny, Hain. Satisfied?"

"It is all that I could hope for," Hain replied, and vanished.

Wuju looked at Brazil, a furious expression on her face. "You gave that son of a bitch *that*? How could you reward that—that monster?"

"Hain gets the wish, but it's not a reward, Wuju," Brazil replied. "You see, they withheld from their newcomer one fact of Akkafian life. Most Marklings are sterile, and they do the work. A few are raised as breeders. A breeder hatches a hundred or more young—but they hatch *inside* the mother's body and eat their way out, using the breeder's body for their food."

Wuju started to say something, then formed a simple, "*Ooooh*," as the horror of Hain's destiny hit her.

"Slelcronian!" Brazil pronounced. "You present me with a problem. I don't like your little civilization personally, and I don't like you much, either. I've adjusted things slightly, so the Recorders now only work with Slelcronians, not with any sentient plant. But you, personally—you're a problem. You're too dangerous to be let loose in the technology of Czill; you know too much. At the same time, you know too much of what is here to go back to Slelcron. It occurs to me, however, that you've really not altered the expedition in any significant way. If you had *not* taken over Vardia, nothing would have changed. Therefore, you didn't—and, in fact, couldn't."

Nothing seemed to change, but there was a difference in the Czillian body.

"So what are you going to do with me and my sister?" Vardia the Czillian asked. As far as everyone in the room was concerned, except for Brazil, the Slelcronian takeover had never happened. Slelcron was merely the funny place of the flowers and the giant bees, and their passage had been uneventful. Even so, the human Vardia had found her sister the Czillian as cold as the Slelcronian had been. She had gone through the same mental anguish as she had before and felt alienated from her sister.

Everything was as it had been before. "Vardia, you are your old self, and no longer your sister," Brazil pointed out. "I think you'd be happiest returning to Czill, to the Center. You've much to contribute, to tell this story the way it happened. They won't be able to make use of what you say to get in, but it may cause the thinkers there to consider what projects are really worthwhile. *Go!*" She vanished.

Now only Brazil, The Diviner and The Rel, Varnett, Wu Julee, Ortega, and the original Vardia were left.

"Diviner and Rel," Brazil said, "your race intrigues me. Bisexual, two totally different forms which mate into one organism, one of which has the power and the other the sensory input and output. You're a good people, with a lot of potential. Perhaps you can carry the message and reach that plateau."

"You're sending us back, then?" The Rel asked.

"No," Brazil replied. "Not to the hex. Your race is on the verge of expanding outward in its sector. It is near the turning point where questions of goals are asked. I'm sending you to your own people on their world with the message I gave you here. The Diviner's gift will distinguish you. Perhaps you can turn your people, perhaps not. It's up to you. Go!"

The Diviner and The Rel vanished.

"Varnett," Brazil said, and the boy jerked as if he was shot.

"What's in that little bag of tricks for me, Brazil?" he asked with false bravado.

"There are degrees of Comworlds, some better than others," Brazil noted. "Yours isn't too far gone yet. Even Vardia's can change. The worst of the lot is Dedalus. It went the genetic engineering route, you know. Everyone looks alike, talks alike, thinks alike. They kept males and females, sort of, but the engineers thought of even that. The people are hermaphroditic—small male genitals atop a vagina below. They breed once, in an exchange, then lose all sexual desires and prowess. Each has one child, which is, of course, identical to the parents, turned over to and raised by the state. It's a grotesque anthill, but it may represent the future.

"They don't even have names there. Obedience and contentment are engineered into them. Yet, the Central Committee retains power. This small group retains its sexual abilities, and the members are slightly different. The population is programmed to obey any one of those leaders unquestionably. The Committee was a perfect target, and they're controlled by the sponge syndicate. That sort of genetic engineering is, I fear, what the spongers have in mind for everyone eventually—with themselves on top.

"I give you the chance to change things. As the Murnies did with me, I do to you. You will be the Chairman of the Central Committee of Paradise, formerly called Dedalus. You'll be the new Chairman. The old one just kicked the bucket, and you're now unfrozen to take command. If you meant what you told me, you can kick the spongers out of their most secure planethold and restore that planet to individual initiative. The revolution will be easy—the people will obey unquestioningly. Your example and efforts could dissuade others from taking the Dedalus course. It's up to you. You're in charge."

"What happens to the new Chairman's mind?" Varnett asked. "And my body?"

"Even swap," Brazil told him. "The new boy will wake up a bat over in your old hex. He'll make out. He's born to command."

"Not *that* madhouse," Varnett chuckled. "Okay, I accept."

"Very good," Brazil told him. "But, I leave you this out. Should you ever want, any Markovian Gate will open for you—to bring you back here, for good. You'll be in a new body, so nobody knows what you would wind up as. You'd be here until you died, but you have that option."

Varnett nodded soberly. "Okay. I think I understand," he said, and vanished.

"Serge Ortega," Brazil sighed. "What in hell am I going to do with an old rascal like you?"

"Oh, hell, Nate, what's the difference?" Ortega responded, and he meant it. "This time you won."

"Are you really happy here, Serge? Or was that just part of the act?"

"I'm happy," the snakeman replied. "Hell, Nate, I was so damned bored back in the old place I was ready to kill myself. It's gotten too damned civilized, and I was too old to go frontier. I got here, and I've had a ball for eighty years. Even though I lost this round, it's been great fun. I wouldn't have missed it for the world."

Brazil chuckled. "Okay, Serge." Ortega vanished.

"Where did you send him?" Vardia asked hesitantly.

"Eighty's about the average life span for a Ulik," Brazil replied. "Serge didn't start as an egg, so he's a very old man. He has a year, five, maybe ten. I wouldn't put it past him to beat the system, but why the hell not? Let him go back to living and having fun."

"And so that leaves us," Wuju said quietly. There was a sudden flicker in the image of the Markovian, then a sparkling graininess. The shape twirled, changed, and suddenly standing there in front of them was the old, human Nathan Brazil, in the colorful clothes he had first worn on the ship a lifetime ago.

"Oh, my god!" Wuju breathed, looking as if she were seeing a ghost.

"The God act's over," he said, sounding relieved. "You should see who you're really dealing with."

"Nathan?" Wuju said hesitantly, starting forward. He put up his hand and stopped her, sighing.

"No, Wuju. It couldn't work. Not now. Not after all this. It wouldn't work anyway. Both of you deserve much better than life's given you. There are others like you, you know—people who never had the chance to grow, as you did. They can use a little kindness, and a lot of caring. You know the horrors of the sponge, Wuju, and the abuse to which some human beings subject others. And you, Vardia, know the lies that underlie the Com philosophy. I've talked to both of you, observed you both carefully. I've fed all this information plus as much data as could be obtained from a readout by the brain while you were in this room. The brain responded with recommendations on what would be best for you. If we're wrong—the brain and I—after a trial of what I'm going to do, then you both have the same option that is open to Varnett. Just get near a Markovian Gate—you don't have to jump into it. Just get passage on a ship going near a Markovian world. If you want, the Gate will pluck you out without disturbing the ship, passengers, or crew. You'll somehow mysteriously vanish. And you'll wind up in Zone again. Like Varnett, you will have to take potluck with the Zone Gate again. Once here, again, there will be no returning.

"But try it my way for a while. And remember what I said about your own contributions. Two people can change a world, if they wish."

"But what—" Wuju started to ask, but was cut off in midsentence.

The two bodies didn't vanish, they just collapsed, like a suit of clothes with the owner gone. They lay there in a heap on the floor.

Brazil went over and carefully rearranged them so they looked as if they were sleeping.

"Well, now what, Brazil?" he asked himself, his voice echoing in the empty hall.

You go back, and you wait, his mind told him.

What about the bodies? he wondered. Somehow he couldn't just vaporize them. Though their owners were gone, they lived on as empty vegetables.

But there was nothing else to do, of course. They were just memories for him now, one a strange mixture of love and anguish. He was prolonging the inevitable.

There was a crackle, and the bodies were gone, back to primal energy.

"Oh, the hell with it," said Nathan Brazil, and he, too, vanished.

The control room was empty. The Markovian brain noted the fact and then dutifully turned off the lights.

ON "EARTH," A PLANET CIRCLING A STAR NEAR THE OUTERMOST EDGE OF THE GALAXY ANDROMEDA

One moment Elkinos Skander had been perched atop Hain's back, looking at the control room and those in it. Then, suddenly, he wasn't.

He looked around. Things looked funny and distorted. He was color-blind except for a sepia tone that lent itself to everything.

He looked around, confused. I've gone through another change, he realized. My last one.

A rather pleasant-looking place, he thought, once he got used to the distorted vision. Forests over there, some high mountains, odd-looking grass, and strange sort of trees, but that was to be expected.

There were a lot of animals around, mostly grazing. They look a lot like deer, he noted, surprised. A few differences, but they would not look out of place on a pastoral human world.

He looked down at himself, and saw the shadow of his head on the grass.

I'm one of them, he suddenly realized with a shock. *I'm a deer. No antlers like those big males over there, so I must be a doe.*

A deer? he thought quizzically.

Why a deer?

He was still meditating on this, when suddenly the grass seemed to explode with yells and strange shapes; great, rectangular bodies with their facial features in their chest, and big, big teeth.

He watched as the Murnies singled out a large doe not far from him and surrounded it. Suddenly they speared it several times, and it went down in wordless agony and lay twitching on the ground, blood running, but still alive.

The Murnies pounced on it, tearing at it, eating it alive.

To be eaten alive! he thought, stunned, and suddenly blind panic overtook him. He started running, running away from the scene.

Up ahead another band of Murnies leaped out of nowhere and cornered another deer, started to devour it.

They're all over! he realized. *This is their world! I'm just food to them!*

He ran narrowly avoiding entrapment several times. There were thousands of them here, and they all were hungry.

And even as he ran in exhausted, dizzy circles, he knew that even if he avoided them today he would have to avoid them tomorrow, and the day after, and the day after, and wherever he ran on this planet there would be more of them.

Sooner or later they'll get me! he thought in panic. *By god! I'll not be eaten alive! I'll cheat Brazil of his revenge!*

He reached the highlands by carefully pulling himself together.

Now that he had decided on a course of action, he felt calm.

There! Up ahead! his mind said joyfully. He stopped and looked over the edge of the cliff.

Over a kilometer straight down to the rocks, he saw with satisfaction. He ran back a long ways, then turned toward the cliff. With strong resolve, he ran with all his might toward the cliff and hurled himself over it.

He saw the rocks coming up to meet him, but felt only the slight shock of pain.

✿

Skander awoke. The very fact that he awoke was a shock, and he looked around.

97

He was back on that plain at the edge of the forest. His shadow told him.

He was a deer again.

No! his mind screamed in horror. *I'll cheat the bastard yet! Somehow I'll cheat him!*

But there were a lot of deer and a lot of Murnies on that world, and Skander still had six more times to die.

PARADISE, ONCE CALLED DEDALUS, A PLANET NEAR SIRIUS

Varnett groaned, then opened his eyes. He felt cold. He looked around him and saw a number of people peering at him anxiously.

They all looked exactly alike. They didn't even look particularly male or female. Slight breasts and nipples, but nothing really female. Their bodies were lithe and muscular, sort of a blend of masculine and feminine.

All of them had small male genitals where they should be, but, from his vantage point, he could see a small cavity beneath them.

None of them had any body hair.

If you did it upside down and the other was right side up, he thought, you could give and receive at the same time.

"Are you all right?" one asked in a voice that sounded like a man's voice but with a feminine lilt.

"Do you feel all right?" another asked in the identical voice.

"I—I think so," he replied hesitantly, and sat up. "A little dizzy, that's all."

"That will pass," the other said. "How's your memory?"

"Shaky," he replied carefully. "I'm going to need a refresher."

"Easily done," the other replied.

He started to ask them their names, then suddenly remembered. They didn't use names on *his* planet.

His planet! *His!*

"I'd like to get right to work," he told them.

"Of course," another replied, and they led him from the sterile-looking infirmary down an equally sterile corridor. He followed them, got into an elevator, and they rode up to the top floor.

The top floor, it seemed, was an office complex. Workers were everywhere, filing things, typing things, using computer terminals.

Everybody else was slightly smaller than he was, he realized. Not much, but in a world where everyone was absolutely identical such a slight difference was as noticeable as if Cousin Bat had entered the room.

His office was huge and well-appointed. White wall-to-wall carpeting, so thick and soft his bare feet practically bounced off it. There was a huge desk, and great high-backed chair. No other furnishings, he noted, although their lack made the place look barren.

"Bring me a summary of the status of the major areas of the planet," he ordered. "And then leave me for a while to study them."

They bowed slightly, and left. He looked out the glass window that was the wall in back of his desk.

A complex of identical buildings stretched out before him. Broad, tree-lined streets, some small parkland, and lots of identical-looking shapes walking about on various business.

The sky was an off-blue, not the deepness of his native world, but it was attractive. There were some fleecy clouds in the sky, and, off in the distance, he saw signs of cultivated land. It looked like a rich, peaceful, and productive place, he thought. Of course, weather and topography would cause changes in the life-styles planet-wide, but he wagered those differences were minimal.

The aides returned with sheaves of folders bulging with papers. He acknowledged them curtly, and ordered them out.

There were no mirrors, but the lighting reflected him in the glass windows.

He looked just like them, only about fifty millimeters taller and proportionately slightly larger.

He felt his male genitals. They had the same feel as the ones he had had as Cousin Bat, he thought.

He reached a little lower, and found the small vaginal cavity.

He spread some papers around to make it look as if he had been studying them. He would, in time, of course, but not now.

He saw a small intercom on the desk and buzzed it, taking a seat in the big chair. At the far end of the room a clerk almost beat the track records entering, coming up to the desk and standing at full attention.

"I have found indications," he told the clerk seriously, "that several members of the Presidium may be ill. I want a team of rural doctors—based, as far as possible, away from here—to be brought to my office as soon as possible. I want that done *exactly* and at once. How long before they can get here?"

"If you want them from as far away from government centers as possible, ten hours," the clerk replied crisply.

"All right, then," he nodded. "As soon as they arrive they are to see me—and no one else. *No one* is even to know that they have been sent for. I mean absolutely no one, not even the rest of the office."

"I shall attend to it personally, Chairman," responded the clerk, and turned to leave. So much for the spongies, he thought.

"Clerk!" he called suddenly, and the other halted and turned.

"Chairman?"

"How do I arrange to have sex?"

The clerk looked surprised and bemused. "Whenever the Chairman wishes, of course. It is a great honor for any citizen."

"I want the best specimen here in five minutes!" he ordered.

"Yes, Chairman," responded the clerk knowingly, and left.

His eyes sparkled, and he rubbed his hands together gleefully, thinking about what was to come.

Suddenly Nathan Brazil's visage arose from the corners of his mind.

He said he'd give me my chance, he thought seriously. And I'll make good on it. This world will be changed!

The door opened, and another inhabitant of Paradise entered.

"Yes?" he snapped.

"I was told to report to you by the clerk," the newcomer said.

He smiled. The world would be changed, yes—but not right away, he thought. Not until I've had much more fun.

"Come on over here," he said lightly. "You're about to be honored."

ON THE FRONTIER—HARVICH'S WORLD

He groaned, and opened his eyes. An older man in overalls and checkered shirt, smelly and with a three-days' growth of beard, was bending over him, looking anxious.

"Kally? You hear me, boy? Say somethin'!" the old man urged, shouting at him.

He groaned. "God! I feel lousy!" he managed.

The old man smiled. "Good! Good!" he enthused. "I was afeared we'd lost you, there. That was quite a crack on the nog you took!"

Kally felt the left side of his head. There was a knot under the hair, and some dried blood. It hurt—throbbed, really.

"Try to stand up," the old man urged, and gave him a hand. He took it, and managed to stand shakily.

"How do ya feel, boy?" the old man asked.

"My head hurts," he complained. "Otherwise—well, weak but okay."

"Told ya ya shoulda got a good gal ta help with the farm," the old man scolded. "If'n I hadn'ta happened along you'd be dead now."

The man looked around, puzzled. It *was* a farm, he saw. Some chickens about, a ramshackle barn with a couple of cows, and an old log shack. It looked like corn growing in the fields.

"Sometime wrong, Kally?" the old man asked.

"I—uh, who are you?" he asked hesitantly. "And where am I?"

The old man looked concerned. "That bump on the noggin's scrambled your brains, boy. Better get into town and see a doctor on it."

"Maybe you're right," the other agreed. "But I still don't know who you are, where I am—or who I am."

"Must be magnesia or somethin'," the old man said, concerned. "I'll be damned. Heard about it, but never seed it afore. Hell, boy, you're Kally Tonge, and since your pa died last winter you've run this farm here alone. You was borned here on Harvich," he explained, pronouncing it *Harrige*, "and you damned near died here." He pointed to the ground.

He looked and saw an irrigation pump with compressor. Obviously he had been tightening the top holding nut with the big wrench and had kicked the thing into start. The wrench had whirled around and caught him on the head.

He looked at it strangely, knowing what it must mean.

"Will you be all right?" the old man asked concernedly. "I got to run down the road or the old lady'll throw a fit, but if ya want I can send somebody back to take ya inta the doc's."

"I'll see him," Kally replied. "But let me get cleaned up first. How—how far is it into town?"

"Christ, Kally! Ya even talk a little funny!" the old man exclaimed. "But Depot's a kilometer and a half down the road there." He pointed in the right direction.

Kally Tonge nodded. "I'll go in. If you get a head injury, it's best to walk. Just check back in a little while, just in case. I'll be all right."

"Well, okay," the old man responded dubiously. "But if I don't hear ya got in town, I'm comin' lookin'," he warned, then walked back to the road.

He's riding a horse! Kally thought wonderingly. And the road's dirt!

He turned and went into the shack.

It was more modern than he would have guessed, although small. A big bed with natural fur blankets in one corner, a sink, a gas stove—bottled gas underneath, he noted—and the water was probably from a water tank near the barn. A big fireplace, and a crude indoor shower.

There was a small refrigerator, too, running off what would have been a tractor battery if he had had a tractor.

He noted the toilet in one corner, and went over to it. Above it hung a cracked mirror, some scissors, and toiletries.

He looked at himself in the mirror.

His was a strong, muscular, handsome face in a rugged sort of way. The hair was long and tied off in a ponytail almost a meter long, and he had a full but neatly trimmed beard and mustache. The hair was brown, but the beard was reddish.

He turned his head, saw that the knot was almost invisible in the hair. Brushing it back revealed an ugly wound.

He died in that accident, he thought. Kally Tonge died of that wound. And I filled the empty vessel.

He stripped and took the mirror off its nail hanger, looking at himself. He saw a rugged, muscular body, well toned and used to work. There were calluses on the hands, worn in from hard farm labor.

The wound *did* hurt, and while he was certain it wouldn't be serious now, it would be better to go into town. It would also help to explain his mental lapses.

He put on a thick wool shirt and work pants, and some well-worn leather boots, and went back outside.

The place was interesting, really. It looked like something out of ancient history, yet had indoor plumbing, electricity, albeit crude, and several other signs of civilization. In the midst of this primitiveness, he noticed with amusement that he wore a fancy wristwatch.

It was not cold, but there was a chill in the wind that made him glad he had picked the thicker shirt. They were short on rain here, he noted; the dirt road was rutted and dug up, yet dry and caked.

He walked briskly down the road toward the town, looking at the scenery. Small farms were the rule, and many looked far more modern than his. There wasn't much traffic, but occasional people passed on horseback or in buckboards, giving him the impression that modern vehicles were either in short supply or banned.

And yet, despite the lack of recent rain, the land was good. The tilled soil was black and mineral-rich, and where small compressors pumped water from wells or nearby creeks into irrigation ditches, the land bloomed.

He came upon the town much faster than he had anticipated. He didn't feel the least bit tired or uncomfortable, and he had walked with a speed that astonished him. The town itself was a study in contrasts. Log buildings, some as tall as five stories, mixed with modern, prefabricated structures. The street wasn't paved, but it went for several blocks, with a block or two on either side of the business district composed of houses, mostly large and comfortable. There was street lighting, and some of the businesses had electric signs, so there was a power plant somewhere, and, from the look of things, running water and indoor plumbing.

He studied some of the women, most of whom were dressed in garb much like his own, sometimes with small cowboy hats or straw broad-brimmed hats on their heads. There weren't nearly as many women as men, he noted, and those that were here looked tough, muscular, and mannish.

The town was small enough so that he spotted the doctor's office with no difficulty and headed for it. The doctor was concerned. He had quite a modern facility, with a minor surgery and some of the latest machines and probes. Clearly medical care was well into the modern era here. The X-rays showed a severe concussion and fracture. The doctor marveled that he was alive at all, as he placed medication and a small bandage on the wound after sewing seven stitches.

"Get somebody to stay with you the next few days, or look in on you regularly," the doctor advised. "Your loss of memory's probably only temporary, and not that uncommon in these cases. But a lot of damage was done. The brain was bruised, and I want someone to see that you don't have a clot in there."

He thanked the doctor, assuring him that he would take care of himself and be watched and checked.

"Settle the bill at the end of the month," the doctor told him.

This puzzled him for a minute. The bill? Money? He had never used it himself, and, back on the street, he pulled out a thin leather wallet, which looked like the survivor of a war, and opened it.

Funny-looking pieces of paper, about a dozen of them. They had very realistic pictures, almost three-dimensional, on them, the fronts showing the same man three times, the others two other men and a woman. The backs showed a remarkably realistic set of farm scenes. He wished he could read the bills. He would have to find out what each one was and remember the pictures.

A three-story log building's lights went on in the coming twilight, and he saw from the symbol on the sign that it was a bar and something else. He didn't recognize the other symbol, and couldn't read the words. Curious, he walked over to it.

There was a rumbling of thunder in the distance.

☼

She awoke, feeling nauseated, and threw up.

The bile spilled on the cheap rug, and in it, as she gagged uncontrollably, she could see bits and pieces and even whole pills of some kind.

The spasms lasted several minutes, until it seemed there was nothing else to give. Feeling weak and exhausted, she lay back on the bed until the room steadied. The stench of the bile permeated her.

Slowly, she looked around. A tiny room, with nothing but a bed much too large for it and a wicker chair. There was barely fifty centimeters' clearance on either side of it.

The walls and ceiling seemed to be made of logs, but the construction was so solid it might as well have been rock. It was dark in the room, and she looked for a light. Spying a string hanging above her, she pulled it, and a weak, naked light bulb suspended from the ceiling flicked on. The glare hurt her eyes.

She raised her head slightly and looked down at her body. Something was definitely different.

Two extremely large but perfectly formed breasts met her eye, and her skin seemed creamy smooth, dark-complexioned but unpigmented.

Her gaze slid down a little more, and she saw that the rest of her body matched the breasts—curving in all the right places, definitely.

She felt—strange. Tingly all over, but particularly in the areas of her breasts and crotch.

She was nude from the waist up, but hanging on sultry hips was a pantslike garment of fine-woven black lace, to which hundreds of tiny sequins of various colors were attached.

She felt her face, and found that she had some sort of hairdo. There were also long, plastic earrings hanging from pierced ears.

She looked around in the gloom, found a small cosmetics case with a mirror in it, and looked at her face.

It is a beautiful face, she thought, and she was not being vain. Maybe the most beautiful face I've ever seen. Cosmetics had been carefully applied to bring out just the right highlights, but the face was so perfect that they seemed almost intrusive on its beauty.

But whose face was it? she wondered.

She noticed a box next to the cosmetics case on the floor, and picked it up idly. It was a pillbox—open, and empty. There was a universal caution symbol on it, but she couldn't read the writing. She didn't need to.

This girl, whoever and whatever she was, had killed herself. She had taken all those pills and overdosed. She had died here, in this room, moments before—alone. And the moment that girl had died, she had been somehow inserted into the body, and the physical processes righted.

She stared again at that beautiful face in the mirror.

What would make someone who looked like this and experienced such feelings as she now did commit suicide? So very young, she thought—perhaps no more than sixteen or seventeen. And so very beautiful.

She tried to get up, but felt suddenly light-headed and strange. She flopped back down on the bed and stared up at the light bulb, which, for some reason, had become fascinating.

She found herself gently caressing her own body, and it felt fantastic, like tingling jolts of pleasure at each nerve juncture.

It's the pills, a corner of her mind told her. You didn't get all of them out of your system.

The door opened suddenly, and a man looked in. He was dressed in white work clothes, like kitchen help. He was balding and fiftyish, but he had a tough, hard look to him. "Okay, Nova, time to—" he began, then stopped and looked at her, the empty box, and the bile and vomited-up pills on the floor and the side of her bed.

"Oh, shit!" he snarled angrily, and exploded. "You went for the happy pills again, didn't you? I warned you, dammit! I wondered why a sexy high-top like you would work this jerkwater! They tossed you out of the others!" He stopped, his tone going from fury to disgust.

"You're no good to anybody, not even yourself," he snapped. "I told you if you did this again, I'd toss you in the street. Come on! You hear me?" he started yelling. "You're going out and now! Come on, get up!"

She heard him, but the words didn't register. He looked and sounded somehow funny, and she laughed and pointed to him, giggling stupidly.

He grabbed her by the arm and pulled her up. "Jesus!" he exclaimed. "You're a hell of a piece. Too bad your insides don't match your outsides. Come on!"

He pulled her out into the hall and dragged her down a flight of wooden stairs. She felt as if she were floating, and made flying motions with her free arm and motor sounds with her voice.

A few other young women peered out from second-floor rooms. None of 'em pretty as me, she thought smugly.

"Stop that giggling!" the man commanded, but it sounded so funny she giggled more.

The downstairs was a bar, some sawdust on the floor, a few round tables, and a small service bar to one side. It was dimly lit, and empty.

"Oh, hell," he said, almost sadly, reaching into a cash drawer behind the bar. "You ain't even earned your keep here, and you burned your clothes on the last flyer. Here—fifty *reals*," he continued, stuffing a few bills in the lace panty. "When you come to out in the street or the woods or the sheriff's office, buy some clothes and a ticket out. I've had it!"

He picked her up as if she weighed nothing, and, opening the door with one hand, tossed her rudely into the darkening street. The chilly air and the hard landing brought her down a bit, and she looked around, feeling lost and alone.

She suddenly didn't want to be seen. Although there were few people about, there were some nearby who would see her in a few moments. She saw a dark alleyway between the bar and a store and crawled into it. It was very dark and cold, and smelled a little of old garbage. But at least she was concealed.

Suddenly the streetlights popped on, and deepened the shadows in which she sat confused. The shock of where she was and her situation broke through into her conscious mind. She was still high, and her body still tingled, particularly when rubbed. She still wanted to rub it, but she was aware of her circumstances.

I'm alone in a crazy place I don't know, practically nude and with the temperature dropping fast, she thought miserably. How much worse can things get?

As if in answer, there was a rumbling and a series of static discharges, and the temperature dropped even more.

Tears welled up in her eyes, and she started crying at the helplessness of her position. She had never been more miserable in her life.

A man was crossing the street, walking toward the bar. He stopped suddenly. Lightning flashed, illuminating her for a brief moment. He looked puzzled, and came toward the alley. She was folded up, arms around her knees, head down against them. She rocked as she cried.

He saw her and stared in disbelief. Now what the hell? he thought.

He reached out and touched her bare shoulder, and she started, looked up at him, saw the concern on his face.

"What's the matter, little lady?" he asked gently.

She looked up with anguished face and started to speak, but couldn't.

She was, even in this state, the most beautiful thing he had ever seen.

"Nothing's that bad," he tried to soothe her. "Where do you live? I'll take you home. You're not hurt, are you?"

She shook her head negatively, and coughed a little. "No, no," she managed. "Don't have a home. Thrown out."

He squatted next to her. The lightning and thunder continued, but the rain held off still.

"Come on with me, then," he said in that same soft tone. "I've got a place just down the road. Nobody there but me. You can stay until you decide what to do."

Her head shook in confusion. She didn't know what to do. Could she trust him? Dare she take this opportunity?

A strange, distant voice whispered in her brain. It said, *"Can you feel it? Fear, greed, horror, ambition, burning within you, consuming you … Perfection is the object of the experiment, not the component. … Don't torture yourself, run away from your fears. Face them! Stand up to them! Fight them with goodness, mercy, charity, compassion. …"*

And trust? she wondered suddenly. Oh, hell! What have I got to lose if I go? What do I have if I don't?

"I'll go," she said softly. He helped her up, gently, carefully, and brushed the dirt off her. He's very big, she realized. I only come up to his neck.

"Come on," he urged, and took her hand.

She hesitated. "I don't want—want to go out there looking like this," she said nervously.

"There's nothing wrong with the way you look," he replied in a tone that had nothing if not sincerity.

"Nothing at all. Besides, the storm's about to break, I think. Most folks will stay inside."

Again she looked uncertain. "What about us?" she asked. "Won't we get wet?"

"There's shelter along the way," he said casually. "Besides, a little water won't hurt."

She let him lead her down the deserted street of the town and out into the countryside. The storm continued to be visual and audible, but not as yet wet. The landscape seemed eerie, illuminated in the flashes.

The temperature had dropped from about fifteen degrees Celsius to around eight degrees due to the storm. She shivered.

He looked at her, concerned, feeling the tremors in her hand.

"Want my shirt?" he asked.

"But then you'll be cold," she protested.

"I like cold weather," he responded, taking off his shirt. His broad, muscled, hairy chest reactivated those funny feelings in her again. Carefully he draped the shirt around her. It fit her like a circus tent, but it felt warm and good.

She didn't know what to say, and something, some impulse, caused her to lean into him and put her arm around his bare chest. He responded by putting his arm around her, and they resumed walking.

Somehow it felt good, calming, and her anxieties seemed to flee. She looked up at him. "What's your name?" she asked in a tone of voice she didn't quite comprehend, but was connected, somehow, in its throaty softness to those strange feelings.

"W—" he started to say, then said, instead, "Kally Tonge. I have a farm not much farther down the road."

She noticed the bandage on the side of his head. "You're injured."

"It's nothing—now," he replied, and chuckled. "As a matter of fact, you're just what the doctor ordered—literally. He said somebody should be with me through the night."

"Does it hurt much?" she asked.

"Not now," he replied. "Medicine's pretty advanced here, although as you know the place is rather primitive overall."

"I really don't know much about this world," she replied truthfully. "I'm not from here."

"I could have guessed that," he said lightly. "Where *do* you come from?"

"I don't think you've ever heard of it," she replied. "From nowhere now, really."

"What's *your* name?" he asked.

She started to say "Nova," the name the man had called her, but instead she said, "Vardia."

He stopped and looked at her strangely. "That's a Com name, isn't it?" he asked. "You're not from any Comworld!"

"Sort of," she replied enigmatically, "but I've changed a lot."

"On the Well World?" he asked sharply.

She gasped, a small sound of surprise escaping her lips. "You—you're one of the people from the Well!" she exclaimed. "You woke up in that body, as I did! That head wound killed Kally Tonge and you took over, as I did!"

"Twice when I needed someone you comforted me, even defended me," he said.

"*Wuju!*" she exclaimed, and an amazed smile spread over her face. She looked him over critically. "My, how you've changed!"

"No more than you," he replied, shaking his head wonderingly. "*Wow!*"

"But—but, why a man?" she asked.

His face grew serious. "I'll tell you sometime. But, good old Nathan! He sure came through!"

The storm broke, then, and the rain started coming down heavily.

They were both soaked through in seconds, and her fancy hairdo collapsed. He laughed, and she laughed, and he picked her up and started running in the mud. Just ahead he saw his shack, outlined in the lightning flashes, but he misjudged the turn to his walk with his burden. They both tumbled into the road, splashing around and covered with thick black mud.

"You all right?" he shouted over the torrent.

"I'm drowning in mud!" she called back, and they both got up, laughing at each other.

"The barn's closer!" he shouted. "See it over there? Run for it!"

He started off, and she followed, the rain getting heavier and heavier. He reached the door way ahead of her, and slid it aside on its rollers. She reached it, and they both fell in. The place had an eerie, hollow sound, the rain beating on the sheet-metal roof

and wood sides of the barn. It was dark, and smelled like the barn it was. A few cows mooed nervously in their stalls.

"Wooj?" she called.

"Here," he said, near her, and she turned.

"Might as well sit it out here," he told her. "There's a pile of hay over there, and it's a thousand meters to the shack. Might as well not go through the deluge twice."

"Okay," she replied, exhausted, and plopped into the hay. The rain continued to beat a percussion symphony on the barn.

He plopped beside her. She was fussing with her lace pants.

"The mud's all caked in them, and the sequins are scratching me," she said. "Might as well get them off, for all the good they'll do as clothing anyway, even if they are all I've got in the world."

She did, and they lay for a while side by side. He put his arm around her and fondled her breast.

"That feels good," she whispered. "Is—is that what I've been feeling? I thought it was still the pills. Is this what you felt with Brazil?"

"I'll be damned!" he said to himself. "I always wondered what an erection felt like to a man!" He turned and looked at her. "I'll show you what it's really like, if you want," he said softly.

"I—I think that's what he wanted," she replied.

"Is it what *you* want?" he asked seriously.

"I think I do," she whispered, and realized that it *was* what she wanted. "But I don't even know how."

"Leave that to an expert," he replied. "Although I'm not used to this end of things." He put both arms around her, kissed her and fondled her.

And he kicked off his pants, and showed her the other side of being a woman, while discovering himself what it was to be a man.

☼

The rain was over. It had been over for a couple of hours, but they just lay there, content in the nearness of each other.

The door was still half-open, and Vardia, still dazed and dreamy from her first sexual experience, saw the clouds roll back and the stars appear. "We'll get you some clothes in the morning," he said at last. "Then we'll tour the farm. This rain should do everything good. I was born on a farm, you know, but not my own farm."

"People—non-Com people—they do that *every* day?" she asked.

He chuckled. "Twice if they're horny enough. Except for a couple of days each month."

"You—you've done it both ways," she said. "Is it different?"

"The feeling's definitely different, but it's the same charge," he replied. "An important part, male or female, is that you do it when you want with someone you want."

"Is that love?" she asked. "Is that what Brazil was talking about?"

"Not the sex," he replied. "That's just a—a component, as he would say. Without the object—without love, without feeling for the other person, without *caring*, it's not pleasant at all."

"That's why you're a man now," she said. "All the other times—they were the wrong kind, weren't they?"

"Yes," he replied distantly, and looked out at the stars. She clenched his hand tightly in hers.

"Do you think he was really God?" Vardia asked quietly.

"I don't know," he replied with a sigh. "What if he wasn't? When he was in the Well he had the power. He gave me my farm, a good, healthy young body, a new chance. And," he added softly, "he sent you."

She nodded. "I've never lived like this," she said. "Is it all as wonderful as tonight?"

"No," he replied seriously. "There's a lot of hard work, and pain, and heartache—but, if it all comes together, it *can* be beautiful."

"We'll try it here," she said resolutely. "And when the fun is gone, if ever, or when we're old and gray, we'll take off for a Markovian world, and go back and do it again. That's a good future."

"I think it is," he responded. "It's more than most people ever get."

"This world," she said. "It must never become like the others, like the Com. We must make sure of that."

At that moment there was a glow far beyond the horizon, and suddenly a bright arrow streaked upward in the dark sky and vanished. A few seconds later, a distant, roaring sound came to them.

"Poor Nathan," he said sadly. "He can do it for everyone but himself."

"I wonder where he is now?" she mused.

"I don't know what form he's in," he replied, "but I think I know where he is and what he's doing, and thinking, and feeling."

They continued to gaze at the stars.

ABOARD THE FREIGHTER *STEHEKIN*

Nathan Brazil lay in the command chair on the bridge and gazed distantly at the fake starfield projected in the two window screens. He glanced over to the table atop the ancient computer.

That same pornographic novel was there, spread open to where he had last been reading it. He couldn't remember it at all, but, he reflected, it didn't matter. They were all alike anyway, and there was plenty of time to read it again.

He sighed and picked up the cargo manifest, idly flipping it open.

Cargo of grain, bound for Coriolanus, it read. *No passengers.*

No passengers.

They were elsewhere now—the rotten ones in their own private hells, the good ones—and the potentially good—with their chances. He wondered whether their dreams were as sweet as they had imagined. Would they forget the lessons of the Well, or try for change?

In the end, of course, it didn't really matter.

Except to them.

He closed the manifest and threw it across the control room. It banged against the wall and landed askew on the floor. He sighed a long, sad sigh, a sigh for ages past and the ages yet to be.

The memories would fade, but the ache would remain.

For, whatever becomes of the others or of this little corner of the universe, he thought, I'm still Nathan Brazil, fifteen days out, bound for Coriolanus with a load of grain.

Still waiting.

Still caring.

Still alone.

The End

www.ingramcontent.com/pod-product-compliance
Lightning Source LLC
Chambersburg PA
CBHW082227140626
46556CB00020B/3371